THE PRUNING

THE
Pruning

AMERICAN DREAMS - BOOK 2

JAN CLINE

WordCrafts

The Pruning is a work of fiction. The author has endeavored to be as accurate as possible with regard to the times in which the events of this novel is set. Still, this is a novel, and all references to persons, places, and events are fictitious or are used fictitiously.

The Pruning
Copyright © 2019
Jan Cline

Library of Congress Control Number:2019944716

Original cover design by Lynnette Bonner

Published by WordCrafts Press
Cody, Wyoming 82414
www.wordcrafts.net

To my sister, Leah.

"*I* am the real vine, my Father is the vine-dresser. He removes any of my branches which are not bearing fruit and he prunes every branch that does bear fruit to increase its yield. Now, you have already been pruned by my words. You must go on growing in me and I will grow in you. For just as the branch cannot bear any fruit unless it shares the life of the vine, so you can produce nothing unless you go on growing in me. I am the vine itself, you are the branches. It is the man who shares my life and whose life I share who proves fruitful. For the plain fact is that apart from me you can do nothing at all."

John 15:1-5
J.B. Phillips New Testament

$$\mathscr{C}hapter\ 1$$

Pasco, Washington, June 1935

After three long days and two nights sitting on a lumpy seat, Clarissa had looked forward to getting off this train, but now all she wanted was to slither into the safety of the grimy locomotive and go back to where she'd come from. Despite a promise of a new beginning, her life was about to fall into an abyss deeper than the sand dunes she had just escaped.

Her throat tightened as she tried to pull in some air. Like the dust storms around their homestead on the Kansas plains, the sight of her husband, Frank, hugging his estranged brother robbed her of breath. If her first impression was correct, another kind of storm brewed before her eyes.

It can't be him. Her gut told her this wasn't her imagination but indeed a cruel twist in her plans for a brighter future for what was left of her family. One more long look at his face, his stature, and any lingering doubt faded.

She turned from the scene and scanned the yard around the clapboard station house. The sheer beauty of the clear skies and rolling hills in the distance should have been her welcome. The sight of blooming flowers and tall leafy trees might have excited her but for the shock of seeing him again.

The train car landing jiggled as the passengers in front of her tromped down the steps. She held tight to Morgan's hand, trying to stand on weakened legs. The breeze tossed his shaggy hair across his forehead. He shook loose from her grip and hurried down the steps without hanging on to the rail.

"Be careful or you'll fall," Clarissa called after him then turned away. Best to stay hidden a few more moments. Time had slowed, but her thoughts raced with questions. What would she say once she joined them?

She hovered in the cramped space at the end of the streamliner car, unable to move. Her hands tingled, and a veil of gray fog dropped through her vision. Fainting now wouldn't exactly make her invisible. Deep breaths brought some relief, and she forced herself to focus on the happy faces of folks greeting loved ones.

"Excuse me, lady." A wiry young man wiggled around her to bound off the train, running to the open arms of a blubbering older woman. She tenderly slid the boy's hat from his head and pushed back his hair. He kissed her cheek, and they walked away arm in arm.

Clarissa's attention darted back to her small family standing below. Another reunion scene, but not the one she expected. It was clear now. William, the brother she had heard so much about, was Will Larson. Her Will. The absurdity of it made it seem unreal, yet there he stood on the ground below her, arms wrapped around Frank, laughing their greetings. With embarrassment creeping up her neck, she imagined them laughing at her. *Nonsense.*

She grabbed the cold steel railing. Her other hand let loose of her satchel, and she dreamily watched it bounce down the steps and roll on the gravel to land behind Frank. He was busy embracing Will, so she could wait to join them, giving her a moment to conceal her horror with a manufactured smile.

"Mother, what's wrong? You're holding up the line." James stood behind her, tugging on her blouse sleeve. He stepped in front of her.

"What? Oh. You go ahead and catch up with your father."

She slipped back into the shadows. People squeezed past her, frowning and huffing. James jumped onto the ground and waited next to Frank.

Your father. Yes, James would catch up with his father today. The scenario she never dreamed she would face was about to hit her head on, and all she could do was cower like cornered prey.

Would he recognize her? Likely.

Her first reprieve was that Frank didn't know James' real father was the long-lost brother he had bragged on for the last one hundred miles of their trip. The second was that Will was equally ignorant of the fact. Her ignorance of this brotherly connection had blindsided her. It wasn't fair.

God, what do I do? Why did you bring me here?

She pulled in a breath of air seasoned with train fumes. Her pulse pounded as the last person to disembark bumped past her. She took one step into the light of the midmorning sun. Its warming splendor reminded her of Black Sunday and the sunshine before the big storm accosted their Kansas county. It seemed another kind of blackness headed her way, one of her own making. She couldn't avoid the damage it would bring. Like Black Sunday, she felt the suffocating wrath of inescapable reality.

James shaded his searching eyes, giving a frantic wave for her to come down from her protected perch. Morgan stood at Frank's side, shaking hands with Will, or whatever his name was. Why had Will changed his name? The irony of it all—she had traveled over a thousand miles to land in the middle of Frank, Will—and James. She thought she had put enough distance between them years ago. If she wasn't so disheartened, she would laugh out loud at God's sense of humor.

You have to go down there, Clarissa. Face your sin, and pray he won't recognize you.

She held her breath until her lungs ached, then breathed out and forced her foot to touch the first metal step. Her stomach lurched to her throat when Frank spun around. "Clary, come here and meet William."

Frank's grin was all she could see, blinding like the sun. Her heart stuttered to think how his smile might be obliterated in the next few seconds—if Will blurted out any recognition.

She landed on the solid rich ground she'd been dreaming about for the last week. She had to look up now, into this man's face—the object of her first fierce love.

Frank inched closer. "William, this is my Clary."

Did he have to look so proud of her, like a trophy he'd won in a contest? She didn't feel much like a treasured possession— more like a consolation prize. She glanced down at her crinkled blouse. She must look as frazzled as she felt, sweaty and wrinkled. Her shoes pinched her feet, and her stockings under her skirt had sagged around her ankles. Frank saw her through the many years of his love for her. William would see a young lady who'd changed into a frumpy, out-of-style woman.

"Hello." William stepped around Frank and held out his hand. His fingers were thick in her sweaty palm.

She kept her eyes down, noticing the tiny cuts dotting freckled arms below his rolled-up shirtsleeves. She looked up to see he had aged gracefully, the passing of time showing in the deep curves around his mouth and the wide branch of wrinkles at the corners of the brown eyes she remembered so well. She dared to meet his gaze. His broad smile greeted her—until he took a good look at her face. Hopefully, the reflection of the girl he knew stayed hidden in her matured features.

William tipped his head to the side for a moment, then his eyes opened wide, still grasping her trembling hand. Her palpitations eased at his remarkable composure. Hers was about to fail, along with her equilibrium. Frank's obvious exuberance at their meeting would be Will's cue to say nothing, and so far he played along.

He loomed over her, tall and broad shouldered. "I'm—William. So nice to meet you." He shot a quick glance at Frank, then back to her. He had to be thinking this was some sort of joke. His grip went from slight to firm as he stared into her eyes. She hoped he saw the frantic pleading in them. She tightened her hold.

"William." She nearly choked on his name, a name she had once cherished. She managed a half-smile, glancing to Frank to judge his expression. Did he notice her trepidation? Surely everyone could hear her heart thumping against her chest.

Frank gathered James to his side, shaking him playfully by the shoulders. "And this is my other son, James."

William's attention lingered on her before reluctantly moving to the boy. "James. Hello." He released her hand and grasped James', searching his face. Would he see himself in James' features? No. He didn't know to look. He couldn't. She never had the chance to tell him.

Oh, God. I'm going to be sick. She slid her uncooperative feet across the dirt, closer to Frank and avoiding William's attempt at eye contact. She inhaled slow, deliberate breaths but couldn't seem to calm the waves of shaking.

The greetings ended, and everyone stood in terrible silence until Frank spoke up. "Well, shall we load up our bags? The rest of our things will be on this afternoon's train."

William hesitated, his eyes shifting from her to Frank. "We'll come back with the truck to get them."

"I know a mail pilot," Morgan piped up, almost singing.

Clarissa exhaled. Everyone laughed as William patted Morgan on the top of his head. She pretended she didn't hear so she wouldn't be expected to laugh. That was asking too much.

William halfheartedly responded. "You'll have to tell me all about him."

James picked up Clarissa's satchel. He turned toward the station house and hollered over his shoulder. "Be careful, Uncle William. You'll get sick of hearing about it."

If there had been anywhere else to go at this moment, any escape from her trap, she would have darted away like a freed prisoner. Of all the ridiculous things to bechance her, she was about to live the worst. They were on their way to William's home. To live. Together.

She closed her eyes and let the breeze blow her hair from her face. A train whistle from down the tracks to the south rang in her ears. She didn't have the strength to be startled, and tuned out the other noises of cars starting and hollered greetings. A slight headache formed around her temples. When she opened her eyes, the boys had walked ahead with William, leaving only Frank by her side.

"Honey? Are you all right?" Frank whispered in her ear. "Your face is flushed. You're not used to any humidity."

Poor Frank couldn't know it wasn't the fine summer day adding color to her cheeks. She willed the crushing shame and panic to go away. Here she would begin a long line of excuses. "I'm just very tired, and I dressed too warm for this climate."

"We'll get you rested up as soon as we get to William's place. You're probably exhausted and hungry. Maybe there's a bathtub at the house. You deserve a good soak." Frank wrapped his arm around her.

She could fall into his chest and cry, but she held her breath to resist. A long bath couldn't possibly soothe the mortification plaguing her, but it would afford her a few moments of peace alone—time to think and adjust. And beg God for mercy.

She leaned close to his stubbled cheek and murmured, "William doesn't know about me—I mean about how we came to be married—does he?" She didn't recognize her own voice, scratched through a dry throat.

Frank pulled back and frowned. "Of course not."

"Please, for James' sake, don't ever tell him." She smiled, but the rest of her plea got stuck in the tears she willed back. She monitored her tone and demeanor. The last thing she wanted was for Frank to be suspicious.

Frank shook his head. "No, I won't. There's no reason for him to know."

No reason. If that were true, the dark misery shrouding her would be replaced with the relief of her new surroundings. Looking through the train car window the last few miles had revealed a land not of torturous groaning but of dark earth and green growth. The lush rolling fields of ripening barley waving in the breeze resembled a shimmering ocean. The train sped past small pothole lakes dotted with boys fishing off the rocky shore. The white billowing clouds in the sky weren't a sign of a dust storm but of lazy summer days to come.

She had imagined the scenery to be a reflection of her rejuvenated soul, a promise of her heart's desires to be fulfilled, of her debt paid at last. Maybe even hope for healing in her own barren body. It wasn't to be, now that William had entered her life again. There might be no reason for him to know, as Frank said, but she faced the very real possibility he would figure it out.

Her peripheral vision caught William stealing a glance at her as he strolled to the auto. She watched him walk—his stride and frame familiar even now. After all these years, she too remembered. With James beside him, she saw the resemblance in their gaits.

Her dreams of starting a new life had taken a cruel turn, rescued from the drought holocaust only to be dropped on the doorstep of another disaster. She couldn't have devised a plot to a tragic novel that was this bizarre. How had she not known they were brothers, and why did he have a different last name when she knew him?

Morgan tugged on her arm, his brow etched with wrinkles. "Mama, does it rain here?"

She looked at Frank. He shook his head and shrugged. She leaned down to hold Morgan's chin in her hand. She knew his question begged assurance.

"Yes, sweetie. It rains here. Wonderful, glorious, wet rain. You'll see." If for no other reason than to ease Morgan's mind, she would pray for rain. William had written Frank that the area got plenty of moisture to grow good grapes. Still, she would pray.

Morgan shaded his eyes and looked to the sky. "I hope it rains soon."

He jogged to catch up with William, who politely listened to the story of Morgan's precious pilot friend. Pilot Billy's visit to Morgan at the hospital felt like a lifetime ago. Everything that had happened back home seemed far away. What were the friends they had left behind doing now? Had they gone, or were they still stuck in that lost land? And where was Elijah now? Was he well?

As Clarissa let Frank help her into the backseat of the auto, she wondered what Elijah would say about her turmoil. She imagined his sympathetic smile and wished he were here.

"All things work together for good, ma'am," he would have gently insisted.

Still, she would keep a close eye on William until she was sure he would keep their secret.

She breathed deep, feeling the warm air pass between her lips. It was time to find the strength she had called upon to get through all the hardships of the last four years. It had to sustain her again, without revealing her weakness. Frank had never known her inner struggles, of her silent anguish over years of toil on the farm and lost babies. He must not know about this blow to her confidence.

William opened the driver's door. The sunlight glimmered off the window glass like a camera lightbulb flash, giving Clarissa's headache a jolt. William climbed in and smiled at James, who had already jumped into the passenger side and settled in.

"Uncle William, this is some auto. Looks brand new." James ran his hand along the dusty ebony dash, then craned his neck to look in the side mirror.

William chuckled. "We call them *cars* here. It's a Ford V8. Got it new last year. Had a good crop, and I don't have a wife or kids to feed, so I splurged." He patted the dash. "It's got the new long chassis, 75 horsepower, and a new kind of paint." He grinned at James' gaping mouth.

Frank slid onto the backseat, next to Clarissa and Morgan. "It's pretty fancy for us midwest folk. But we'll get used to it." He laughed and winked at Clarissa.

She felt the urge to cry, but stuffed it down. She would have to be patient with Frank's exuberance.

"Uncle William, I had dust pne… pneumonia," Morgan blurted out.

William started the engine. "Really? When?"

Clarissa interrupted before Morgan could start the usual lengthy explanation. "It was just a few weeks ago, and I think we should get Morgan to the house so he can rest."

The reflection of William's eyes staring at her in the rearview mirror made her flinch, remembering how she used to long for him to look at her.

"Sure, we'll get going. It takes about 30 minutes to get to the place." He shifted the gears.

Thirty long minutes. She leaned into Frank and took off her hat to fan herself, feeling the salty perspiration on her lip dry up. She wilted more by the minute and hated feeling weak. Perhaps William's house would be cool.

The numerous possibilities for calamity loomed over her like a rain cloud all the way to William's vineyard. It would take every ounce of character she could muster to live there with him. It would never be an acceptable permanent arrangement.

What should have been a happy day was anything but that. At least Frank would be elated, working side by side with his brother. Until he discovered the truth.

It was only a matter of time.

The dirty white wicker rocker on the front porch beckoned her to sit awhile. She welcomed a chance to breathe in the fresh cool breeze coming off the river far below the vineyard. She would enjoy the quiet until James and Morgan finished their studies in the kitchen, and Frank and William returned from the station with their long-lost trunks. The last of them had been diverted to a town up north called Spokane. Frank had spent an hour at the station office that first afternoon, but assured her that her belongings were on their way.

She dusted off the seat and listened to the creak of the porch planks as she rocked, a lullaby much like the sound of the windmill back home. Clarissa examined the porch posts and clematis vine–covered railings. Like the inside of their new little home, the outside needed a good scrubbing. No bother—it was better than cleaning up after William in his house.

"I hope you don't mind not being in the big house. It's just not ready for company," William had said that first day.

Mind? A cottage of their own among the lilac bushes and shady aspen trees? A pardon from the sentence of sharing a dwelling with William? A chance to escape the past staring her in the face on a daily basis? This gift from heaven lifted a heavy weight from her chest, and now she could rest in her own space, away from him. So far he had respected her signals to be left alone. She could only guess how long that would last.

Set in the backdrop of lush grapevines and endless rows of budding apple trees, the white clapboard cottage offered respite from the drought and dry lands of home. The green shutters needed painting—one hung crooked where a nail had come loose. And Frank would have to remove the layers of last fall's dried leaves from the roof. A much lighter task than shoveling the drifts of Kansas sand.

She had cried tears of relief the day they'd arrived and opened the front door. Like stepping into a time capsule, she noted the delicate décor of gauzy cobwebs. Moderately furnished with an overstuffed faded sofa and a paint-chipped kitchen table and chairs, the cottage seemed to be waiting for her. A framed still life of roses hung on the living room wall, remnant of a woman's touch. Two of the three small bedrooms had double beds, complete with squeaky bedsprings and brass headboards, and a single bed filled the smallest room, perfect for Morgan.

In the humble kitchen, wedged between two counters, sat an electric stove. She'd made an immediate mental list of items she would need to bake the goodies her boys missed. She could already smell the aromas of cinnamon and brown sugar. A small window brought light in above the white porcelain sink with a tarnished faucet. They would have running water in the house at last.

The overgrown garden in the backyard and graveled pathways around the place begged for a nurturing touch. Her fingers itched to plant the seeds she'd been saving for several years and had carried all the way from Kansas. If they would still sprout, this summer they would have corn, squash, beans, and later she would plant seed potatoes. It would take some convincing to get the boys to eat potatoes again. The steady diet of the vegetable for the last year had ruined any appetite for them.

As she rocked, her thoughts drifted, and sleep teased her behind closed eyes. The quiet dissipated with the rumble of the truck motor sputtering up the drive. It would be like Christmas to unpack the last of their things.

"They're back. Let's go," she heard Morgan holler at James as his shoes tapped toward the front door. She would never get them back to schoolwork now.

Morgan pushed open the screen door, rushed past his mother, and halted at the edge of the steps. He turned to give her a sheepish smile—the one that always melted her heart and her resolve.

"You said we could quit when Daddy got home. Can we go now?"

James stood next to her. "We got most of our reading done anyway."

She nudged James' arm. His pleading eyes broke her. It was as good a time as any to set them free from schedules for the day.

"You can go. But you have to stay within earshot, just like back home."

Morgan stopped at the bottom of the steps and stretched out his arms. "This *is* home."

His voice of truth made her shudder. It might be home to Frank and the boys, but despite being pleased with her surroundings, she hadn't found an anchor here. Not even a little. She couldn't make a lasting home here as long as William stayed entangled in their lives. It was her fault. She had brought this all on herself. If only they had some other place to go. It was too late, for Frank had fallen in love with the place.

The boys darted off toward the enormous faded-red barn at the end of the yard. They would be entertained for hours chasing butterflies, throwing rocks at roosting crows, and piling hay for William's lone horse.

The truck skidded to a stop in front of her. William nodded in her direction through his open driver's-side window. As the dust from his abrupt halt filtered past her, she could swear she saw him wink. He couldn't have been so bold. Still, her arms shivered and she stood on tiptoes to see the bed of the truck.

Frank jumped out of the passenger side. "It's all here. At last." He pulled three boxes and one trunk from the back of the truck while William waited behind the wheel. Once he set everything on the ground, William sped off.

Frank waved after him. "Thanks for the lift!"

She clenched her teeth. It was the first of many *thank-yous* they would owe William from now on. Such a shame they would have to owe him anything. For a fleeting moment she wished they had left more belongings at the homestead—just in case.

As soon as Frank dumped the last box inside the cottage door, Clarissa rolled up her sleeves and tightened the strings on her apron. After she served their meager dinner of stale bread and warm cheese, she would dig out the necessities for setting up housekeeping on a farm filled with life. She embraced the fleeting moment of freshness and hope as she watched Frank.

New life danced in his eyes, which sparkled with boyish excitement as he pushed the last trunk through the door. He scurried around the living room and hall, rummaging through the boxes stuffed with their mementos. She unstrapped the trunk and opened the lid. If her little clay pots had survived the trip, she would plant seeds right away. Here her plants would live—even thrive.

"No more watching things die for this family," Clarissa declared to the empty room as she unwrapped the unharmed clay pot.

"I found it," Frank hollered from their bedroom.

"Found what?"

Instead of answering, he sauntered down the hallway with the square wrapped parcel of her mother's painting. After stashing it away in the largest satchel they'd carried on the train, Clarissa had checked on it often during the trip. Once they'd arrived, all her mental energy went to William, forgetting about her treasure packed away. As much as she'd loved giving her sister one of the pair, she wished she had more of her mother's legacy.

Frank tore the wrapping off and held it up, then removed the rose still life and gingerly hung the framed gem as if it were a Rembrandt. It hadn't graced a wall in so long. Clarissa cried as she dusted the corners, making visible the distinctive signature from her mother's hand.

She pressed her lips to his cheek. "Thank you." The pride in his eyes didn't miss the mark of her heart.

"Once we get your studio set up and you have a chance to paint, I'll hang your artwork too." He returned her kiss. "Gotta go. William wants to show me the orchard. He went on ahead, so I'll need to catch up."

She bristled at the thought, but checked herself on knowing William was the boss. Sharing Frank would take some getting used to. She would rather he and Will hated each other.

She called after him. "Don't be late for dinner."

He bounded down the hall and let the back screen door slam behind him. She didn't mind the solitude. It was her chance to hang the wet shirts and towels still sitting in the ringer. Getting all the dust from their clothes had proved to be a challenge, but she had finally rid them of any reminder of Kansas dirt.

She hauled a basket of wet clothes outside and dropped it under the makeshift rope clothesline. The pure joy of being outside in the sun faded the looming issue with William. Still, she glanced over her shoulder to his porch to make sure he wasn't there watching her. The railing on the steps sagged, and the flowers in a large pot on the top step were wilted and dry. William must not be as handy as Frank at fixing and tending.

Her wild curiosity about the inside of the big house grew each time her eyes caught sight of the two-story brick structure. She imagined a grand, well-stocked kitchen, and fine velvet sofas and chairs in the sitting room. Perhaps when she knew William was away, she would sneak inside to experience it all.

She draped and pinned several shirts and pants while daydreaming about the little graveyard behind the Kansas homestead, wondering if Timothy and Sarah Margaret were lonely. Silly, of course. They were in heaven. Years of emotional investment were buried there with them, a burden she couldn't seem to lay down. She had promised Frank to make an effort to be happy here. And she would—for now.

"Need any help?"

William's voice shook her. She grabbed the rope to keep from faltering. Every muscle she needed to turn and face him froze up. She exhaled all the air in her lungs to free them.

"Oh, no. But thank you." She hated hearing her voice shake. Her side vision revealed he stood his ground. The moment she had been dreading gripped her core. "I thought you and Frank were off touring the orchard." She turned to search the yard, praying for a glimpse of Frank. "Where is he?"

"He wanted to look over the perimeter of the property. I walked back and left him the truck." He shifted from one foot to the other. "I'd like to talk to you for a moment, Clarissa."

No. I don't want to talk—not even for a moment. It was no use. Where was Elijah when she needed him? He had always been there to rescue her, watch over her. She was on her own, a torture of her own making.

She would try the innocent act first. "What about?"

He stuffed his hands in his blue jeans pockets, his face flushed. He squared is broad shoulders. "I think you know what about. I can't believe it's you standing there. It's been so long, yet it seems like yesterday."

If only it were yesterday. She would not have given in to her desperate love. Her father would not have kicked her out in shame, and she wouldn't have endured those devastating years of drought and storms. She would have had no debt to pay for her fall from grace. Then again, she wouldn't have James or Morgan. Or Frank.

She dropped Frank's wet shirt into the basket. "I don't want to bring up the past. I'm having a hard enough time dealing with my present."

He looked down and toed the ground with his boot. "I guess I just wanted to apologize for leaving town back then without telling you. I did write to you, but never heard back. I would have sent for you, Clarissa. You must know that after—"

She held up her hand. "Will… William. It's all over and done. We both have our own lives. We obviously weren't meant to be together." She paused to swallow with a dry tongue. "I really need to finish hanging the wash. If you'll excuse me." She blinked hard. If wishing had any power, he would vanish, but when she opened up her eyes, there he stood.

William stared at her like he had done all those years ago, only now his lips pursed into a smirk. She turned away. Her blood cooled to feel his gaze on her. The fluttering in her stomach told her what she already knew. It would be impossible to live near him and too risky to have him near James. How ironic that William had the power to give Frank what he dreamed of, and also had the power to ruin all their dreams. She shuddered to think William might have figured that out too.

"If that's the way you want it…"

His voice faded, and she risked one look to make sure he left.

His eyes found hers. "You know, you didn't have to run off with Frank so quick. Guess you didn't care for me like I thought." His jaw twitched.

Yes, I did have to go with Frank. You'll never know why.

He had his back to her by the time she thought to make a request. "Will?"

"Yes?"

"Are we agreed that Frank will not know about us?"

He paused, squinting. She would have to stake her bet that William wouldn't want to jeopardize his relationship with his brother. Her stomach knotted.

William's gaze traveled to the yard. She followed it to see Frank inching the truck toward them. She cleared her throat, and William finally turned his face to her.

"Sure, I guess so."

His gruff tone startled her. "Thank you, Will." It was the last time she would call him that, but there was one more thing she had to know. "May I ask why you didn't think it strange that Frank married a girl named Clarissa?"

He shrugged. "Our father didn't mention your name when he told me about Frank running off to get married. Didn't know you two knew each other."

"I see."

She returned to her basket of laundry when he stepped away. Her hands shook as she attempted to use a clothespin. She didn't know this man anymore, and in the deepest part of her, she questioned trusting him. Her tense muscles relaxed some when she heard the friendly exchange between the two men she watched with one eye.

"William, you have quite the spread here. Wandered around till I got to the edge of the vineyard. That's some cliff. I'll have to warn the boys about it." He shook his head. "It's so great to be on a functioning farm again."

"Glad you all are here. I'll need the help come harvest. Hard to be a one-man show." William glanced back at Clarissa and patted Frank on the back before heading for the big house.

She had to read William better—to know what kind of man he had become and what his plan might be. Her skin prickled when he looked at her. Surely he wouldn't risk losing a brother's love by betraying her secret. It wasn't as if he wanted her for himself. He didn't still care for her after all these years.

He couldn't.

Frank knelt next to William, feeling his knees sink into the soft earth. Since they'd arrived, he hadn't stopped deep-breathing in the rich sandy loam. That first day he had walked to the edge of the vineyard and stooped to grab up a handful of moist brown dirt, rubbing it between his palms. Never had he seen such productive soil. He wouldn't forget the gift it was to be here.

He had done his best to make something out of nothing—to make crops grow in powder-dry ground. His love of farming had faded long ago, but now he had been given renewed strength to go on.

"You clip it right here. See?"

Frank tucked his head under the vines, focusing where William placed the end of the slender shears. He had only a short time to learn the vineyard business before the harvest. Knowing how to trim the vines was one step of many to becoming a grower of grapes. Someday he hoped to have vines of his own to prune.

He focused on William's shears. "Yes. Why there?"

"You see the next row? You want that shape and density of your vines. Those were pruned last winter. I'm only showing you how it's done. Won't do it again till winter sets in and the plants are dormant."

Frank craned his neck and studied the shape and size of the vines in the row. "Yes, I see. What happens if you don't prune?"

William scooted out from under the branches and sat on the ground, resting his elbows on his knees. "Well, if you let the vines just continue to grow, they'll produce dense shade but little fruit. Heavy pruning provides the greatest quality of grapes. Knowing how to prune grapes can make the difference between a good crop and a bad one. You want to cut off as much of the old wood as possible to encourage the growth of new wood, which is where the best fruit is produced."

Frank sat opposite of William. "Wow. So much to learn." He scratched his head. "It's a good spiritual lesson, isn't it?"

William frowned. "What would that be?"

"Well, we have to keep ourselves pruned of the old man so the new man in Christ can flourish with good fruit. Otherwise, we're just a show of leaves with nothing good to offer anyone." He paused, wondering if William had forgotten their mother's teachings. "Like the stories Mom used to tell us." The memory of William's resistance to churchgoing flashed in Frank's mind. He would have to be careful with William's feelings about religion.

Tension floated in like a fog between them. William only stared at him, glassy eyed. Even though he'd argued his way out of attending most church services, Frank had thought his little brother understood the things of God. The grown man in front of him must have chosen a different path.

William pushed himself up from the ground. "Well, I'll leave such lessons to you. They never did much good for me."

Frank jumped up, keeping any further words about God for another time. They had so much to talk about, so many questions about how their lives had gone since they'd parted. Frank had always envied his risk-taking brother, especially when William suddenly left their hometown to chase bigger and better opportunities, sure and ambitious. If William had to get away from his father, Frank couldn't blame him. He would have done the same, as he never bonded with his ill-tempered stepfather. He'd never understood why his mother had married the man.

Frank scanned the vast acreage and spied the back of the cottage in the distance. The scene was something out of one of those fancy magazines on the newspaper stands in town. Except this was real, and he was a living part of the beauty, all thanks to his brother's generosity. He would work hard not to let him down.

He caught up to William. "I bet you never get tired of enjoying all this splendor."

William stopped. "What splendor?"

"This place. It's so beautiful."

William's lip curled up. "Just a way to make a living. Don't pay much attention to the—beauty, as you call it."

Frank tipped his head. "Really."

"You're too sentimental, brother. Always have been."

Frank chuckled but felt a twist in his stomach.

They strolled in silence down the next row of vines until Frank touched on a question that had burned in his mind. "William. Why did you leave town? We didn't hear much from you afterward. And you changed your name. Was Mom behind that?"

William slipped the shears into his back pocket and removed his straw hat. He didn't answer right away, his eyes darting as though he was filing through scenes from his past. After a few moments he faced Frank, his jaw twitching.

"I don't like thinking about those days. My decision to leave town was a mistake. Nothing worked out, and by the time I returned—there was no one—nothing left for me. Mother had passed on, you were gone and married, and dad—" He slapped his hat against his leg. "Well, he had been drinking himself to death for some time. We never did get along, and it only got worse when I came home broke and without a job."

Frank's chest burned. He hadn't realized things were bad after he'd left. The story sounded much like Clarissa's sister, Treena, and their father. He wanted to reach out and touch William's shoulder, but his arm hung tight to his side.

"I'm sorry, William."

"I took your name—Mother's name—because I hated him. He would come home drunk and want a fight. I was afraid to defend myself for fear of killing him. So I had to take a few licks until he passed out." He wiped his brow with his sleeve before replacing his hat. He chuckled and shook his head. "That man could make me so mad." He looked up to the sky. "When he died, I was glad. That's when I became William Wilding instead of Will Larson." He looked down the row of vines. "I still hate him. He did nothing for me except leave me a name that had a bad reputation in town. So I changed that."

"I wish you had written me a letter and explained all that, instead of just sending a telegram about Dad. I would have understood. I didn't like him much myself, but for Mom's sake, I pretended. He was the only father I ever really knew, so even though I wanted to like him, I just couldn't. I guess most stepsons feel that way."

Frank searched William's eyes. Yes, fiery anger blazed in them. Frank's throat thickened. He didn't know his half brother very well, but the book of his life opened just in the last few minutes. Frank felt a pang of guilt over being the lucky one. Lucky to have Clarissa and the boys. Even though the last four years were a challenge to his very soul, he at least had family. William had no one, a fact that stung Frank's sense of fairness.

William's eyes narrowed. "So how did you come to marry Clarissa? I didn't even know you were seeing anyone before I left. I just got settled in Chicago, and the next think I hear is that you married some pretty little thing. She didn't waste any time—I mean, you didn't."

A shiver crawled up Frank's arms at the chill in William's voice. It was almost as if he knew. But he couldn't possibly. He hadn't known Clarissa. Thanks to Clarissa's controlling father, she and Frank had only been distant friends, at least for her. She'd been more than that to him from the moment he laid eyes on her. He had been ready to give his whole heart, but she made it clear there was someone else in her life. Later, when she came to him and told him about her situation, his heart had burst with pain and love for her. She'd forbidden him to ask any questions.

Frank shook off the pity for his brother. "Just blessed, I guess. You might say it was a whirlwind romance. You had already left town by the time I convinced her to marry me. She's a prize for sure." It was all he could say. He had promised her not to disclose their history. It would only serve to make Clary unhappy if William was in on the secret. There was no reason for him to know.

William tipped his head while searching Frank's face. "Well, it's just curious that it happened so fast, but I guess it was for the best. She seems happy enough. And you seem content. You drew the long straw, I suppose. If I remember right, you always had the better luck of the Wilding men."

There it was again, that cold edge to William's voice. Frank supposed it was only natural for another man to envy his happy family, but he didn't like how the tone of the conversation had turned.

William strode ahead of him toward the big house. "I'll let you get to dinner with the boys. I can smell something good cooking from here." His long-legged steps quickened as he turned away from the path to the cottage. Frank waved him on, but his conscious nagged him. Why hadn't William ever married? He never had female companionship that Frank was aware of. It didn't seem right for him to be alone.

Frank stopped. "Why don't you join us?"

Without breaking his stride, William hollered over his shoulder. "Not today. See you in the morning."

Frank wiped perspiration from his forehead with his shirt-sleeve. How would he get to know a man as closed as William seemed to be? When he had met them at the train station, William seemed so happy to see them. Now Frank had a sliver of doubt his brother was still delighted they were there, and couldn't imagine what had changed. Perhaps he had inherited his father's moody ways.

The alluring aroma of meat cooking dissipated his doubts. He meandered to the cottage, planning ways to show William that he cared about him. Perhaps Clarissa would join in the quest to win him. Before their isolation over the last few years, she'd eagerly reached out to people in need, and William was in need.

"Hello." Clarissa stood in the open doorway, her face smudged with flour. Still a *pretty little thing*, as William put it. Any man would be envious.

Frank poked his nose in the air and filled it with savory smells. "What smells so good?"

"Roast chicken. The boys are about to burst, waiting for you to get back so they could eat." She brushed flour from her apron. "Even made fresh biscuits. Where were you?"

Frank brushed by her, wiping the powder from her nose. "With William, learning about vine pruning."

Her smile fell. "Oh. How is he doing with us here?"

"Great, I think." Frank sank into the kitchen chair. "Honey, I think he's a hard man. He's had a lonely life. I should have stayed in touch with him more."

"Lots of people are lonely. Looks like he's done well for himself. I wouldn't worry."

But he did worry. When Clarissa got to know him better, she would too.

Chapter 2

The morning clouds parted, letting sun shine through the streaked kitchen window. Clarissa frowned to think she had missed cleaning it. Her arms already ached from polishing the panes on the front of the house. She never used to tire so easily.

The constant huffs and sighs from the boys at the kitchen table rubbed on Clarissa's nerves. James finally verbalized a protest.

"Why do I have to know this stuff anyway?"

Clarissa pitched back the same old argument. "Because. If you're going to be a pilot like you always say, you'll need to know your arithmetic—and geography."

"Hey," Morgan chimed in. "*I* want to be a pilot. Like my mail pilot, Billy."

"He's not *your* mail pilot." James nudged Morgan with his elbow.

Although Clarissa had no intention of encouraging either of her sons to fly, she tossed the books in front of them at the kitchen table. "You'll both need arithmetic then. Get busy."

James mumbled just loud enough for her to hear, "Elijah didn't have no schooling, and he does just fine."

"Didn't have *any* schooling."

James peeked over his book and smiled. "Okay, okay. But I'm tired of sitting at the table with a stack of books."

Morgan scrunched his face as if to reinforce the sentiment.

She would have the same itch to move about if she were the one tied to schoolwork on such a nice day. They'd had such little opportunity to play outside the last several years. She longed to see them run and enjoy the usual boyish fun.

She waved her hands in the air. "All right, scoot." The birds chirping outside gave her permission to be lenient today. Besides, the bright sky beckoned her as well.

She followed as they scampered toward the door, pulling on shoes, likely headed for the barn. The immense structure had become their favorite place to take a break from book learning. She giggled to hear them whooping through the yard as she wandered down the path to the back of the cottage. After only a few minutes, the sun's hot rays penetrated her pale skin. She wound toward the garden and groaned at how the persistent weeds had popped though the rich soil since her last pulling session. What she guessed to be milk thistle and some sort of wild sage thrived with the occasional rain showers that rolled over the nearby Blue Mountains. A battle with weeds seemed petty compared to having no garden at all.

"As long as the yellow marigolds and strawberries come up, I'll pull weeds." It had been so long since she'd had hope for any life to grow at her hand. It seemed the only thing she could cultivate these days were lies and secrets.

Clarissa cringed at the prospect of continuing her charade, but for everyone's sake, she had to try. So far Frank had forgotten about their agreement to tell James that the father he loved was not his by blood. Only she knew the consequences of exposing the truth now. It would have to be a life or death matter before she would reveal anything on her own. She had to stick to her plan. If Frank mentioned talking to James, she would put him off. Suppose William discovered James' birthdate and figured out James could be his child? *So many ifs.*

Each time she heard William's voice, her stomach twisted.

The last several days had been a welcome relief from fear of running into him. He had taken a business trip to Spokane, leaving Frank to manage the place, working long days, hardly seeing the boys. She didn't mind, and took the opportunity to catch the boys up on schooling, hoping they would be ready for their appropriate grade come fall. *If* they were still here. Every day she prayed for somewhere else to live. It would take a miracle, or a tragedy, to move Frank.

She knelt to clear a large square of dark earth and lined it with rocks from the rows of apple trees behind the barn. The soil squeezed between her fingers like a soothing balm. The seed packets she kept in her apron pocket would finally be planted in moist soil. The vegetables the boys so desperately needed would soon grow, tall and green. They needed to be planted as soon as possible. She closed her eyes to imagine the bounty. Even William would get his share.

William. She sat down on the cold ground and stared at his big house. She would be living there if things had gone differently—if she had mustered up the courage to tell him back then she carried his child. The hair on her arms bristled. She wouldn't have been happy. Not with William. God had seen to it that she married a good man. She would spend the rest of her days in gratitude.

She closed her eyes to clear her head. Footsteps tromped to her right.

"Didn't know you were such a gardener."

William stepped in her line of sight, close enough that she could see perspiration on his forehead. When would he stop sneaking up on her? She slid her seed packets out of her apron pocket and onto the dirt in front of her, pretending to organize them. She took deep breaths to calm her racing heartbeat. She had become an expert at hiding her emotions in front of him.

"Hello, William. I didn't hear the car come up the drive."

"It didn't come up the drive. Ran out of gasoline back at the road. Had to walk."

She stood and brushed off her trousers.

His hands rested on his hips as he glanced around the yard. Sweat stained his gray shirt. "Where's Frank and the boys?"

"Frank's over at the end of the apple trees, resetting the limb props. I'm sure he'll be here any minute."

It wasn't true. Frank had several rows to tend to. She hoped her lie deterred William from hanging around. "The boys are playing in the orchard. I should call them back. I promised they could help me plant the seeds."

William smiled. "Never thought I would see you in trousers, getting your hands dirty. I remember you were always dressed so nice. You were such a delicate girl. Now look at you." He tipped his head to the side, still smiling.

Clarissa's face burned, but not from the sun. She hated him bringing up the past again. Her days of delicate girlhood were long gone. If she could leave them behind, he should.

"I'm not the same, William. Nothing's the same." She brushed back her loose strands of hair with her wrist. Her fingernails were crusted with dirt. He had been right about her changing from a city girl to a farm wife and mother. That was all he needed to know.

She looked toward the barn. "Guess you'll be fetching some gasoline for the car. I need to go look for the boys. Nice to see you."

"Is it?" He took one step closer.

She backed away, tripping on one of the rocks. She righted herself just as he reached for her. She felt his touch on her arm. In her momentum, she kept walking toward the barn, leaving William standing there. She didn't care about being rude. Distance was her aim, even if she had to stumble all the way across the yard.

Morgan met her halfway, running from the barn door. "Mama, come see what James found. Hurry."

He spit out the words and then bent over, coughing. Clarissa sprinted to his side. "Hands above your head, and slow breaths."

Morgan nodded and obliged. She held his scrawny arms and glanced over her shoulder. William stepped out of the shed, red gasoline can in hand, taking long strides toward the road.

"Easy. Better now?" She rubbed his back.

Morgan nodded and squirmed his hands away from her grip. "You have to see this thing. It's in there. Come on." He waved his arms.

She followed him after one last look at William trudging down the drive toward the road.

Clarissa couldn't keep up with Morgan. He had gained back just enough strength since his bout with dust pneumonia to stay well ahead of her. Once inside the weathered double doors, she searched the shadows for the boys. The midday filtered light played tricks on her line of sight. Three steps in, she saw Frank come in the other set of double doors opposite her. She opened her mouth to call to him, but he beat her to it.

"Clary, stay there." He dropped his tools and pointed to her while moving toward the corner of the barn. "James, stop!"

Clarissa's heart thumped. "What is it, Frank?"

Frank moved out of her sight into a shadow. She wasn't about to wait. Her adrenaline surged, dissolving her patience. She stepped into the partial darkness just in time to see James stuff his slingshot into his back pocket. He and Frank gazed up to the rafters. Morgan clung to his father's waist.

Clarissa crept up behind Frank. "What is it?"

He put fingers to his lips, then pointed up and to the far right. "We have a visitor."

James piped up. "I was gonna shoot him, but Daddy said not to. The thing looks so mean."

Frank scratched his head. "They usually roost in trees. Guess he likes the barn. Probably grabs up the mice in here."

After scouring the dirt floor for mice, Clarissa searched the rafters again and finally spied the object of the commotion. A beautiful hawk perched on the far end of a rafter, the color of his mottled feathers blending with the weathered wood tones. The creature blinked his steely gray eyes, as if to see right through her. Even in the filtered light she could see black talons gripping the thick beam. His head feathers were white like milk.

Frank pulled Morgan and James back a few feet. "It's a hawk. They're good to have around. They keep the birds from eating the fruit. But they aren't harmless, not with those sharp talons."

Clarissa slipped her arm through Frank's. "I'm with James. He looks mean. Could he hurt the boys?"

Frank shook his head. "Probably not, but it's best to leave him be."

Morgan scratched his head. "Sure is a pretty thing. I like him. I think I'll name him—Elijah."

James leaned down. "What? That's dumb."

Clarissa grabbed Morgan's hand. Her softhearted son still hadn't accepted saying goodbye to Elijah. "I think it's appropriate to name him after Elijah. It will remind us of our friend, right, Morgan?"

Morgan sighed. "I miss Elijah, Mama."

Frank and James turned and strolled toward the door, James shaking his head.

Clarissa's heart ached to talk about him. She couldn't imagine how hard it was on James. "I do too, Morgan."

"I wish he was here."

"Me too, dear."

Frank jumped out of bed at the sound of someone pounding

on the cottage door. The thuds resounded through the hallway. He pulled the table clock close to his face. Three a.m. He darted to the door, leaving Clarissa upright in bed, wide eyed and silent.

When Frank cracked the door open, William stood on the other side, buttoning his shirt.

"Temperatures dropped in the night. We need to check for frost. Late June is pretty rare to have one, but we need to find out for sure. Get dressed and meet me in the yard."

Frank slipped into the bedroom and dressed as quietly as he could. It was bad enough William had awakened Clary. The boys would never get back to sleep if they stirred.

Clary pulled the covers up around her neck. "What's going on?"

He pulled on his pants and whispered to her. "Have to go check for frost. Be back in a bit." He shook himself awake and grabbed a lantern from the screened porch on the side of the cottage. He lit it and set it on the rickety table by the screen door and buttoned his jacket. As he looked around, a fleeting idea passed through his mind. *The porch would make a great place for Clarissa to paint. With an easel and clean windows…* The picture faded when he heard William's voice.

"Frank, you coming?" Frank glanced out the dirt-smudged window to see William waving to him from the yard, holding his own lantern.

He wondered how they would ever be able to see in the dark with just two lanterns until he glanced up to see a bright moon and twinkling stars. The clear night and low temperatures were the combination for frost William had told him about.

He dashed down the yard to catch up with William. If they found frost, they would need help to set some smudge pots. It dawned on Frank that he had never seen hired help on the place since they'd arrived three weeks ago. Surely it wasn't possible to run a vineyard and orchard with just two men.

Frank followed William down the first row of vines. William held his lantern high in the air, inspecting both sides of the row. His forehead above his intense eyes creased with deep lines. Frank remembered feeling fear like that. Fear of losing another crop, another animal. Fear that another storm would steal your livelihood. Or your child.

"You go down a few rows and take a look. I'll head over to the apple trees." William turned from Frank and jogged toward the grove along the cliff.

Frank hollered at him. "Be careful. Don't fall over the edge in the dark."

"Just get going. We need to move fast."

He had often wondered why there wasn't a stretch of fence along the cliff's edge. The drop to the river was steep and rocky. Not the best place for children, and he had warned the boys several times to stay away. Besides, the rocky terrain was home to rattlesnakes who liked to bask in the thermal warmth.

Frank rounded the corner of another row of vines. He raised his lantern and scanned for any sign of crystals or a glassy covering on the leaves. His pulse pounded in his ears to think he might see something amiss. What could two men do against Mother Nature? He had learned the hard way that when she came upon you with vengeance, only God could salvage the damage.

William called from the distance. "It all looks good back here. You see anything?"

"No. All—"

William's cry split through the still night air. It echoed down the gulch, sending chills up Frank's back.

He knew exactly what had happened. He broke into a sprint, his lantern giving off jiggling light rays ahead of him. He reached the edge of the cliff to see William's lantern on its side in the dirt. Leaning over the rim, he could see William's hands clinging to a branch a few yards from the top. Each time he struggled, his grip slipped. He dangled above the steepest part of the ravine face, with sharp rocks looming below. Frank shuddered at the possibility of William losing his hold.

Frank set his lantern down and righted William's, placing it near the edge to light the ravine. He flopped onto his belly and stretched his arm as far as he could reach. A sharp rock dug into his side, but he stretched harder.

"Grab my hand!"

William stilled and took a deep breath. His hand crept toward Frank's until their fingers touched.

"Reach, William!"

Frank could feel William's fingers shaking as he attempted to take hold of Frank's hand.

"Come on!" Frank wiggled his torso until he was able to extend his arm farther. The rock under his ribs scraped his skin through his shirt. Dirt and rocks tumbled again as William slipped a foot away. Frank couldn't see what was directly below now. William needed another rock to brace his foot on, or he would continue to descend.

A few seconds ticked by, then William grunted and thrust his arm up to meet Frank's hand. Dirt and gravel ground into Frank's elbow as he grabbed William's arm and pulled him closer. Frank winced at the sound of rocks rolling down the ravine. He bumped the lantern with his elbow, and the glow shed light on William.

"I can see a crevice by your left foot. Can you feel it?"

William slid his foot to the spot Frank described and dug his boot in, thrusting himself up to the top. Frank pulled with all his strength to drag him the rest of the way over the rim. William's body landed hard next to him, and they both lay in silence for a moment.

William panted between coughs. "That was close, huh?"

"Yep." Frank's arm quivered—as did his heartbeat.

"William, what would you have done without help?"

"Don't know."

William lay on his back as Frank stood and gathered the lanterns. He held up the light to see William's face. "You okay?"

William stood and brushed off his trousers. "Am now. Thanks."

They strolled toward the yard through the vines, William with a slight limp. The sun peeked over the horizon as if to check on them, easing Frank's pounding heart. The adrenaline had given way to a calm gratitude. If he hadn't been there… He didn't want to imagine.

Frank breathed in the fresh morning air. How blessed William was to have sunshine and wet earth to grow things. A world far away from the dust and drought, a contrast of abyss and paradise. Seeing the sun come up over the hills each morning, he knew he had done the right thing by coming here. Besides, William needed him, and he knew what it was like to need help and not get it.

"Do you usually have hired hands around this time of year?"

William turned to smile at him. "I wait as long as possible to hire help for the season. Don't want to pay wages for those people to just sit around doing nothing. It's nice to have you here though. Extra hands are well appreciated."

Frank wondered who *those people* were. Did he mean migrant workers, or was he thinking more specific? The phrase soured him, but also gave him an idea. Why hadn't he thought of it before?

"Well, I might know of someone who wouldn't cost you much, and he's great help."

William huffed. "Frank, James is a little young for this sort of work." William patted Frank on the back as they entered the yard.

"No, not James. There was a drifter fellow that came by the homestead while I was away for a few weeks. He helped Clary and the boys a lot. I owe him a debt. I think he would come for room and board."

"Don't like having strangers around. But maybe if you'll vouch for his character—"

"Oh, he's trustworthy. And the boys love him." Truth was, he didn't know Elijah very well himself. He hesitated to say more, but Clary and the boys would never be so crazy about someone who wasn't a good man. The overall proof of Elijah's character had been in the way he stuck by Frank's little family through all the storms and helped more than could be asked of any man—especially a homeless drifter.

William parted from Frank and stopped at the back steps to the big house. "I'll think about it." His tone didn't spark hope in an ultimate affirmative answer.

Frank refrained from trying to sell Elijah's good points. The suggestion had been a generous offer, and it would be up to William to decide. "Sure. Night—or rather, morning."

William waved and disappeared through the door. Frank yawned and stood to admire the cottage. Clary was right—it needed some care. He trudged to the side porch. The door squeaked as he gently shut it. He plopped down on the wicker-backed chair and slipped off his boots. No sense stomping the house awake. He reached to touch his side. It stung, and he pulled his hand away to see a slight smear of blood. Something he would have to hide from Clary.

Elijah's face came to mind. Wouldn't it be something for him to show up and surprise Clary and the boys? If William agreed, he would send for him. William couldn't possibly understand how hard things were for them in Kansas, and what a help Elijah had been. His only concern was that Elijah had moved on from the Johnson place.

The glow of a rising sun filtered into the porch. He leaned back and let it soak the walls of the cottage with warmth and hues of gold and pink. Cobwebs glistened in the corners where the frame of the screens met the stone. Piles of dusty boxes and stacks of old newspapers filled one end of the room. It wouldn't take much to turn the area into a nice painter's studio. The concrete floor could be washed easily, and he could board it in for wintertime. If Elijah were here, they could finish it up in no time.

"Elijah here. Wouldn't that be something?" he whispered into the stillness.

The sound of rattling dishes and a cupboard door shutting drew Frank's attention. He left his muddy boots and tiptoed to the kitchen doorway. Clary was still in her nightgown and robe, making the morning coffee. The bread she'd baked last evening was on the counter, ready to be sliced and jellied.

He had teased her as she kneaded the dough. "Aren't you going to make cornbread anytime soon?"

Her shoulders shuddered. "Never. Or at least not for a long, long time. The boys and I have eaten enough cornbread to last the rest of our lives."

He knew she was thankful for her new stove, and as far as he was concerned, she need never bake cornbread again. She had a way with baking, and she had always hoped for a little girl to hand down her recipes to. Perhaps someday a daughter-in-law would fill the gap in her heart.

He snuck up behind her. "Smells good." He nuzzled her neck to smell lavender soap.

She jumped back and into his arms. "Frank. Don't *do* that."

He stifled laughter and kissed her cheek. "Sorry. I'm going back to bed. Tell me when the coffee's done."

She frowned, nudging him away. "You'll smell it. I'm going to sit at the table and answer Treena's letter."

"She still in Kansas City?"

Clarissa nodded as she pulled the envelope from her robe pocket. "Far as I know, she never made it back to New York."

Her sister's letter. He had forgotten about the will. Clary would be coming into some money soon, but taking care of their father's estate wasn't the only reason Treena stayed in Kansas, or so Clary had voiced as suspicion.

Frank yawned again. "Tell her hello from me."

"Go to bed. But be quiet and don't wake the boys," she whispered.

The sun sneaked in through the window, lighting up her darkening blond hair. She seemed content at last. Leaving her precious homestead had been hard for her. She deserved a nicer place than this, but it would be years before they could do any better—and they would never be able to afford a house like William's.

Frank dropped his trousers and crawled under the covers. His eyelids fell shut. He lay and envisioned the studio for Clarissa on the back porch. If she wasn't happy yet, she would be when she saw her painting room. Getting back to her talents might soften the pain of leaving her babies behind. He would make it a nice space so she would want to stay here for a long time.

Even though they hadn't talked about their future much, he hoped she would want to make this their permanent home.

He certainly did.

The cottage danced with an excitement Clarissa couldn't explain. She stood still at the door to the porch as she had been instructed. The tweed rug scratched the bottom of her bare feet. Morgan wiggled beside her, giggling like a little girl. Her skin itched under the blindfold James had wrapped around her head. She didn't dare remove it after a strict admonishment not to.

Morgan tugged on her arm. "Don't peek, Mama."

She grunted. "I'm not peeking. Can we hurry this up? Dinner will burn." She felt for the top of his head and patted it.

"Who cares about dinner?" Frank called from the other side of the door. "Be patient."

She had a vague idea what was going on, but decided to go along with the game Frank and the boys had cooked up. She had been after Frank to clean up the screened porch so they could sit out there on nice summer days and have dinner. Her vision of curtains and a few house plants sent her heart soaring with gratitude for this place to live—this clean green countryside. If only they could stay.

A breeze from the door opening brushed her face, then Frank's voice came near. "We're ready." He scooted close to her and touched her elbow, guiding her over the threshold and onto the concrete floor of the porch. She could smell fresh paint. Why? Her eyes strained to find a flaw in the blindfold, some pinpoint of light to see something—anything. Wrinkling her nose didn't help. Frank's strong hands on her shoulders guided her in position.

"Ready to take off the blindfold?"

She huffed and rested her hands on her hips. "Yes, yes."

Frank's hand touched the back of her hair as he untied the knot of the scarf. It slid down her face and down to the floor just as the boys shouted in a chorus.

"Ta-dah!"

Her blurred vision focused as she blinked. Before her was the room of her dreams—not for sitting or eating dinner. For painting. Her knees buckled, and she grabbed James' shoulder to steady herself. A large easel towered in the corner, below it a stool made of smooth pine. Next to that, on a small three-legged table, were mason jars filled with brushes and pencils of all sizes and colors. She shuffled over to the arrangement and ran her fingers over the framed empty canvases leaning against the freshly painted wall.

"Mama, don't you like it?" Morgan was suddenly beside her, his eyes pleading.

She wanted to speak the words of gratitude bubbling up from her chest, but tears clogged her throat. She nodded and wrapped her arms around Morgan's shoulders and pulled him close. The rest of the room was clean and polished. In the other corner of the room were two chairs made of honed tree branches, and a table to match.

Frank strolled over and sat in one of the homemade chairs. "Now you know why I locked up the porch and why me and the boys kept disappearing on you the last few days. We had a real furniture-making plant in the barn." He slapped the arm of the chair. "Not the most comfortable, but we figured you could make—"

The dam of burning tears broke through. Her hands found her face, and she sobbed into them, tears dripping off her chin. Frank stood behind her while she cried and laughed at the same time, his arms tight around her shoulders. Small hands patted her back. Morgan always hated seeing her cry. She opened her eyes to see it was James who comforted her. She let go of Frank and twirled around to hug James and then tucked Morgan under her other arm.

The room mirrored her mother's small studio. Memories of canvases and sketches washed over her, the best long days of her youth spent watching her mother's mastery—the hours ticking by like a tired clock.

"Thank you all so much for a perfect studio."

"Whew." Morgan wiped his forehead in a grand gesture. "I was afraid you were mad, the way you were carrying on."

James wiggled out from under her embrace and into one of the tree-branch chairs.

"Mama never gets mad. You should know she's just happy." He frowned at Morgan.

Never got mad? Is that what James thought? She must have done well at hiding all the times back home when she'd battled anger toward Frank and his absence—when she'd screamed at the approaching storms and balled her fists to see the piles of sand on her front porch. *Mad?* Yes, more often than they knew.

"Well, I'll show you how mad I can get if we don't get in the kitchen to eat dinner." She shook her finger at Morgan, then turned and winked at James.

Frank raised his hand to his forehead in a salute. "Yes, ma'am."

The boys raced each other into the kitchen. Clarissa grabbed Frank's arm as he tried to follow. She pulled him close to her.

"You and the boys did a fine job. Thank you," she whispered.

"Welcome," he whispered back. He pushed her to arm's length. "Why don't you take a minute and make sure we thought of everything you need. I'll dish up the boys."

His weighty tone confirmed what she knew about Frank. He truly wanted the room to be just right for her. At the homestead he did everything for her, trying his best to please her. Hauling rocks to place around her dying flower beds, the new green paint on the front porch, and even the white picket fence around her babies' graves had been engineered to her specifications.

Her stomach knotted. The meager thank-yous she had offered him then were inadequate payment for his acts of love. Proof of his love wasn't in surprising her with the studio. It was in his presence—the essence of his gift to gather his family together. She had missed seeing it but wasn't about to miss appreciating it from now on.

She picked through the clear jars filled with brushes and examined the colored pencils. Her mother would have made a masterpiece with tools like these.

"What if I can't do it?"

You can. Just try. Take a risk.

She let go a tension-filled breath. Laughter and men's voices rang from the kitchen. As she stepped in to see the source of the commotion, there stood William with his hand on James' shoulder. Frank pulled up another chair to the table.

No.

All pleasant anticipation of a family meal melted away— the laughter that should have been hers to enjoy stolen by an intruder. The sight of William with James was enough to ruin her joy over the painting room. She had to stop thinking of this man as her enemy, but every time he came near her son, she felt the pinch of past pain and the fear of future disaster.

"Honey, we talked William into joining us for dinner. It's all on the table. Come and sit."

She forced her lips to curl up. Eating with her guts churning would be a trick. Entertaining William without showing her disdain would be nothing short of a miracle.

"The boys tell me they made you a painting studio." William crossed his arms on his chest. "Didn't know you were an artist too."

If her scowl could have shot daggers, they would have at this moment. She froze, searching faces to see if anyone caught his meaning.

"What do you mean—too?"

Frank's frown iced her hands.

William glanced at Frank and then back at her. "Well, I meant that she does so many other things well, I was surprised she could paint too." His voice wavered as he shot a cold glance at Clarissa.

Liar.

Clarissa fought the urge to say something sarcastic. Instead she smiled.

"Why thank you, William." She sauntered toward the table.

William jumped to pull the chair out for her.

She avoided his eyes and pulled her chair close to Morgan.

"Mama, will you paint something soon?"

In her peripheral vision, she saw William sit at the end of the table. He dare not say another word that might give her away, or he would see just how fast he would be uninvited.

James set a pot in the middle of the table. "You could paint the hawk in the barn."

"Good idea." Morgan stuffed his napkin in his shirt. "Could you, Mama?"

She tousled his hair. "Sure."

William leaned his elbows on the table and shook his head. "Didn't know there was a hawk in the barn. Don't like the things."

Silence stilled the air. The look of horror on James' face prompted Clarissa to break in.

"So, James—why don't we work up a study on hawks for your next school lesson?"

Frank stepped up next to the boy and nudged him. "Another good idea."

William leaned back in his chair and smiled at Clarissa. She didn't care. He wasn't a part of this family, and if wishes came true, he never would be.

Chapter 3

*S*he couldn't remember the last time she had precious hours to herself. Hours to do whatever she wanted. With the men and boys all in town for the day, her chance to be productive had been fruitful. Her new art room sparkled from dusting and scrubbing. The slender paint brushes and freshly sharpened pencils leaned against each other in the mason jars she'd tied with ribbons. The gauze fabric she'd hung on the south window filtered the brightest light, turning the room into a studio fit for creating without glare.

She finished organizing with just enough time to sketch a likeness of the cottage for her first composition. With the last stroke of the pencil, she stepped back.

"Mother would like this." She glanced to the wood tray holding a dozen tubes of various vibrant colors. Frank and the boys had done well to pick the richest colors for her surprise art studio. All the supplies explained the mysterious trip to town Frank and the boys had taken last week. She reached for an unopened tube.

"She always started with green."

Her hands shook as she opened a tube of the deep-olive hue. Sketching was one thing—attempting to paint as well as her mother was something she had longed for since she was a child. Sneaking into her mother's studio was like stepping into a candy shop. Canvas images, many half-finished, leaned against the walls and tables. The pungent smell of oil paints and turpentine sometimes made her dizzy, but she would cover her nose and mouth with a handkerchief in order to stay. She'd have done anything to spend time with her mother and avoid her father—a fact she hadn't realized until now.

"You'll get used to the smell," her mother would say.

Clarissa's hand shook as she held the paint-laden brush above the sketch. One mishap and her picture would be ruined. No, just not as perfect as she needed it to be.

She stepped back from the canvas. "Every artist needs to accept flaws in their work. That's what Mother always said."

But it wasn't so simple. She had to take a break. Just finishing the sketch was enough for now. She would have to work up more nerve to actually put oils to the canvas. The turpentine-soaked cloth turned deep green as she squeezed the paint from the brush. Everything tucked back in it place, she placed a drape over the evidence of tentative talent.

She enjoyed the view through the screen for a few minutes, and when her eyes scanned the yard and landed on the big house, her whim took flight. She found herself standing under the walnut tree next to William's back steps. She looked to her left and her right.

Don't do it, Clarissa. It's not right for you to snoop.

Despite the truthful sentiment, her curiosity burrowed in deep and set her feet in motion. She made one last inspection of the yard to make sure she wasn't seen. "A quick peek can't hurt."

The copper doorknob turned hard but was unlocked. She pushed the weathered five-panel door until it creaked all the way open, the sunlight exposing the dirty yet intricate tile flooring. She had never seen such a unique pattern, even in the city homes around Father's house.

She ventured in as far as the archway to the dining room. "Oh my word."

It was as regal and ornate as she had imagined. A gilded chandelier hung heavy with crystals from the center of a matching circular medallion on the ceiling. The room was dark and cool. She rubbed her bare forearms. Something more than the coolness of the room sent shivers onto her skin.

"You shouldn't be in here. You're trespassing," she whispered into the immense space.

She backed her way out of the room, catching sight of the parlor to her left. Just one peek and then she would go back to the cottage before the men got home. The last thing she needed was for William to see her in his house.

Hurry up and soak in the glamour. It's the last you'll see of it.

She planted her feet just inside another archway and leaned in to survey every cobwebbed corner. Taking in the velvet furniture and large secretary desk, she tried to imagine herself living in such luxury. William didn't seem the type to appreciate such nice things. They didn't even belong to him. The landlords must trust him to—

Her heart skipped a beat as her eyes focused on the west wall. There, hanging on top of the gaudiest green-and-gold wallpaper she had ever seen, was a simply framed painting. A garden scene so familiar to her, it bathed her in warmth. Her knees wobbled as she stepped closer to the artwork. Creeping along the woven Persian rug, she was finally close enough to see the signature: S. M. Tate.

"What? Mother?"

Incredulous, she blinked and looked again. Yes, it was her mother's name by her hand. And yes, she recognized it as the one hanging in the hallway near her mother's bedroom. She hadn't paid much attention to it then. It had been hung just before her mother died and everything fell apart. Her mind raced with possible scenarios of how it had ended up in William's house.

Well, it really isn't William's house. He says he has landlords. Does that mean this is their house? Then Mother's painting belonged to them. It explained nothing.

The faraway rumble of the truck coming up the drive took her breath. No time to examine the picture more closely. She spun around and ran to the back door. Pulling it shut behind her took all her strength. It stuck just short of latching. The truck was closer. Any second it would come through the shadows of the locust trees. She held on and leaned back hard. The latch clicked, though not solidly. The screen door slammed as she stumbled down the steps and into the yard, the vision of the painting etched in her mind.

Get your breath. Act casual. She straightened her shirt and strolled toward the cottage, as if coming home from a leisurely walk through the vineyard.

The truck ground to a stop just a few yards from her. Morgan sat in the cab between William and Frank, and he leaned across Frank to wave the huge, colorful candy sucker in his hand. "Mama, look. Uncle William bought it for me."

She forced a grin, but her eyes glared at Frank, who peered through the window of the truck door. His sheepish smile satisfied her that he was remorseful, or at least apologetic.

"Don't you eat all of that at once. Just a piece for now and save the rest for tomorrow." Her insides shook from her near miss at being caught poking around William's house. If she hadn't, she would never have known about the painting. Now to figure out the answer to the mystery. The only one who could explain it was William, and if Frank saw it, the mystery would be irrelevant in the culmination of her ever-hovering fears of exposure.

Leave it alone. Act normal.

James crawled out of the back of the truck with a brown paper bag in his hand.

Clarissa tilted her head to one side. "Don't tell me. You got a bag of candy to ruin your teeth too. Same rules go for you, young—"

He held out the bag to her, face frozen in blankness. She knew the look. She had made him mad.

"It's all right, James. You don't have to give it to me. I trust you to manage it."

"Take it. It's for you." He stepped closer, the bag dangling from his outstretched hand.

Frank leaned on the truck door. William rested his elbows on the hood, staring and grinning. James' face also broke into a broad smile.

"What?" She gingerly took the sack from his grip and glanced once more at Frank, hoping for a clue to what was happening. The last time James brought her something was the scrawny turkey he'd shot while hunting with Elijah. She wanted to revel in the memory a bit, but curiosity set in.

She untwisted the top of the bag and opened it, keeping her face at a distance in case of a prank. The sweet smell of brown sugar and butter escaped, and the aroma found its way straight to her heart. She peeked in to see if her senses were correct.

"Raisin spice cake! Where did this come from?" She reached in and pinched a crumb from the treat she had loved as a child. She often told the boys and Frank of her grandmother's special recipe. She slid the bite onto her already salivating tongue and savored the rich cinnamon, the spongy texture.

Morgan clapped his hands. James winked at Frank, who stepped up beside Clarissa.

Frank laughed. "It was the boys' idea. We saw it in the window of the local bakery and couldn't resist. Of course the candy shop was next door."

Morgan licked his candy. "Mama, you should have seen all the stores that had to close because of the de—depress…"

Frank finished for him. "Depression." He looked at Clarissa. "It is sad. So many people having to move on. Just like at home. Banks closing—it really is tough for some people." He nodded at William. "So glad we have a place to live and work."

William ignored Frank's remark and addressed Clarissa. "How's the cake?"

She pinched off another morsel and fed it to Frank, then turned to the boys, purposefully slighting William. "I love it. Thanks, boys. I guess you can have all the candy you want for bringing me this." She saw William out of the corner of her eye. He still stared but had lost his smile.

If he knew what she had been up to, he would likely be furious. If she thought bribing him with the rest of her cake would get him to tell her about the painting, she would gladly give it up, no matter how sweet it tasted.

The sunlit ground turned dark. Everyone looked to the sky.

William grabbed a bag of groceries from the bed of the truck and slammed the driver's-side door shut—shouting orders. "Looks like a squall of rain coming. James, take the groceries in the cottage. Frank, open the barn door for the truck."

Clarissa reached for Morgan's arm and pulled him through the cottage door. James marched close behind, juggling two large sacks. A torrent of large drops pelted the ground just as they shut the door. Morgan ran to the window and gazed wide eyed at the deluge.

He waved James over. "Have you ever seen so much rain?"

James set the bags on the table and sauntered over just long enough to give a casual glance out the window. "Of course I have. You were too young to remember. It's just rain. It'll stop soon."

Clarissa watched his face. In his expression was etched the dry harsh reality of his words. It had been so long since they'd experienced the wetness and chill of a soaking rain. She hated that her boys had missed so many simple pleasures others took for granted. James could pretend all he wanted, but she knew he was as excited as his brother.

Morgan scowled at James. "No it won't. It's going to rain for a long time. Maybe forever."

James fired back. "You'll see. It won't last long. It will probably just make a muddy mess."

He looked toward the window, and Clarissa wondered if he remembered the days before the drought when the rains made mud for him to play in. He would bring the packed patties into the kitchen and ask her to bake them. He'd been around five—so long ago.

Morgan turned and flopped into the chair by the window. His joy seemed to have vanished with James' words. He jumped up and ran into her studio, slamming the door between it and the kitchen. Clarissa opened her mouth to stop him, but let him have his solitude. She imagined he would sit by the door and watch the rain as long as it lasted. If he were a well child, she would let him go outside to play in it. Morgan deserved some mud pie time too.

She took one more bite of her cake before placing the sack on the top shelf in the cupboard. She caught James by the shoulder as he headed for the bedroom. "You shouldn't argue about little things with your brother. He's so sensitive, and he doesn't always know not to take you seriously."

"I know. Sorry. It's just that he's such a baby about some things." He trudged into the bedroom.

Clarissa brushed the crumbs from her shirt and shook her head. James was growing up so fast, and the distance between him and his brother would also grow. Morgan's attachment to James would be tested soon. He'd been trying so hard to keep up with his big brother. Her only hope was that this would be a time for Morgan to find his own way, whether here or in their own place away from this vineyard.

She opened the door to the porch and scanned the studio. Morgan had disappeared.

He's outside in the rain.

She opened the screen door to see Frank and William walking from the barn.

"Frank! Morgan is out there somewhere. Will you find him and bring him in the house?"

Frank's face echoed her rising panic. Morgan's vulnerability to colds and respiratory illness signaled her stomach to quiver.

"I'll find him," Frank hollered back. He looked around for a moment and turned to run toward the shed.

William hesitated, watching Clarissa for a few seconds, then marched to the back steps of his house. Wasn't he going to help? She hadn't seen his lack of compassion when they were young. It wasn't likely a new development to his character—just proof of her blind devotion back then.

She shut the door and hurried into the kitchen to strike up the stove to heat the small space. The clouds and rain had done their job, adding dampness to the cottage. Morgan would be soaking wet and in need of extra warmth. He must have been intent on his mission, risking a chest cold. She rubbed her temples to push away the same old worry over her youngest.

What in the world was he thinking, running off that way? She thought back to their conversation. It must have been something James said.

Something about the rain going away.

Frank tried not to let the frantic feeling in his gut take over, but finding Morgan walking around behind the shed shook him to the core. The boy's clothes were drenched and his body already wrenching with coughs. Frank swooped him up in his arms and jogged to the house, not taking time to scold.

He burst through the back door and deposited Morgan on the kitchen table. Frank couldn't tell if his son was crying or if a wash of rain covered his face.

Morgan's whole body shivered. "I'm sorry, Mama."

Clarissa peeled off his clothes and hung them over a chair. She wasn't speaking at all, just working quickly to dry Morgan, her lips pursed. She wrapped him in a blanket, and Frank sat him in a chair, moving it closer to the stove.

Clarissa leaned down to tuck in the blanket around his hips. "Are you warmer now?"

Morgan nodded. His bluish lips stuck to his chattering teeth. He kept his chin down, but his eyes moved from one parent to the other. Frank held back a reprimand in favor of asking why Morgan had run off in the rain. Clary seemed content with nurturing rather than scolding.

Still, Frank needed to ask. He knelt beside Morgan. "Son, what were you thinking, going out there to get soaked?"

Morgan's lip quivered. "I had something I needed to do." His cough boiled up, shaking his thin frame.

Clarissa stood and squinted at Frank, shaking her head slightly. He wouldn't press the boy anymore. It wasn't important.

"Where's James?"

Clarissa motioned to the bedroom door cracked open a few inches. Strange that James had remained in his room instead of checking on his brother. Frank took off his wet boots and meandered to James' door. He tapped twice, then pushed it open. James lay on his bed, reading a book.

"Hey, James."

"Hey, Dad." James didn't look up as he turned a page.

"Morgan's fine, if you want to know." Frank bit his lip. It wasn't exactly what he wanted to say, but his patience waned. His relief opened up the dam of fatigue he'd been holding back the whole long day. The week had been demanding on his muscles.

James' jaw twitched.

Frank took the clue to inch closer to the bed. Not only did he not know why Morgan had run off, but he had no idea what was eating James. Fine father he was. He had failed his promise to Clary to spend more time with the boys. Yet hadn't the day in town with William meant anything?

He sat on the edge of the bed and tugged at the book. "Something bothering you?" He used his softest tone. "Want to tell me?"

James let the book come to rest on his lap. He turned away and stared out the window. The rain still streaked over the windowpane, like a soothing shower. The air hung thick with dense humidity and proximate tension. Frank waited for James to explain his mood. Maybe there was no explanation. He remembered what it was like trying to become a man, stumbling through the dark maze of questions and emotions.

"Well, if you ever want to talk, I'm here." Frank stood and took a few steps to the door.

"You're hardly *ever* here."

James' voice could barely be heard over the spattering of rain drumming on the window. Frank spun around. It was true. He had felt it in his heart the last few days. Here, but absent. Off trying to make things happen for this family instead of letting God place his steps in the path already imprinted for him.

Frank shuffled to the edge of the bed. "You're right, son. I'm sorry."

James tossed the book aside and pushed himself up to sit. "I don't want special attention like Morgan gets. I just thought that when we got to Washington, we would at least do things together. You're always working with Uncle William, and Mother is either fussing with Morgan or working on the cottage—like it's something special." He turned to the window again. "It's not even our place. It's not even Uncle William's place. He lives alone in that big house, and we're cramped up in here."

Frank's temples pulsed. He hung his head, trying to conjure up words to satisfy James' disappointment. What words did the boy need to hear? He hadn't expected James to go through the usual adolescent phase of selfishness and rebellion. It would have been logical that the years of growing up with demanding expectations would have matured him faster. Now Frank had to deal with James' thoughts of entitlement.

"James, we can't just barge in and expect to live in the big house. I'm just a hired man around here."

Frank paused. No response. "We've all been through so much in the last few years. Your mother and I had been caught in the middle of something we didn't know how to deal with. No one could. The drought and terrible storms kept us down, and we just couldn't seem to find rest. Then when Morgan got so sick, we knew we had to stop trying to fight life on our own. We thought coming here was leading us to a better life for you boys." Frank positioned himself to be face to face with this soon-to-be man. "You must admit we are better off here."

James' eyes brimmed with moisture. He nodded curtly. At least he was listening.

"We don't always do things right. We haven't—I haven't always given you the attention you deserve." He paused to swallow down tears. "I guess I need to slow down and watch for that leading more often. I'm a stubborn man. You probably will be too."

Or would he be? Who knew what traits James had inherited? He might turn out to be someone Frank wouldn't recognize. The realization made his heart thump against his chest. Should he tell him now? He could call Clarissa in and—

Clarissa pushed the door open. "Frank, I need your help with Morgan. His cough is bad."

Her face paled before his eyes. Frank's instinct was to jump up and run out of the room, but he couldn't move. There was something he still needed to say to James.

"I'll be right there."

Clarissa's eyes shifted from Frank to James, panic glistening in them. She backed out of the bedroom and shut the door. He knew what she was thinking. He couldn't have this talk without her permission. It would have to wait.

James scooted to the edge of the bed and swung his legs over. "It's okay. Morgan needs you."

"I'm not leaving until I tell you something. I love you, James. You're a fine young man, not a boy anymore. I'll make certain we have good times together from now on. We need it, don't you think?" Frank nudged James hard. He waited for an answer, hoping for more than just an ambiguous nod.

James locked his gaze on Frank's face. "We sure do need it." He stood and straightened his shoulders. "Maybe I could teach you how to hunt with slingshot. Elijah taught me."

Frank let out all the pent-up air in his lungs. He detected a slight curl of James' lips. He stood and put his arm around him. "I'd love that. It's about time you taught your old man something, and about time for some rabbit stew."

"I'll teach you how to make one, just like Elijah taught me."

He felt James' arm reach around his waist. It had been too long between embraces. They walked together into the kitchen.

Clarissa knelt next to Morgan at the kitchen table with a bucket of steaming water. She had covered Morgan's head with a towel and helped him bend over to breathe in the soothing heat.

Frank let go of James and knelt next to Morgan's chair. "How you doing, son?" He stole a glance at Clarissa. Her cheeks were red, her usual sign of worry. He stood and took her chin in his hand. "Go sit down for a bit. I'll sit with him, then we'll put him to bed."

She blinked, and a tear escaped. She shuffled to the front of the open room and sat in one of the big overstuffed chairs. She seemed to melt into it, wiping her eyes with her apron. James took a few steps toward her. Frank took the opportunity to reach out to him. "I could use your help." He raised his brows and looked deep into James' eyes.

James glanced at his mother. "Sure. What can I do?"

"Fill the kettle with more water and start it heating. We'll replace the water in the bucket as it cools."

James nodded and went to work. While he filled the kettle, he spoke to Morgan.

"Remember that time Elijah took Amos down to the cellar during a storm? We had a heck of a time getting him out, didn't we, Morgan?"

Frank smiled at James' attempt to cheer up his ailing brother. Morgan tried to giggle before another cough erupted.

Clarissa leaned over the side of the chair. Her smile was the stamp of approval he hoped for. Frank's tired muscles twitched with new energy. This was where he needed to be at this moment. His striving had to stop for his family's sake. William would have to understand. Frank would speak to him about making more family time. They needed him now even more than back on the homestead.

There was another they needed also.

The mud must have been two inches deep after another morning rain today. Clarissa loved the smell of it and waded through the slippery slop from the mailbox to the cottage. The driveway from the road still harbored shallow puddles jiggling in the breeze, making it impossible to avoid sinking into the mire. At least the sun had appeared, and temperatures soared toward the seventies. She imagined the boys working with Frank in the orchard, getting mud-caked from head to toe. She had protested Morgan going with Frank, but his cough had subsided, and he had no fever.

"You bring him right home if he starts feeling bad," she had instructed Frank.

She kicked off her slimy boots and left them on the front porch. Her stomach fluttered just holding another letter from Treena. The return address was marked Kansas City. She hoped this envelope held more than just chitchat about Treena's escapades. She didn't mind her sister's ramblings, but more news of an inheritance would be an encouragement to her plan to leave the vineyard.

"She must have decided to stay there permanently." She tossed the few pieces of random mail on the table and took the letter to the big chair. The legal-sized envelope felt thick and heavy. Treena had promised to mail a copy of their father's will, so this had to be it. She slid her fingernail under the flap and pulled out a bundle of papers stapled together. Unattached to the rest was Treena's handwritten note to her. She laid it on the arm of the chair.

The heading on the top page sent shivers up her arms. *Last Will and Testament of Marcus J. Tate.*

Her hands shook to hold it. The emotion of his passing had long worn off, or so she had thought, until now. She hurried to read through the first page. On the second page, her tears erupted, making the words blur into a sea of black and white. It was a list of all his possessions, monetary gifts to charities, and then a few paragraphs of cold legalities. Still nothing about his daughters.

She let go of the papers and wiped her eyes. *Take a deep breath. He can't hurt you anymore.*

The last page, after all the legal dissertation, simply stated her father's wishes.

Once all debts have been satisfied, any remaining estate shall be divided equally between my two daughters, Treena Seamore and Clarissa Wilding. Payment of said amounts to be determined by and distributed by the law office of Daniel M. Brower.

"That's it? No chiding or withholding his money to teach Treena and me a lesson?"

Her tense muscles relaxed. It was possible her tyrant father had given up the fight with his righteous principles in the end. If only he had forgiven her and let her stay with him, he would have had her gratitude and a grandchild to dote over.

"You had to have your own way, Father. It cost you the love of you daughters."

She sighed hard to let the last of her tension go. All the other antagonistic memories from those days had been quenched in her spirit. The will was closure for her. She hoped it was for Treena too, although they both had more demons to rid themselves of.

Treena's letter teetered on the chair's arm, tempted to flitter to the floor by the breeze coming from the open window. Clarissa snatched it and settled in to read her sister's news of what was left in the estate. The depression holding the nation's financial world hostage couldn't have done his investments any favors. She braced herself for the possibility that there could be nothing left.

Dear Clary,

I'm still here in Kansas City and will probably stay for good. I have met a nice man, and we are getting serious. Yes, he is a man of faith and has even taken me to church. Imagine that. I am very happy and have no desire to return to New York as I planned and as you must have read between the lines of my last letter. I do miss you and the boys. And I often think of Elijah, and hope he is well.

He did impact my life, even though I resisted his influence for all the wrong reasons.

Clarissa lowered the paper to her lap. Elijah. She thought of him every day and sensed he must be praying for this little family whose lives he'd touched. She knew the boys missed him terribly. Their parting had been too abrupt.

I hope you all are well. You will be much better soon, when your part of the inheritance arrives in the mail. The attorney said he would issue the check as soon as Father's bank could round up enough funds to cover it. For some institutions, large sums of cash are still hard to come by these days. You will be surprised at the amount. I won't tell you now. You'll see when the check arrives. I know—I'm such a mean sister. Father was very wise with his investments, and though he lost some, much of his estate was salvaged.

I want you to know I have made my final peace with Father. Knowing he resisted leaving us out of his will helped me see he must have loved us in his own way. Poor man just didn't know how to show it. Now it's too late for him, but not too late for us to move on and find happiness.

Please give the boys a squeeze from me, and I will write again soon. I will have a better place to live soon, and a telephone too, so I'll send you the telephone number where you can reach me. Who knows. You might see my happy face in Washington someday.

All my love,

Treena

"And how does she think I will call her—with a tin can attached to a string?"

As she folded the papers and stuffed them into the large envelope, her hopes rose to think she would come into some substantial money. Over the last several weeks, she had contemplated what she would do with it. Her original stubbornness not to accept Father's inheritance had faded the more she plotted to convince Frank to move into town, where she wouldn't have to see William. Without money to relocate, she would have little chance at succeeding. He would surely question her desire to leave anyway. She would have to take that risk—as soon as the money arrived.

"Lord, I don't like being deceitful. Help me find a way to get out of here."

Morgan pushed open the front screen door, his face smudged with traces of mud. "I'm hungry."

Clarissa gasped and looked at his feet. James was right behind him, holding up his hand to her. "Don't worry. I made him take off his boots. I knew you'd be mad as a hornet."

She relaxed into the chair and smiled. "James, you're a good big brother. And I would indeed have been mad as a hornet."

"What's a hornet?" Morgan looked up at James.

"A big mean bee. We used to have them back home, before the storms came."

Clarissa stood and tucked Treena's letter in her apron pocket. "What do you want for lunch?"

James smiled back. "Anything but tomatoes and cornbread."

A funny but sad remark. Their steady diet of cornmeal and canned goods had left a sour memory that might never go away. James hadn't complained much back then. He deserved to be sarcastic now. She could handle the bad memories as long as her sons continued to grow and thrive.

"Where's your father?"

Frank stepped through the door, also in stocking feet. "Right here."

Clarissa waved him over. "Come sit at the table and talk to me while I fix up lunch. I have leftover beef stew."

The boys ran down the hall to wash up while Frank scrubbed the mud from his hands in the kitchen sink. He wiped his hands on a towel and cleared his throat. "Had an interesting talk with William this morning."

Clarissa's heart lurched. She had dreaded the day Frank would come home to say William had exposed his past with Clarissa. This could be the day. If it was, all the inheritance in the world wouldn't soothe the wound about to be opened. She steadied her voice, but her knees buckled.

"What about?" The bread knife jumped in her quaking hand. She casually laid it on the counter and turned her back to Frank to stir the stew.

"You'd be surprised at what I now know." He sat down at the table.

What was his tone? Hard, angry? *Don't turn around.*

Her ears rang so loud she could barely hear him. Even her stomach rolled as if it would empty itself. It was over. Her secret was out for sure this time. She closed her eyes, her back still to Frank. His silence grated on her insides and brought the walls in on her. Was he waiting for her to turn around and face him, shame and all? She couldn't. He would have to break the news without the satisfaction of seeing her reaction.

"About what?" She managed to keep a calm inflection, but held tight to the edge of the stove.

"Well, I always wondered about how William kept a vineyard going during prohibition. Now I know."

Her wobbling legs stabilized. She let out the breath she'd been holding and stepped away from the stove. "Oh? Do tell." Surely he could see how shaken she was.

"He got a special permit to grow some of the grapes for sacrament wine. You know, for the churches who use it in communion. The rest of the vines he had to plow under for that orchard growing there now. But he managed to survive well on grapes and apples. He bought more mature apple trees from the neighbor and had a crop the second year. Isn't that something? Pretty smart, huh?"

It was something all right. Another reprieve from the truth

was more than something to her. She couldn't care less about William's clever ways to stay in business. Her only thought was to get away from this place.

"Still kind of hard to believe he could make so much money through those times."

He looked tired and in need of some good news.

"Well, I have some interesting news too."

She handed him Treena's letter. "Take this and go sit in the comfy chair."

She returned to the stew. She would let the inheritance information soak into his brain for a while before bringing up her idea to move. Once they got away from here, and when Frank could find work without William, she would tell him the truth about who James' father was.

He had always been a reasonable man. And more than fair to her. She would hold that thought as long as she could. After a few minutes of silence from the living room, Clarissa turned around, spoon in hand, to see Frank's eyes closed and his mouth open a sliver, with soft snores whistling through it.

Everything in Clarissa relaxed, except her stomach, which pestered her with modest nausea. All would be fine, especially if she could manage to eat some stew.

Frank's news could just as well have been disastrous. There might still come a day for bad news. As soon as he woke up, she would start some dialogue about being on their own. It was a risk—one she had to take. It was time to broach the subject of moving to town.

As soon as he woke up.

Chapter 4

*F*rank hovered over the engine of the truck, checking spark plugs and anything else he could think of to get it running again. His knowledge about 1931 Ford Model AA trucks could be held in a thimble. He welcomed the chance to do some mindless tinkering. He had promised Clarissa last night he would think about the secret feelings she had expressed, but he hadn't planned on her idea to move dominating his thoughts and grinding into a headache. After coming all this way to start a new life, she surprised him with her discontent. After weeks of trying to rebuild their marriage, he was clueless about what could really be eating her.

The dark tone of the reels turning in his mind had to be extinguished. Self-blame and doubt had crept into his thoughts even after they arrived in Washington. He should never have let Clary make the decision to stay so long on the homestead— letting Morgan get sicker by the year. His ability to lead the family had withered with the crops, and he didn't get it back in time to save two of his children. The courage to obey God's voice had dwindled each time he looked into Clarissa's face and saw the fear she harbored about leaving Kansas. He couldn't understand her need to stay. Now he couldn't comprehend her wish to leave here. How could he have missed such important clues?

He stood up straight and threw his oily rag on the ground.

Scanning the rolling green hills beyond the vineyard and far across the river beyond, he felt his hopes and dreams soar over the treetops, looking for a place to land. He had gladly left his precious yet heartless dry earth behind, and the memories of strife and exasperation lingered as an ache in his chest. When he stepped off that train a month ago, his feet had landed on fertile earth. He was free at last. If only Clarissa had felt the same. He thought she had. Her sudden and unexplained change of heart puzzled him.

"What are you doing with the truck?"

James' question startled Frank. He forced himself not to chuckle at the cracking octaves of the young man's voice.

"You know, I'm not sure. William knows how to take things apart and put them back together again. Even when we were kids, he got in big trouble tinkering with Father's tools. Our dad didn't seem to be proud of our natural abilities." He paused at the vision of William receiving another beating from their father because he took apart the family radio to try and fix it.

He put his hand on James' shoulder. "I hope you know I'm proud of you, James." His sentiment was especially meaningful since he wasn't James' real father, but again, this was not the time to share anything so life changing. He was beginning to wonder if there ever would be a good time.

James toed the ground with muddy boots. "What for?"

"What for what?"

"What are you proud of me for?"

Frank placed his wrench on the fender of the truck and leaned his back on the grill. He had missed many opportunities in the past to encourage James. This chance rose up like a neon sign flashing *Affirming Words Needed.* His vision for such signs had cleared considerably in the past weeks.

"Well, there are many things. But I think the thing I'm most proud of is how you took over for me on the homestead while

I was away. You took charge of Morgan and the chores and became the man of the family. You're a natural-born leader, Jimmy. That's a great thing."

It had been quite a while since he'd called him Jimmy. He was afraid James would take it as a condescending tag instead of the term of endearment it was meant to be. He hadn't shown love to the boy the way he should have. This was the time to do it, the perfect setting for bringing James in close. The vineyard could be a place where they could work together and grow a father-son relationship. He had to convince Clary to stay.

James' face flared crimson. "I'm no leader." He gazed off to the horizon as if he wanted to be somewhere else at this moment or talking about something else. Frank had seen James stuff feelings deep. Not this time.

"Yes, you are. We all have trouble seeing our strengths. Sometimes we need someone else to tell us. Trust me, you proved yourself back home. Your mom needed you, and you came through."

James smiled and tipped his head. "Well, Elijah helped a lot." He looked off in the distance. "I think Elijah and me have some things in common."

In common? "Like what, son?"

James avoided Frank's inquiring eyes. "Oh, like not feeling like you belong anywhere in particular. Like feeling different from everyone else."

"You feel different? Different from who?"

"From Morgan… you." He shook his head. "I don't know. It's silly I guess."

Frank froze for a moment. This boy had strong instincts. He hadn't seen it before, and James' feelings would need to be addressed soon. If only Elijah…

Frank snapped his fingers and pushed away from the truck. He had nearly forgotten to go into town to check for a reply to his telegram to Mr. Johnson. He looked away from James.

"I'm sure Elijah had a good influence on you. We need to talk about things like that. Man to man, right?" Frank nudged him with his elbow. The talk would have to wait. "Well, I have to get this truck back together. Have to get to town for something."

James leaned under the hood and peered at the motor. "Can I come?"

Great. How are you going to say no?

"James!" Clarissa called from the cottage. "You promised to finish your chores."

James rolled his eyes. "Dad, will you tell her I have to come with you to town?"

"Nope. You go do your chores so your mother doesn't get the idea to do them for you. I'll bring some fresh roasted peanuts back for you and Morgan. You can go next time."

He silently hoped the next time would include bringing Elijah from the train station to their home. It would all depend on the reply. It was very likely Elijah had moved on from the Johnson's place by now. His telegram might be answered by Mr. Johnson, saying Elijah was long gone, ruining his plan for Clarissa and the boys. Best-case scenario would be that Elijah's presence at the vineyard would be enough to make Clarissa feel more at home.

Then again, Frank had a good feeling about this. Elijah himself had said he never knew where he would end up next. A man of surprises. And mystery.

While Frank said good night to the boys, Clarissa took one last look at her artistic efforts of the day. Her arms were finally used to reaching to the canvas, and she had made more progress than she thought possible. Letting go of her insecurity was good medicine.

The likeness of the barn she captured pleased her. William said the building had to be at least one hundred years old. Its roof sagged on the south side, and the red stain had long been faded from the sun and chipped off by the rain and occasional winter snowfall. The structure leaned slightly to one side, like a man with one leg shorter than the other. This summer evening it stood proud against the setting sun, its tired silhouette saying good night to another day.

Clarissa had sketched it a week ago but had been inspired this morning by the sky behind it. All day clouds had swirled above, in between showers, flirting with the tops of trees in the distance. The changing backdrops had been hard to choose from, and she could complete the scene tomorrow, replicate the lines and colors from memory, then fill in the emotion and story of the painting. Just a few more strokes before letting it sleep for the night.

Frank stood in the doorway. "It's looking good. Almost as good as the one of the cottage."

Clarissa turned her head just enough to see him sip on a cup of steaming coffee.

"You'll be awake all night with that coffee."

Frank raised his brows and tipped his head toward her. "You're the one who can't drink coffee at night. Not me. And it's too hot to drink it during the day, so I'm having my fix now, if that's okay with you." He winked and took another sip.

She held her breath to make the last two strokes of the amber color on her brush. Stepping back to scrutinize, she shook her head. The same old doubt haunted her.

"I'll never be as good as Mother."

"You don't have to be. You have your own style. Go with it." He closed in on her. "I like it."

"You're supposed to say that. And you're biased."

"If you say so." He pulled her close and kissed her neck.

"I need to clean up. The turpentine is making my tummy turn a bit." She wiped the soaked brush on a cloth and put the lid on the turpentine jar. Come to think of it, her stomach had been twirling since breakfast.

Frank flipped on the light switch as he passed by the doorway. "It's getting dark in there."

"At least I had some time to view the sunset." Clarissa pulled her painting apron over her head and hung it on one of the coat hooks on the wall. Morgan's jacket hung on the next hook. One of his pockets bulged. She smiled, wanting to investigate what treasures Morgan might have been gathering. He often disappeared behind the cottage and into the trees beyond, singing and talking to himself. She sometimes heard him talking to Elijah as if he were standing right there, telling him all about his new life in Washington. He had gone missing during the last two rains, coming home unconcerned about being drenched and cold.

Frank sauntered into the kitchen and grabbed a newspaper from the table. Clarissa resisted the urge to snoop through Morgan's pocket and turned out the light after taking one last look at her studio. Strange how one small room could bring such joy and satisfaction. Did every artist have a relationship with their special painting place? The canvas and brushes seemed to know they belonged here, belonged to her. She would do her best not to let them down.

Frank sat at the table, but instead of reading the paper, he stared off into the darkness on the other side the kitchen window. His right brow dipped. She had come to know his expressions, the nuances of his mood and movements. Her guess would be he was mulling over her revelation about leaving here. She would give him more time before bringing it up again.

He lifted his chin and turned his head to her. "Clary, can we talk?"

Her queasy stomach lurched. She might be about to get her answer. She pulled out another chair and slid into it.

The silence only lasted for a few seconds, but to Clarissa it seemed an eternity. She folded her hands in her lap, clenching them so tight, they ached. *Please say we can move.*

Frank pushed his coffee cup away from him. He glanced at the boys' bedroom doors. Both shut tight, just like Clarissa's jaw.

Frank sighed hard. "I've been thinking over what you said about a place of our own away from the vineyard. I don't understand why you want to leave. I'd like for you to tell me more about your feelings. Do you have something against William? I was hoping the two of you would get along—be family. But you seem to dislike him, and I don't know why." He leaned back in his chair. "Is it that you want a bigger house? You know I can't afford something of our own yet."

Clarissa forced her jaw to loosen. She couldn't lie, but she could certainly not spill her true feelings about William. A simple explanation was the only way to keep a lid on things. Like her painting waiting for her to fill in the details to create the full picture, Frank would have to be content with a sketch of her reasoning.

"Frank, I don't dislike William. He's your brother, and I'm grateful for his generosity. I would like a place of our own closer to town. I know we can't afford to buy something, but we could rent. There must be lots of empty houses from all the poor folks moving away. I could do some baking and sell pies at the general store. I might even be able to sell a few paintings if I get good enough." She looked away. "Besides, it's not all that safe around here for the boys. The barn is ready to fall down, and the bluff at the end of the vineyard is a constant worry for me. You know how Morgan wanders off, and…"

She heard herself rambling, ruining her simple explanation.

Frank stared into her eyes. If he looked deep enough, he would see her manipulation and excuses.

"And what, Clarissa?"

"Well, how will we get the boys to school come fall? We're miles from town."

Frank put his elbows on the table and rubbed his face with his calloused hands. After a moment, he leaned back and crossed his arms over his chest.

"We can work through all that. I think we could be happy here if you gave it a chance. I understand your concerns, but we haven't been here long enough for you to get adjusted. You haven't been feeling great lately, and I think it's because you're unsettled."

"I'm fine."

Frank smiled and laid an open hand on the table, reaching for her. She unlocked her grip and placed her hand in his palm. Her heart had slowed, knowing what he was about to say. Her pleas had been ineffective. Only the whole truth would free her from this place. But it would also do irreparable damage to Frank and the boys. Yet if they stayed, it was only a matter of time before discovery caused them all pain.

God, don't ask me to submit.

Frank squeezed her hand. The warmth of his skin felt good against her cold fingers.

"Clary, let's give it another six months. If you still feel the same after that, we'll reevaluate. I'm asking that you do this for me—for our family."

Her cheeks were wet by the time he finished. For lack of words, she nodded, her energy drained. Poor Frank couldn't possibly know the emotional disasters that could besiege them in six months. Frank pulled her up from the table and held her close.

"You'll see. Things will work out. William isn't so bad, and I know he likes you. Let's see what happens, all right?"

She buried her face in his shoulder. She could think of no

defense. For now she had to give in and pray things would change. "All right."

"Would you make more of an effort with William?"

More of an effort? He didn't know what he was asking of her. It didn't matter anyway.

"Sure."

Frank let go of her. "Let's get some sleep."

The night had warmed more than usual, especially in their cramped bedroom. Clarissa's body ached, and throwing off covers didn't help. The moonlight filtered through the curtains, making lacy patterns on the wall. The shapes and shadows caught her artist's eye. Diving into sketching and painting again had boosted her creative awareness. It was the one thing working for her at this place she had yet to call home.

Lying next to Frank, she studied her mental notes, numbering the things she would need to do to prepare for the next six months. At the top of the list was finding a way to secure her secret from Frank. And from William.

If only Elijah were here to referee. She should have written down Mr. Johnson's address so she could write to him. She needed his wisdom to keep her from disaster, even if it meant the risk of losing his respect. Considering all things, she was bound to lose respect from someone, maybe everyone.

Clarissa squirmed in the front seat of William's car, which Frank had borrowed to go into town. She had begged him to let her stay at the cottage and finish her barn portrait. He insisted, even using a commanding tone to get her dressed and into the car. The boys already occupied the backseat by the time she donned a hat to cover her mussed hair. Being nauseous all morning had taken its toll on her appearance according to the bathroom mirror.

"Why is this all so mysterious? Can't you at least tell us exactly where we're going?"

"Nope."

Morgan leaned forward and chimed in the argument. "Just a hint?"

James pulled Morgan back. "He's not going to tell us, so quit pestering."

Frank laughed. "That goes for you too, Mother."

"It better be worth our while." Clarissa checked her pocketbook for the pewter powder compact Treena had given her. Her lack of sleep last night showed in the whites of her eyes. A little face dusting wouldn't cure the bags underneath, but might help to disguise them.

"I think you'll be happy you came."

Frank's smirk scraped her irritability like nails on a chalkboard. She struggled to cover the agitation in her soul during breakfast. Even fixing oatmeal had turned her stomach.

The car lurched as Frank drove it into the train station parking area. He stopped and turned off the motor.

"Train station?" She raised her brows. The memory of the last visit to the station brought shivers to her back—her first encounter with the ghost of her past overshadowing her thrill of stepping foot on Washington soil.

"Who's coming? A visitor? Aunt Treena?" Morgan bounced in his seat until James grabbed his shoulders.

Clarissa's heart skipped. Was Treena here to visit? How wonderful and terrible at the same time. Clarissa didn't need extra chatter and pushy sentiments right now. And what would happen when Treena connected the dots about William? Still, seeing her sister's face could bring some clarity on her dilemma and a shoulder to lean on.

"Come on." Frank opened both doors and waited for her and the boys to get out of the car, his arm outstretched.

Thick crowds lined up next to the train, people weaving in and out, searching the faces pressed up against the passenger car windows. People saying goodbyes and hellos milled about like players on a stage. Each one had a role to assume—happy or sad. If only she knew what role she would play here today.

Frank took her and Morgan's hands and wove his way through the sea of people toward the second-to-last train car—the one with only a few windows. It looked to be a special car of some kind. There were no crowds waiting at this car, and all disembarking passengers were colored. Frank halted several feet away from the steps. He turned to Clarissa and grinned wide. James and Morgan squeezed in between them.

"What's going on?" James finally protested. "Are we coming or going?"

Frank patted his head. "Just keep your eyes on the doorway."

Almost before Frank had finished speaking, a tall figure appeared on the landing. His salt-and-pepper hair stuck out from under his old brown hat, and the twinkle in his eyes penetrated the air, just as always. Clarissa's legs wobbled, and she held on to Frank as she tried to call out. "Elijah."

Morgan tugged on James' arm. "Look! It's Elijah!"

Clarissa's feet seemed frozen to the ground, but Morgan broke loose and galloped to meet Elijah at the bottom of the stairs. Elijah dropped his small satchel and wrapped his arms around Morgan's shoulders.

James stood still, his eyes filled with moisture. Clarissa wanted to nudge him in Elijah's direction, but James' Adam's apple bobbled, and his posture straightened. The sounds of reunion between Morgan and Frank and Elijah couldn't tear her from James' face. She had misjudged the depth of affection he held for this drifter.

Soon Elijah was at her side. "Hello, ma'am."

"Elijah. It's so good to see you." She rested her hand on his chest. He wasn't a dream. "I can't belief you're here."

Elijah turned to James, who stuck out his hand, but then flung himself at Elijah. No words were exchanged. Everyone stood motionless for a moment until Morgan took Elijah's hand and pulled him toward William's car. James took Elijah's satchel from him and toted it beside him. Clarissa thought she heard a sniffle from her oldest son.

As the boys each took a side of Elijah, Clarissa slipped her arm through Frank's. She pulled him in close. "You just made something wonderful happen. Thank you."

Frank grinned. "It was pretty easy. I sent a telegram, and the next thing you know Mr. Johnson replied saying Elijah would be on this morning's train. He even paid for the ticket. Said Elijah had been a godsend to them, but they were leaving Heartland's misery, and it was time to send him where he was most needed."

"I guess we do need him. I just didn't think you knew it."

"I knew. It was written on all your faces each time you spoke of him. Besides, William said he could come for room and board if he helped out. And that's saying a lot for penny-pinching William."

Clarissa bristled at the thought of William being a part of this special time. She would give him no credit. Frank was the one to arrange it. He did it out of love. A love she determined never to take for granted again.

Elijah had been given the grand tour of William's car. He seemed hesitant to get inside, but the boys coaxed him in.

"My first train ride and now my first ride in a fancy car. My, my. Ain't this somethin'?"

Frank looked at Clarissa. They must have been thinking the same thing. Had this man been that sheltered? Had he walked on foot all over the south? Frank led Clarissa to the passenger side and shut her door. He looked at Elijah and shrugged a shoulder before he resumed his seat behind the wheel.

"Well, Elijah, I'll try and give you a smooth ride."

"I thank you, Mr. Wilding. And thank you for invitin' me up to Washin'ton. In all my travels I never saw such beauty."

The car filled with chatter and laughter all the way home. Memories and stories flew back and forth between Elijah and the boys. Clarissa would have been more cheerful had it not been for the returning nausea. She hadn't seen a doctor in years and didn't want to start now. Even through all the physical hardships of the last several years, she never once required a doctor's care.

While the boys helped Frank clean up the car inside and out, Clarissa gave Elijah a peek at the cottage and her painting studio.

"It's sure pretty. I know you'll paint lots of nice pictures in here," Elijah said as they stood in the studio. He moved closer to the painting of the barn still on the easel. "I think you have a gift, ma'am."

"Well, I don't know about that, but I'm enjoying it all the same."

He tipped his head to one side. "If you don't mind me sayin'—I hope you don't spend too many hours in here without the window open. The fumes wouldn't be good for your condition."

There was that sparkle in his eyes—the eyes she had come to use as a compass as sure as a guiding star. What on earth was he talking about?

"My condition?" She pulled up a shade and cracked one of the windows open.

"Forgive me if I overstepped. Are you not with child?"

Every muscle in her body twitched. Her hand moved to her abdomen. She immediately rejected the notion and fought annoyance at Elijah for mentioning it. Of course she couldn't be expecting. She had dried up in the drought, carried and lost too many children. Her time was over, and her body had told her so by refusing to bleed anymore.

"I—I have no reason to think that I am."

She opened the door to the outside and walked through. Elijah followed.

"I'm sorry. I thought I saw somethin' in your eyes. I did overstep."

"It's all right, Elijah." She wasn't about to stand there and discuss a personal and impossible scenario with him, even though he had never led her astray before. She pointed to the barn.

"You'll want to see the rest of the place. I'm sure James and Morgan are anxious to show you around. Why don't you wander over while I rustle up some lunch?" Her hand shook as she lowered it to her side.

"Don't go to no trouble for me. Mrs. Johnson packed some food for me to eat on the train. I finished the last of it yesterday."

Yesterday? He hadn't eaten since yesterday and was willing to skip lunch because it would trouble her? Elijah was back just as he was when they'd left him.

Her wobbling legs took her as far as the kitchen chair. She had to muster energy to fix a meal. Her mind raced with the words of Elijah's ridiculous notion. She just needed to eat better and get a good night's sleep. Still, everything the man ever said to her before always made sense. Even Treena saw his special wisdom.

Not this time. He had to be wrong.

Chapter 5

The old tack room attached to the back of the barn had a cot and a window—just the right size for one person. Thankfully, William had agreed on Elijah using the space. The boys had rounded up a chair and small table, and Clarissa made an effort to clean it up, but Elijah would have none of that, insisting she do no more than sit and watch. She supplied him with bedding and left the men to do the work.

Frank remembered Elijah's helpful eagerness on the homestead, but he didn't remember him so protective of Clarissa. Frank knew how much she wanted to make a nice place for her friend, but Elijah insisted she not lift or sweep. Clarissa's stories about his unselfish ways were evident.

Frank hurried to fix the latch on the door. William wanted him back to work as soon as possible. It was clear his brother thought of Elijah's arrival as an interruption in the day's work schedule, and there were things to be done before William had to leave on a supply trip.

He had reproached Frank after their return from the station. "I'll be honest—I never was much for hired help. Most of them can't be trusted. Just remember, he's not a guest. He's here to work. We have a lot to do before harvest."

As Frank pounded the last nail into the door hinge, William's words replayed in his head. Boyhood memories of being bossed around by a younger brother gave weight to his hammer.

Elijah stepped through the barn door holding a lantern.

"Mr. Wilding, I found this hangin' outside. Mind if I use it? Would be handy for gettin' to the outhouse after dark."

Frank cringed at realizing there was no electricity or toilet in the barn or tack room. Elijah wouldn't mind, but Frank did. In time, he would ask William about continuing the electric lines from the main house to the barn. For now, a dusty old lantern and leaning outhouse would have to do.

He nodded to Elijah. "Sure thing. I bet it hasn't been used in years. Is there fuel in it?"

"Yes, sir. And more in a can over yonder." He pointed to the shelves on the side of the old horse stall. "I appreciate it."

Elijah joined the boys inside the new space. Frank listened to the banter about how fine it looked now that the cobwebs and straw were gone. He shook his head. *How could a man be so content in any circumstance?* A good man to model himself after. If he could be as good example as Elijah, maybe Clarissa would see she could also be content here, especially since their friend had joined them.

"You coming?" William poked his head around the barn door. "Got to get those limbs propped up today, Frank."

"I'm coming. What do we need?"

"Grab those two-by-fours stacked in the corner, and I'll make sure we have enough strapping." William glanced at the closed door of the tack room. "Your man can finish setting himself up. I need you with me." William disappeared.

My man? He has a name.

Frank bristled at William's gruff tone. Still, his brother was the boss around here. It was time to get used to how it felt to be a hired hand. He didn't like the implications, but it was better than being a slave to the drought back home, even as the owner.

He gathered up the lumber and stacked it in the back of the

truck. He tugged at his gloves to relieve his sweating palms and watched William rummage through a large box of tools by the pump house. It was just like the toolbox inside their barn in Kansas. Frank missed having his own things. He recalled the tightening in his gut as he buttoned up his tools and other belongings in the root cellar. He was sure they would never return, but couldn't bear to sell off everything. No one had money to buy him out anyway.

Elijah had explained how more families had left their homes to go to California. The Wilsons, the Martins, and the Gundersens had all packed up what belongings they could and headed for greener lands. Elijah shed a tear telling Frank the sad tale of empty farmhouses overtaken with mountains of sand, and cattle being slaughtered to save them from slow starvation. Frank's heart shuddered to think of what it would have been like if they hadn't moved away.

"Ready?" William tapped the hood by the driver's door.

They both slid onto the truck's worn leather seats. Before starting the motor, William turned to Frank. "I hope your man will be ready to work tomorrow. I don't mind him helping Clarissa sometimes, but he'll be of more use tending the orchard and vineyard. I'll leave it to you to teach him what he needs to know. Agreed?"

"Yes." Frank grit his teeth. He couldn't hold back the irritation anymore. William was his brother, but Elijah deserved respect too. "Do you think you could call him Elijah? I'm not comfortable with you calling him *my man*. He's his own man."

William's lip curled up on one side. "Sure. Elijah it is. At least I don't have to call him *Mister* something." He started the motor and steered down the rutted road to the heaviest-laden trees.

Where had William acquired this attitude? Their mother used to sit with them on the front porch and watch people go by. They would each take a turn guessing where they all came from and where they were going. Black, white, brown, yellow—their mother would say everyone was the same inside. It was a game to the boys, but when he grew to manhood, Frank realized the significance of her clever teaching methods.

William shifted gears to low for descending a steep hill. "Anyway, it seems Clarissa is quite fond of the fellow. Weren't you surprised to find he had been at the farm while you were off looking for work?"

Frank shook his head. "No, not really."

"I was under the impression that Clarissa had a stricter upbringing—more proper and uppity, you might say."

"She did, but she is also independent and has a very inclusive heart. It never surprised me that she would have Elijah around. And it was a mutually beneficial arrangement." He tipped his head. "How did you know about Clary's upbringing?"

William didn't answer for a long moment. Frank thought he saw a glimmer in William's eye.

"She must have said something to me sometime." He slammed on the brakes. "Here we are. You start on the east end, and I'll work my way toward you. Holler if you need help."

William unstrapped the lumber and slid four two-by-fours onto his broad shoulders. Frank hesitated, wondering if he could carry that many. He would start with three and come back for more.

His boots sunk into the muddy path as he trudged along with a heavy load. Something William said pounded in his head. William's description of Clarissa's upbringing didn't sound like the kind of words she would use. Clarissa would never tell a perfect stranger about her past. Yet William seemed to know. She must have felt free enough around him to divulge feelings it took her years to explain to Frank.

An unfamiliar pang shot right through his ribs. No time to entertain ridiculous notions and stir up something out of nothing. He ducked under a low limb of a Red Delicious apple tree. The ripening fruit clung in tight clusters among the large green leaves.

"William said it would be a banner crop this year. This must be what he meant."

He worked as fast as he could, trying to get his rows done and meet up with William. His muscles ached as he pushed up the lowest hanging limbs with the notched boards. He grunted and tightened his abdomen to give a hard shove on the third two-by-four. He surveyed the next few rows.

"One down. Looks like a dozen or more to go."

He sprinted to the truck and hoisted four boards this time. He couldn't let William have the upper hand for this job. Or with anything from now on. He didn't care about the physical consequences at the end of the day. All he knew was that an uncomfortable spark of competition grew deep inside.

The afternoon crept up on her, making it too hard to concentrate on much of anything other than staring out the back door at the garden. She took in the sights and sounds before anyone else stirred—the sun and dew on the growing plants, birds chirping, and a glimpse of a rabbit making off with a few leaves of cabbage. All morning she'd tried to fight her lazy disposition, but the orchard had called to her, begging for a leisurely stroll under the shade of the drooping branches.

She arrived home to find the breakfast dishes washed and drying on the counter. The empty house only encouraged her to go back to bed, and she would have if not for the persistent roiling in her tummy. The clock ticked away toward noon.

"Lunchtime already." She peeked out the front window to see if the boys were on the porch. "I must be the only one who doesn't want to work today." She turned quickly from the window and had to swallow down a rise of nausea. It subsided as she edged to the kitchen to pull sandwich makings out of the refrigerator.

Despite struggling with a queasy stomach over the last week, her belly had rounded ever so slightly. From the time they left till a few weeks ago, she had noticed a weight gain. Regular meals and fresh air had worked its magic for her and the boys. Rosy cheeks and shiny hair had been a testament to better health, and she was grateful.

But this wasn't usual for her—to be thick in the waist. The only time it ever happened was when she was expecting a child. She and Treena both had been blessed with their mother's petite figure.

As she cut bread and meat for Frank's lunch, her thoughts raced. Elijah had seen it. She thought it was nonsense then, but her doubt diminished with each passing day.

She tucked the wrapped chicken sandwich into a brown paper bag and folded the top. Her hand moved to her belly. She stroked it, praying for an answer. Time would tell.

Give it another week.

The front door rattled with a loud knock. Elijah stood on the other side of the screen, pulling his hat from his head.

"Ma'am. Mr. Wilding sent me for his lunch. He went off to the other side of the vineyard and wants me to bring it to him."

"Come in, Elijah." If she knew William's ways, and she had come to know them over the last three months, he would have Frank out there all day and not care a lick about food.

"Yes, ma'am."

She knew better than to try and get Elijah to call her Clarissa, or even Mrs. Wilding. She had come to think of the word *ma'am* as her special name. Just having him back in their lives had given her emotional stability. He still surprised them daily with little miracles of hope and sustenance. A baby bird for

Morgan to nurse back to health, a bundle of showy stickweed for her garden, or a stash of firewood for winter from the grove of white pines down the road.

She pointed to a chair at the table. "Sit down while I fix another sandwich. You'll be hungry too, I'm sure."

"No need to—"

"Elijah, no arguments. Sit."

"Yes, ma'am." He removed his hat and wiped his brow.

She sliced more of the fresh loaf of bread. The boys would be back from their walk to the meadow anytime and would be ravenous. She would make a stack of sandwiches to satisfy them.

"I haven't had a chance to ask you how you liked your time with the Johnsons. Were they good to you?" She smothered the bread with butter.

"Oh, yes. Mighty fine people, the Johnsons. But I sure missed y'all." He stared out the window. "Your garden needs tendin'. I'd help you, but Mr. William says he wants me to be in the orchard much as possible."

Clarissa pursed her lips. If William thought he had acquired a slave, he would find out soon enough it wasn't true. She would make sure he understood Elijah was his own man. If he wanted to tend a garden, he could do just that. She slapped a large piece of roast chicken on the buttered bread and wrapped it up. Once it was in the bag with Frank's sandwich, she huffed.

"Well, I don't think Mr. William would mind if you helped me with a project now and then. As a matter of fact, I have something in mind to surprise the boys with if you would help me."

Elijah's eyes brightened. "Sure will, if you think it's all right with the boss."

"I think I can persuade him to spare you for an hour or so." She wasn't confident of her statement, but there had to be a compromise with Elijah and William's expectations. He wasn't paying him, and she knew by his silence about their past that he had some compassion. She would show Elijah the project and ask William later if Elijah could do the task.

"Here's the lunch." She handed him the bulging sack. "Let's go out back, and I'll show you the job before you go back to Frank."

She untied her apron and spun around to walk down the back hallway. The room swirled in circles for a few seconds. She grabbed the wall to steady herself.

"You all right, ma'am?"

"Yes, of course. Come this way."

She was not all right. If she turned so Elijah could see her face, it would worry him. She felt it flush as she took her first steps to the door. *Don't think about it. Breathe.*

She pushed open the door and took deliberate care to maneuver the steps to the ground. Elijah followed her in silence as they swished through tall grass and weeds for about 15 yards to the old stone pump house. Beside the structure was a small area surrounded by quaking ash trees and two sad-looking lilac bushes. The foliage had overwhelmed the ground and climbed up the wall of the pump house. She stopped and wiped her moist forehead with her apron. Elijah held the sack to his chest as he scanned the scene.

"I'd really like to make an area for the boys and me to have a picnic here. Do you think you could clear it and build us a table to eat at? It's so picturesque and quiet. We could even do their schooling here." She rested her hands on her hips, breathing in the wetness of the greenery.

"Why, that'd be a nice idea. I can sure do that for you. The boys will be blessed for it."

The rumble of the truck motor caused Elijah to spin around. They both tromped through the weeds to the yard. William stopped the truck in front of them and leaned out the window.

"Need you out there… Elijah." He wagged his thumb to point behind him. "I'm sure Mrs. Wilding can spare you. Frank is waiting for his lunch, but you'll have to help me load some metal stakes first. You can ride in the back when we're done."

"Sure thing, Mr. William." Elijah jogged to the truck and threw the lunch sack onto the seat. He glanced at Clarissa and gave a nod before jogging off toward the barn.

She had gotten him in trouble. Elijah must think he had to be subservient to William for her sake. She had to come to an agreement with William about Elijah before there was another embarrassing incident. She hated feeling as though she were in a tug of war over another human being.

She stepped up to the passenger window of the truck. Before she could open her mouth to ask the favor, William removed his hat and turned his head to face her.

"Have you been taking the mason jars off my back porch?"
She stepped back. "What?"
"Every once in a while a mason jar goes missing off my porch. I wondered if you were taking them. Don't know who else would need something like that."

She stood dumbfounded. Her arms clung tight to her sides. He couldn't be accusing her of stealing. His pursed lips answered her. Yes. He was.

"All you had to do was ask, Clarissa." He slipped his hat back on his head.

She loosened her tongue. "I didn't ask because I don't need any jars. I did not take them. If you have a thief, it's not me." She swung herself around and took two paces before stopping. "And don't get any ideas it was Elijah." Two more steps and a turn around. "If I were going to steal something, it would be my mother's portrait hanging in your parlor."

This time she marched all the way to the cottage side door

and slammed it behind her. Her breath gone and heart pounding, she leaned against the wall until she heard the truck pull away. She felt her way along the hallway back to the bathroom. As she grabbed the sides of the cold porcelain toilet, everything she had eaten that day erupted into the bowl. Beads of sweat dripped from her chin as she steadied her shaking arms on the floor.

Elijah was right. She was pregnant. Her burst of anger was confirmation her emotions had turned on her, so much so that she had betrayed herself with William. It was just a matter of time before he confronted her on snooping in his house.

Frank wouldn't be happy about any rift it might cause between him and William—and between them. She had to lay low and keep away from her brother-in-law.

But a baby? Now?

Success in avoiding William for the last two days had come at a cost. Frank noticed Clarissa's reclusiveness and pressed her on her apparent negative attitude. She needed time to think about what to do about many things. William must be wondering how she knew about the painting in his house. The explanation was obvious, but she would have to make a confession sometime that she had snuck into his house.

To appease Frank, making up the excuse that she had caught some kind of persistent stomach bug would buy her a few days, but soon she would have a hard time hiding her pregnancy. Better to keep her secret until she knew she would carry the child past the first several months.

Her secrets were piling up like fireflies in a jar. If she didn't keep them under wraps, they would shine to expose her. She wasn't ready to tell him.

She stood in her studio as the sun rose toward noon, staring at the nearly finished painting of the barn. *God, why have you complicated my life with a baby, William, and making Frank be his brother's hired man? We need to get away from here. Please.*

Elijah appeared at the open doorway. A large basket rested on his shoulder. "Excuse me, ma'am. Mr. Wilding thought you might use these unripe apples that been fallin' from the trees. I told him they're good for makin' pectin for jelly." Elijah chuckled. "Now he wants you to try makin' some."

Clarissa shook away her deep thoughts. "Well, I've never made it, but if you could show me how, I'll try. Bring them into the kitchen." She held the door to the kitchen open for him, looking down to make sure her blouse wasn't too tight against her belly.

Who are you kidding? He knows.

"Just put it on the table and I'll sort through them later." She had to confide in someone. Elijah was the only one she couldn't fool anyway. His eyes always reflected truth.

"I'll be happy to tell you how to make the pectin." Elijah hoisted the basket on the tabletop.

Her throat felt like it was lined with sandpaper. She had nothing to fear from this man standing before her. His new overalls hung on his slender frame. Several pockets were stuffed with shears and rags. He would never give away a secret, and she could use one of his spiritual analogies about now.

"Elijah, I want to tell you that you were right. I believe I'm expecting."

His eyes twinkled. "That's a blessin', ma'am."

"Frank doesn't know—yet. I don't want him to be disappointed if…"

Elijah's smile faded. "Don't think you need to be worryin' about that. God will bless you."

"But He took my other babies." She inhaled a deep breath to keep the pain away.

"The Lord didn't take those children. The drought did. In His mercy, He received them into heaven. You'll see them again. This child was meant for this time, for a purpose."

This time? It seemed like the worst possible time to her, but Elijah was firm in his conviction. His pulled-back shoulders, and hands clasped to his chest confirmed the authority in his voice, and she sensed a certain agreement inside her.

Clarissa peeked inside the basket. A project for another day.

"Do you have a few minutes now, Elijah? I have some ideas for that area out back I showed you."

"Yes, I think so."

"Let's go look."

Once outside, they made their way to the side of the pump house. The sun streamed in through the tree branches, revealing the weeds in the tall grass. She breathed in the earthy freshness of the shade under a crooked maple tree. This would be the perfect spot for an outdoor studio. It was as if whoever planted the many varieties of trees long ago had in mind a special place.

"I'm concerned about the overgrowth up against the pump house. Do you think it would be hard to clear away? And I wonder what kind of damage it might have done to the wall." She tugged on a thorny vine that had climbed all the way to the roof and beyond.

Elijah pulled a pair of gloves out of his back pocket. "Let me pull that away and we'll see."

Clarissa stepped back and let Elijah grab a stalk of the vine. The plant must have been there for decades, spreading and creating pockets where animals could hide. She shivered to think of providing a hiding place for skunks or raccoons. Elijah rolled up his sleeves and tugged for several minutes, pulling away at the smaller tendrils to loosen the thicker vine that held on to the wall. Sweat beaded on his temples, and he tried in vain to untangle the mess.

"I'll try the other end."

She followed him to the end of the pump house. Elijah planted his feet firm, ready to pull with vengeance. He grabbed hold of a branch and folded it back onto the rest of the plant. Clarissa tensed to see his face contort into a frown, his eyes wide. Did he find an animal? She stepped back, ready to run.

"Ma'am. What do you make of this?" He waved her over.

"Elijah, don't scare me with a dead something."

He chuckled, so she peered around him. On the ground were six mason jars with lids, filled with a clear liquid. Her mind flew immediately to images of bootleg liquor she had seen in a newsreel years ago.

She glanced around before whispering to Elijah. "You don't suppose it's whiskey, do you? It hasn't been that long since prohibition. I wonder—I mean, after all, this *is* an orchard."

"One way to find out, if you don't mind me takin' a sip."

Clarissa giggled. "Just a sip, Elijah. Don't want to ruin your reputation."

As he reached for one of the jars, a puzzle piece connected for her. "William's mason jars," she mumbled to herself.

If William was a bootlegger, why would he hide it here? And why would he accuse her of stealing the jars?

Elijah stood, gripping a jar. He glanced around before opening the lid. He brought it close to his nose and sniffed.

"No smell." He raised his brows. "You still want I should taste it?"

"Hmm." Clarissa didn't want him to drink something that might harm him. But if it had no smell, at least it wasn't turpentine or gasoline. "I think so, if you don't mind. Just taste it and then spit it out."

He nodded and held the jar to his lips. He hesitated, but then tipped the jar until he had a mouthful.

He swallowed, then smiled. "Water. Jus' water. Tastes like rainwater to me."

"Water? How can you tell it's rainwater?"

"Jus' has that rain taste, I guess. Can't explain it, but I been drinkin' rainwater all my life. My mama used to collect it in case we had a drought. Kinda silly, and it was in a bucket, but that's what she did."

Clarissa's mind raced with questions of who around here would collect rainwater. William said the jars had only disappeared in the last few months. She knew it wasn't Elijah, unless he was a good actor. It had to be Frank or one of the boys.

But why? What good did it do to catch the rain?

Chapter 6

*F*rank held his head in his hands as he sat on the back porch of William's house. He took advantage of the solitude and thought through all the issues facing him and Clarissa. They would have to have that talk with James about his parentage. And William would have to know that they could be moving on if Clarissa still wanted to leave after their six-month agreement. His brother would be less than pleased if Frank couldn't persuade his wife to stay, but Clarissa was the one he had to make happy. She had endured more than her share of heartache, and he was responsible for her, even if it meant he would have to leave a job he liked.

He thought back in time to their first year on the homestead. So many firsts. A first crop, a first child, a first time for Clary to tell him she loved him. It was so good in the beginning. Green and easy.

Then came the drought, lost babies, and buried affections. When they left the farm, he vowed never to close himself off again, especially to Clary. If she wanted a home of their own near town, he had to find a way to give it to her. If it meant leaving William or traveling back and forth, he would make it work.

His eye caught the plume of dust from a car coming up the driveway. William could be back from town early, but it didn't sound like his vehicle. Perhaps Clarissa and the boys had hitched a ride back from their hike to the park by the river. He had expressed his protest that she stay home and rest from whatever was exhausting her.

"I'll be fine," she had said. "Believe me, the exercise will do me good."

He wasn't convinced and wished it were them coming up the drive, but the car that appeared was far from the type to pick up strangers and bring them home. If he wasn't mistaken, this was a Cadillac convertible. Candy-apple red. The kind he had seen on billboards in town. He pulled in a deep breath and held it till the auto stopped in the yard 20 feet in front of him.

He jumped up and brushed off the dust from his overalls, removed his hat, and ran his fingers through his hair. He glanced down a couple rows of vines to see if Elijah was nearby. Facing fancy visitors alone was not his forte. No doubt they were looking for William.

"Hello." A man in a brown tweed suit emerged from the driver's side and tipped his hat.

Frank nodded. "Hello. What can I do for you?"

A woman opened the passenger door and swung out her legs. As she stood, Frank had to grit his teeth to keep his mouth from falling open. Her golden hair tumbled out from under a wide-brimmed straw hat with artificial fruit cascading down the side. Her hair rested on the shoulders of a puff-sleeved, peach-colored dress that hung just below her knees. Her creamy complexion made the perfect backdrop for her peach lipstick and deep-blue eyes.

The man slipped his suit coat off and then removed his hat and tossed it on the front seat. He wiped his brow with a handkerchief. "Hot day, isn't it?"

The woman didn't seem the least bit crumpled or bothered by the heat. She shaded her eyes and scanned the area, smiling.

"George, it's not changed much, has it?"

"Nope."

So they had been here before. Relatives? Not a chance. Friends of William? He stepped closer to the car. "I'm Frank Wilding, William's brother."

The man made his way around the car and reached out his hand to Frank. "George. George Tanner." He gestured to the woman. "That's my sister, Felicity Greenwald."

Frank shook the man's hand and smiled at the lady. "Nice to meet you. Are you looking for William?"

"Yes. Is he here?" Felicity slammed the door. Her pouty lips pursed. She crossed her arms and leaned against the car.

Frank blinked and pulled his gaze from her to George. "No, I'm afraid he's in town for the day. Is there anything I can help you with?"

George rubbed the back of his neck and raised his brows at his sister. She nodded.

"We're William's landlords. We were anxious to have a meeting with him. It's too bad he's not here. We've come a long way, and there's some important information we need from him today." He stepped closer to Frank as his eyes shifted to Felicity again. She removed her hat and fanned herself. A few grapes fell from her hat, and she stooped to pick them up.

Frank's throat tightened. He had no idea when William would be back. William had told him he was in charge if something came up, and William couldn't be reached. This would be a test of his brother's trust.

"What is it you need? I can certainly tell William, and he can send it to you or call you on the telephone."

Felicity stepped forward. "I'm afraid the matter is urgent. It's just some figures William forgot to give us. It's all in his ledger in his office inside the house. I assure you, he wouldn't object if we had a look—just to confirm some business dealings. You understand."

That was just it. Frank didn't understand anything about landlords. He had always been his own boss and never had to be business partners with anyone. William did tell him once that his landlords were sticklers for profits. Plus Frank knew where the key was to William's house.

"I suppose William would want you to have the information if it's urgent." *Make sure they are who they say they are.* "Would you by any chance have identification on you, since we've never met?"

Felicity's eyes widened, but George planted himself in front of her and pulled out his wallet. "I have one of those new driver's licenses. Will that do?"

Not proof, but good enough. "Sure."

Felicity squinted her eyes at Frank. He smiled back, but she stayed firm with straight posture and set, yet slender, jaw. He wondered how Clarissa would look in a pretty new dress and hat. She deserved one. He couldn't recall her ever wearing anything but hand-sewn clothing. As soon as William paid him for the month, he would go to town and surprise her with a dress like this one. Maybe in blue.

"Here you are." George handed Frank the license. *George Tanner, 22 Green St., Everett, Wash.*

Frank held it out for George to take. "Good enough for me. Thank you for understanding. Follow me, and I can let you in."

Felicity dashed ahead of him toward the door. "No need. We have a key. It's technically our house." She scrunched her nose.

Frank jerked his head to George, who shrugged his shoulders. "True. Just didn't want to barge in without explanation. Thanks for your trouble. We'll get what we need and be on our way."

City folk. He never cared much for them, and these were the kind of people they would have to live among if Clarissa got her way. He sat under the maple tree to wait for them, but he barely leaned back before Felicity bounded out the door and down the steps. George followed, locking the door and slipping the key into his pants pocket.

Felicity clutched a thick book with a frayed binding under her arm. "We'll be back to return this as soon as we can."

George stopped and stretched out his hand to Frank. "Thanks again. Tell William that we'll be in touch." His lip curled up on one side.

Frank thought he heard him chuckle.

He held back the urge to stop Felicity. "Are you sure William won't mind you taking that book? I don't want to get in trouble."

George shook his head. "We're not merely business partners, Mr. Wilding. William works for us. We have a right to the ledger. William knows that." He opened the car door. "Good-bye, Mr. Wilding."

They both slammed their doors. The motor revved, and George wasted no time turning around in the yard and speeding away. Frank's stomach fluttered. Had he done the right thing? He really had no choice. If there was a problem, William would have mentioned it. Still, his stomach tensed. He didn't want William to be angry with him.

Every muscle in her body ached. Clarissa's decision to hike that far with the boys yesterday was a poor one at best. She should have listened to Frank and stayed home. Her efforts to avoid a discussion with him had succeeded, but at a price. She was too old to be traipsing around the countryside.

But not too old to be pregnant. You could have endangered the baby.

She would have to tell Frank about the child today, as soon as he returned from town. Whenever that would be. For now she would busy herself in the garden, pulling the relentless weeds.

She had pouted when William sent a message with one of the neighbors early last evening. The car had broken down while he was in town and had to be worked on. William spent the night in town but had summoned Frank to bring the truck to him first thing this morning. The plan would have been acceptable, except William came home with the truck and left Frank in town to tend to the car's repair. She didn't like her suspicions about his motives.

Frank seemed to be more like a hired hand than a brother to William. Her chest tightened each time she witnessed William letting Frank do most of the work. Frank insisted it was not a problem. Maybe not for him, but she knew William better than he did.

"I'm learning the business and how to care for the vineyard. Who knows what the future might bring. Knowledge is always a good thing, Clary," Frank had explained.

If only she had the knowledge *she* needed right now. Getting an answer from Frank about moving off the vineyard had proved harder than she'd expected. They were both avoiding facing the truth—she with the pregnancy and dislike for William, and he with his feelings about leaving here and telling James about his parentage.

She had confided to Elijah about the new baby, but he knew nothing about how William fit into her past—and James'. She had been tempted to seek his counsel but feared he would tell her to face her demons. He would be right.

"But do you have the stomach for it, Clarissa Wilding?" She sat on her haunches and spoke out into the expanse of wildflowers and blooming lilac bushes.

She could see puffs of dust from William's truck bumping along the road in the west field. She followed the plume, tracking its path to the house. *Where are Elijah and the boys?* She stood and searched the corners of the apple-laden tree boundaries but saw no one to come rescue her from being alone with her brother-in-law.

William drove the truck into the yard as she brushed off her trousers and treaded for the back door of the cottage. He hadn't spoken much to her in the last week, just pleasantries when Frank was around. She shouldn't have exploded and revealed that she'd been in his house and seen her mother's painting. He was either still mad, or scared of what she would do about it.

She reached for the handle on the screen door, hoping William hadn't seen her.

"Clarissa."

She closed her eyes and sighed a long breath. Her grip on the handle tightened, then she let go, dropping her arm to her side. She turned to see William marching toward her.

"Good morning, William." The words stuck in her throat.

"I'd like to talk to you."

He's going to yell at you about going in the house. What are you going to do?

She stood still on the step, slowing her breathing to calm her racing heart. If he confronted her about her snooping, she would fire right back with questions about her mother's painting hanging in his parlor. Before William said another word, Morgan appeared, running through the rows of vines, screaming.

"Mama!"

Clarissa jumped off the stairs and ran past William toward Morgan.

"Morgan, what's wrong?" Clarissa and Morgan nearly collided. She grabbed his shoulders to steady him. "Are you hurt?"

Morgan erupted in a cascade of cries and jumbled words.

She shook him. "Tell me!"

Morgan gasped for breath. His blotchy red face alarmed her. She knelt beside him and rubbed his back. "Breathe slow.

Tell me what happened. Where's James?" She glanced over Morgan's shoulder to search the rows.

William came closer.

Morgan grabbed his mother's apron. "James—he fell." Another gasp. "Bleeding."

Clarissa shuddered from head to toe. William's voice broke through Morgan's cries.

"Get in the truck. We'll find him. Morgan, show us where he is." William picked up Morgan and lifted him onto the seat.

Clarissa climbed up next to him, hoisting herself from the sideboard. Her hands trembled as she stroked Morgan's head.

"He's—he fell off the cliff at the end of the orchard." Tears streamed down his dirty face.

Clarissa wiped at the stains with her shirtsleeve.

"It's my fault. I—I made him chase me."

He coughed so hard Clarissa feared she would see blood in his spittle.

"Slow your breathing, Morgan. It will be all right."

He dropped his shoulders and turned his head to look into her eyes. "Mama, there is so much blood." His wheezy tone calmed, and he buried his head quietly in her side.

William glanced at Morgan, then at Clarissa. His eyes darted back to the road. Why hadn't she brought something to wrap James in, or something for bandages? He would need water. What was the matter with her? What if he died? No. God would never take another child from her.

Morgan's soft sobs wet her shirt. Each bump of the road jostled her away from him, and she had to pull him close.

"Can you go any faster?"

"No. Not unless you want to be bounced right out of this truck." William nudged Morgan. "Which way?"

Morgan lifted his head, his face white and tear stained. He pointed to the left. "Over there. Where Daddy always tells us not to go." His voice shook, but he leaned forward and held on to the dashboard, searching. "There! Down there!"

William slammed on the brakes. Clarissa braced herself with her hands. She made herself slow down to step to the ground. She already felt her head swimming and saw darts of sparks across her vision. By the time she reached the edge of the dirt and rock cliff, William was already partway down the side, hollering for James. She wanted to yell too, ease her way down the rocky edge. What if William fell too?

"Stay here, Morgan." Clarissa took two steps, and her foot slid. *Don't do it. Think of the baby.* Deep breaths cooled her compulsion to move. Her mind raced with questions. Did James have boots on and long pants to protect his skin? She rubbed her forehead to think of what he had been wearing when he left the cottage. She should have paid more attention.

Seconds ticked by like hours until William's voice bellowed up from below.

"I have him. He's bleeding bad."

Bleeding. Adrenaline surged as Clarissa ran to the truck, scanning the cab for anything to use as a bandage. Only greasy rags and tools lay on the floor. She caught sight of her white shirt sleeve. It would have to do. As Morgan kept watch at the cliff's edge, she pulled at the seams where the sleeves met the bodice. After a couple tugs, one sleeve was off, ripped but usable. A few more tugs on the other side and she had two long sleeves to tear into whatever they needed to stop the bleeding.

She ran to stand next to Morgan and saw William trudging up the sharp rocks and sand with James half slung over his shoulder. She planted her feet firm and reached out to pull William's elbow. Then she saw James' leg—his jeans soaked in blood that dripped onto the rocks. His ashen face and closed eyes sapped her already wobbling legs. James' arms dangled.

He didn't speak. Only the sound of Morgan's sobs and falling stones filled the air. William stumbled on solid ground away from the cliff but held tight to the boy in his arms.

By the time William laid James in the back of the truck, blood had dripped a trail on the ground. James only groaned, his face now void of color.

"You'll have to ride in the back with him," William spoke in close proximity to Clarissa's face. "It will be rough, but if you let him lay in your lap, you can bandage him while we go." He tipped his head to see into her eyes. "We have to get him to the hospital fast, Clarissa. He's bad off. Do you understand?"

Her brain played tricks on her. She heard his words but could only think of the smell of coffee on his breath. All other senses had numbed. She nodded, trying to absorb his instructions. He helped her up onto the bed of the truck and grabbed Morgan's hand.

"You'll ride up front with me, Morgan."

Clarissa regained her breath and ripped her sleeves into four strips and found the wound—a five-inch gash on the inside of James' lower right thigh. Frank had taught her what to do about cuts and gashes, in case something ever happened to him on the homestead. She tied a tight knot around James' leg above the cut. The pulsing blood drip stopped almost completely. She pushed herself against the truck cab and grabbed James by the armpits to pull him onto her lap. Blood had pooled beneath him, and now her own trousers were stained red.

Her stomach rolled as she propped his leg up on the side of the truck bed. She breathed deep through her mouth. Vomiting now would be a disaster.

James moaned and nuzzled his face into the crook of her arm.

"James? Can you hear me?"

Groans were his only answer. The truck hit a rut, sending Clarissa airborne several inches. Her rump hit the metal bed with a jolt up her spine. She checked James' face. White and wincing with pain.

God, keep James safe. And my baby.

William slowed as they rolled into the yard. Elijah stood by the cottage. Clarissa pounded on the cab window.

"Stop! I want Elijah to come!"

William looked over his shoulder, scowling. She feared he wouldn't stop, but he eased the truck to a halt.

He waved his arm to Elijah. "Get in!"

Elijah hurled himself into the back of the truck just as William hit the gas again, throwing him hard onto the bed. Clarissa reached for Elijah's arm.

"Pray, Elijah. Pray!"

Elijah reached to run a finger over James' cheek and frowned, bracing himself as the truck jostled them. He looked up to the window where Morgan's stricken face was pressed against the dusty glass. Elijah placed his palm on the glass, and Morgan touched his palm on the other side.

A man who could comfort everyone at once is a rare find. If only Frank were here.

Even though temperatures had climbed into the 80s outside, Clarissa shivered as she leaned her bare arm against the cold white walls in the hospital waiting room. She dared not sit and close her eyes or she would faint. Besides, she didn't want to see the images of James' trauma that appeared behind her lids. Standing was the only way to fight the fatigue and fear. Her body still shook from the violent ride in the back of the truck. She couldn't tell how the baby had fared.

William jogged down the hall in her direction and was soon at her side.

"Morgan is with Elijah just outside. He'll be fine."

"No he won't. You don't know Morgan. He will sit on the steps and feel guilty."

"Clarissa, it's better than him being here in the thick of it." William reached to put his hand on her shoulder.

She pulled away and shuffled to the swinging doors to the emergency rooms.

"I should have been watching them. Frank will never forgive me if something—"

"Nothing's going to happen to James. And if anyone should have been watching them, it was me. I was out in the orchard. I could have checked on them. No one is to blame. It was an accident." William plopped into a chair down the hallway and stretched out his long legs in front of him. His trousers were stained with James' blood.

Clarissa tuned to stare at him. What did he know about blame and children and losing a child? He didn't even know how to be a good brother. She wondered if he was thinking that James could have been his child. Maybe he didn't remember those days.

"Mrs. Wilding?"

Clarissa spun around at the mention of her name. A young man in a white coat stood behind her.

"Yes. I'm Mrs. Wilding. How is my son?"

He stuck out his hand. "I'm Dr. Moray. I've been looking after your son. He's doing better but lost a lot of blood. I'm afraid he needs a transfusion immediately. Since we don't have time to test his blood, our best bet is a mother or father." He looked Clarissa up and down. "You are very thin, Mrs. Wilding. Perhaps his father should donate. Then we will want to keep him overnight to watch for infection." He glanced William's way.

William stood with a start and opened his mouth. Clarissa held up her palm to William.

"How important is a transfusion, Doctor?"

The man looked to the floor and then up at her. "He could die without it. As I said, he's lost a lot of blood and is still in shock."

Clarissa's breath caught, her ribs threatening to squeeze the life from her. The moment she'd dreaded for years pressed in on her.

The doctor checked his watch and squinted at her. She knew her hesitation must have seemed unlike a normal response from a mother.

He looked back and forth between her and William. "I'm sorry to have to do it this way, but our hospital isn't yet prepared to house a blood supply for patients. We are working on it, but—"

"If you'll go prepare, one of us will be ready when you come back, Doctor."

The doctor pursed his lips and slipped through the doors. William was at Clarissa's side before she could turn around.

"What are you doing? You'll have to donate, thin or not. There's no way Frank could make it here in time."

Clarissa's throat was so dry, she didn't know if the words would come. They had to come. It was James' life at stake. She let her arms drop to her sides and closed her eyes for a short prayer.

"Did you hear me?" William's voice rose.

She bit her lower lip, then looked straight into his eyes. "I heard you, William. You will have to give blood for James. I can't because I'm pregnant."

William took a step back, then turned his gaze to her belly and back to her face. "Okay, so you're pregnant. The best bet is his father, but are you willing to risk waiting for Frank to come?"

The wrinkles on his tanned brow deepened. She felt a pang of pity for him. He was about to hear news that would change his life. If only it didn't have to be said. If only it wouldn't change her life so drastically too.

"William. *You* are James' father." She choked saying it. "You have to do it."

William let his jaw fall open. He stood so still, not even a twitch rippled his sweat-stained shirt. She had given him the keys to his future, a son to carry his name. At the same time Frank's legacy had just deflated. Another child taken from him.

"Do you understand, Will? James is your son, not Frank's."

She had meant to whisper it, but her voice come out flat and loud. She swallowed down the sour taste in her mouth.

William's face paled. His hands clenched into fists. "Why didn't you tell me before? This is—"

"Mr. Wilding? Are you ready?" The doctor stood halfway through the door, staring at William. He turned to Clarissa and handed her a clipboard. "Sign this for permission to give James blood."

She scribbled an illegible signature and handed it back as William scowled at her.

Clarissa touched William's arm and whispered in his ear. "Will, please. He could die without you."

William's eyes locked on to hers—cold and moist. "We'll talk more when I get back." He jerked his arm away from her touch and slid through the doors with the doctor.

Through the round window she saw him roll up a sleeve as he walked.

Her ears buzzed while the floor seemed to move beneath her. She placed her palms on the wall and took deep breaths. A nurse approached her, leaning in close to her face.

"Ma'am, are you all right? You should sit down." The woman couldn't know that sitting down wouldn't cure the mess she had made of things.

"I just need some fresh air. I'll be fine if I can join my other son out front."

She would never be fine again. No one in this family would be the same after today. She thought her sin had been atoned for, her punishment over. A foolish assumption she would never make again.

Morgan ran up the steps to meet her. "Is James okay, Mama? Is he coming home? Where is Uncle William?" His red eyes proved her intuition about his worry.

She nearly bawled at his questions. Elijah stood at the bottom of the steps, his kind eyes looking her over. She wanted to fall against his chest and cry it all out. *Not in front of Morgan.* She sat on the far end of the top step and pulled Morgan to her. His little arms wrapped around her neck so tight she thought she would choke.

"He'll be all right. Uncle William is helping the doctor fix him up. But he can't come home till tomorrow."

Morgan's grin seemed foreign and out of place. Everything in her was crumbling, and yet the innocent young smile somehow reassured her heart.

"Oh good." Morgan jumped down to where Elijah stood. "James is getting all fixed, Elijah. God answered our prayers, didn't He?"

Elijah squatted to be face to face with his little friend. "Yes, the Lord is takin' good care of our James. You did good to pray."

Morgan waved to Clarissa. "Can I go play on the grass now, Mama?"

"Sure."

Clarissa stood and took the steps one by one. Her feet were heavy, and she still felt like dropping to the ground.

"Ma'am, you look tired. Maybe you should lie down inside. I'm sure the nurses would find a place for you to lay your head."

Clarissa shaded her eyes to watch Morgan doing cartwheels on the lush grass. The sky was void of clouds, letting the July sun heat the concrete pavement and steps. Her bones ached despite the warmth. She would have to go inside soon if she wanted to see about James' arrangements for the night. Of course, she would stay by his side.

She sensed Elijah staring at her. She had forgotten to answer him.

"Elijah, what am I going to do? Today is the day I must tell my husband who James' father is. How do you tell a man that his son really belongs to his only brother?"

Elijah's face softened. "Beg pardon? You mean—Mr. William—James' daddy?"

She would have felt better if Elijah had pursed his lips, maybe scolded her or turned away. She would expect that from anyone else. Elijah would never do any of those things. He was the constant, the forgiving, the unsurprised.

"Yes. William knows now. He's in there giving blood so his son can live. Something Frank could never do. He'll be hurt over that—over everything it implies." She let the tears fall down her face. "I don't want to hurt him, Elijah."

"You'll have to let God ease his pain. Ain't nothin' God can't mend. You know that by now, ma'am. You jus' need to take care of yourself and that baby."

Clarissa laughed through her tears. "How funny God is to give me a baby at a time like this."

"His timin' is always perfect." Elijah looked past Clarissa, his smile fading.

She turned to see William tucking his hat on his head and taking the steps slowly. He reached Clarissa and then glowered at Elijah.

"Would you mind checking on Morgan?" Clarissa whispered to Elijah.

He tipped his hat and strolled to the lawn, avoiding William's steely eyes.

William fidgeted with the gauze on his inner arm. "Doc says James will be fine now. They gave him something to relax him, but he wants to see you."

"You didn't—"

"No. I didn't tell him." He cleared his throat. "I'm going back to the farm. I'll take Elijah and Morgan with me and send Frank back for you. I won't say anything to Frank. Not yet." His face reddened, and his jaw twitched through a tortuous silence.

"I'm sorry, Will. Thank you for giving your blood."

He jerked his head to look at her. "He's my son. I'm just glad I was here." He took the last step down and spoke without looking at her. "This is a real mess, Clarissa. I won't be left out anymore. You shouldn't have run off with Frank all those years ago. You should have waited."

She shuddered at his tone. Maybe he was right, but she'd had no choice.

He sneered at her. "Just so you know—I paid the hospital for today and for an overnight stay. I'm his *father*, so I took care of it."

She lost her breath to call him back as he walked away. Frank would never allow it, especially once he knew the truth. In the distance William talked with Elijah and Morgan. Elijah nodded to her and Morgan waved.

"Goodbye, Mama. See you tomorrow."

Elijah paused before following William and Morgan to the truck. His smile reached her, calming and reassuring. He ran to catch up and jumped in the back of the truck. He would be praying all the way home. Praying for Frank to understand.

One prayer God might not be able to answer.

Chapter 7

"What? Is he all right?" Frank's knees weakened when he heard what William blurted out.

"He's going to be. They're keeping him at the hospital tonight. Clarissa is there, and you can take the car to join her. It is fixed, isn't it?" William wrung his hands and stomped around the outside of the car.

Frank wasn't sure he heard the question. "What?"

"Fixed. Is the car fixed?" he shouted from the back of the vehicle.

"Yes. Yes, they found the problem. Where's the hospital? I need to go now." He turned to Elijah, who stood with Morgan on the porch of the cottage. "Elijah, will you watch Morgan for me till we come home?"

"Yes, Mr. Wilding. Sure will. Don't you worry."

Thank God Elijah was here. He couldn't possibly have left the boy with William. Whatever was irritating his brother couldn't be more important that James' health. William walked around the other side of the car and strode toward the big house, handing Frank a piece of paper as he passed.

"Here's directions to the hospital. You know I should have... Just get back here as soon as you can tomorrow. There's work to be done."

The thick tension between them only added to Frank's confusion. He fought the urge to confront William about his agitation. He took the paper and ran to hug Morgan. "Be good for Elijah, okay?"

"I will." Morgan sniffled and then clung to Elijah.

"We'll be back tomorrow."

Elijah leaned over to Frank. "See if you can get Mrs. Wilding to rest. She sure is worn out."

Frank felt his stomach twist. *Poor Clarissa. I should have been here.* He ran through all possible scenarios all the way into town. Once in the parking lot, he looked in the side mirror to see the orange glow of the setting sun. He groaned to see his reflection. He was a mess, but it couldn't be helped. Clarissa needed him.

He took the front steps two by two until he reached the double doors into the entry. He stated his case to the charge nurse and followed her down the darkened hallway.

"The lights have been dimmed for the night. I'll show you his room," she whispered.

Frank stopped just inside the door of James' room. Clarissa sat in a chair, one arm draped over James' chest, her head resting on the mattress. James' form was silhouetted under a white blanket. His eyelids fluttered as if he were dreaming, and he groaned.

Clarissa jerked her head up and reached for James' forehead. Frank took another step, and she turned to him. A tear escaped her dark-circled eye, and she gave him a desperate smile.

"Hi," she squeaked.

Frank crept across the concrete floor to her side, keeping his eye on James. He knelt by Clarissa and laid his head on her lap. "I'm sorry you had to do this alone. I came as soon as William told me."

"Told you what?"

"That he was…" He pointed to James.

Clarissa held up her hand. "It's okay. I'm just glad you're

here now. He's sleeping. They gave him something for the pain. He's been twitching and groaning a lot. Did William tell you he can go home in the morning?" She looked away and stroked James' arm.

"Yes. That's good." He touched Clarissa's chin and pulled her face toward him. "Are you all right? You look pretty tired—and worried. He'll be better soon, and you need to rest."

He stood and surveyed the stark white room. Nothing there was appropriate for her to lay on. He would have to talk to the nurse about a cot.

"I'm fine, Frank."

Her voice didn't convince him. "I'll be right back." He tiptoed out to the hallway just as a young man in a short white coat hurried past him.

"Excuse me," Frank called to him in a grinding whisper.

The young man stopped and turned around. "Sir?"

"I need a cot in my son's room for my wife to lay down. She's been here all day and needs some rest."

"Well, I'll see if it's allowed." He fidgeted with the pockets on his coat.

"It's important. I'm sure you can make it happen." Frank nodded to him and spun to return to Clarissa.

She stood near the small lamp on the bedside table. He stopped just inside the doorway to assimilate her posture and countenance. She had gone through many changes since they'd come to Washington. Most he took joy in—the color of her skin had reflected her time spent in the sunshine tending her garden. Her thin arms and hollow cheeks had filled in with some much-needed weight. Even though her shape was changing, she was still the most beautiful woman he had ever known. The slight fullness through her waist did prompt sadness about her lost babies, but she seemed to have reconciled her loss. They would have to settle for two wonderful boys.

Frank moved close to her and wrapped his arms around her shoulders from behind. "He'll be all right."

She nodded. He could feel a deep, long sigh fill and then leave her chest. He wanted desperately to know the whole story of James' accident, but Clarissa seemed far away. Her shoulders shook under his arms.

"Are you cold?"

"No. I'm fine."

It was then he noticed her bloody clothes. His heart skipped. Why hadn't he thought to bring her a change of clothing? He let go of her and led her back to the chair, easing her down with firm hands.

"I've asked for a cot for you. I want you to try and sleep, at least for a while. Then we can talk about James' accident and how we're going to manage caring for him at home. I should have brought you fresh clothes. I'm sorry. I was just so worried about my son, I guess."

Clarissa burst into tears. He knelt beside her, and she thrust her face into his chest, sobbing. Heat ran up his neck. Either she was more exhausted than he'd first surmised, or there was something she held back about James' condition.

She took some deep breaths and then pulled away from him, searching his eyes. "I'll rest awhile. Then we need to talk."

Her somber tone sent a chill up his back. Frank's stomach tightened. Questions swirled in his mind, but he resisted the compulsion to find out what was really on her heart.

The door swung open, and the young man from before entered, laden with a cot. Frank jumped up and helped him position it in a dark corner of the room. Before Frank could ask for a pillow and blanket, an elderly nurse appeared with both items in her arms and handed them to the orderly.

"She'll want these, poor thing." She leaned in to Frank to whisper. "She seems to be taking this awfully hard. I'm glad you're here. You'll have to sleep in the chair, I'm afraid. No room in here for another cot." She patted Frank's arm. "Let me know if you need anything. I'll be back in an hour to check on your boy."

Clarissa settled in on the cot. The orderly handed her the pillow and then hurried out of the room. The nurse's words echoed in Frank's head. Clarissa did seem to have reacted strongly to James' injury—more so than she used to when one of the boys got hurt.

Frank slipped through the door to catch up with the nurse. She and the orderly were just outside the door. He made sure the door was shut, then caught the nurse's attention. "Can you tell me how serious my son's injury is? My wife seems distraught. I wondered if there was something I needed to know. He is going to be all right, isn't he?"

She smiled and nodded. "Your son is going to be fine. I was told once he received the blood transfusion, he perked up. He'll be in pain for several days, but we'll give him some medicine to help." She leaned in. "Your wife has taken it hard, but it could be because of the pregnancy. Women who are expecting are more emotional. You just need to get everyone home and rested."

Frank's knees weakened. Why would this silly woman think Clarissa was pregnant? He tapped her shoulder just as she turned to walk away.

"My wife isn't expecting. It must be something else making her so upset. Are you sure James isn't in any danger?" He glanced to the door of James' room to make sure Clarissa couldn't hear.

The nurse frowned. "Well, she asked to get an appointment with one of our obstetricians, so I assumed—"

Frank didn't hear the rest of her explanation. The ringing in his ears overshadowed everything in his sight and hearing. *Clary, pregnant?* That would account for her emotional state and her physical changes. The fatigue and stomach upset made sense now.

"Mr. Wilding?" The nurse touched his arm.

"I understand. Thank you."

He had to talk to Clarissa. There had to be a reason why she didn't tell him. Fear would be his first guess. Losing another child would be more than they both could bear.

She was asleep by the time he approached her cot. James groaned and twitched.

He would have to take the weight Clarissa had been carrying and be diligent to help care for James when they got home. William would have to understand. He didn't have any children of his own, but surely concern for his nephew would win over his need for Frank to work as much.

Frank slid onto the chair and stroked James' forehead. He watched the boy's chest rise and fall. Clarissa stirred. Frank squinted in the darkness to see her tossing in her sleep. She ended up on her back. Frank could see in the shadow the small bulge on her tummy. *It's true.* Frank's heart leapt. He would have to make sure she took better care of herself this time. It would mean time away from work.

He turned his gaze to James. Thank God William had rushed them into town and that the hospital could give James blood.

William had been a good brother. He was a reasonable man. He had to understand. Frank closed his eyes and leaned over to rest his head near James' arm. As soon as they got home, everything would be better. They'd make some adjustments and deal with the situation. As always, everything would be fine.

It had to be.

Clarissa sat at the kitchen table wishing the wind would stop. The leafy branch scraping on the window grated on her already tethered nerves. Why hadn't she told Frank about the baby—or the fact that William was James' father? She'd had every opportunity as they waited at the hospital. Frank had been so quiet all the way back to the farm, the eerie silence between them like a shadow of unsaid words.

Now that James was settled into his bed, his leg propped up with throw pillows from the wicker chair on the porch, she could send Morgan off to play to give her some privacy with Frank. It had to happen soon—before William broke open the secret she was forced to share with him. She had to expose it all to Frank. Now.

"Mama, is James gonna die?"

Morgan's question startled Clarissa from her thoughts. Poor young Morgan had seen so much tragedy in his short life, it was no wonder his tone sounded incurious. She glanced into the bedroom where Elijah stood next to James, telling him a tall tale. Morgan plopped onto a kitchen chair and looked up at her, waiting for her answer.

She brushed back his hair. The sunshine of the last months had birthed freckles on his nose—much like her own complexion. "Of course not. What gave you that idea?"

"Just wondering. He's never got hurt before or had to stay in a hospital like I did. You thought I was going to die in the Kansas hospital, didn't you?" He scratched his head, keeping eye contact with her.

Not sure how to answer, she pulled another chair next to him. "Why do you say I thought you were going to die?"

He shrugged and picked at his fingernails. "I heard you out in the hall talking to Daddy. You were crying something awful, and you said you were afraid I was going to die." He sighed and leaned back.

Clarissa's thoughts swirled to remember the conversation, but those days were all a blur now. Morgan might have dreamed it, but it was likely she did express the horrible fear she'd lived in then. It hurt to know Morgan had carried her words all this time.

"Well, you didn't die, and neither will James. He just needs some rest and time to heal. You might have to help with his chores. Will you?"

She pinched his chin.

"Sure, Mama. And I'll help Elijah too."

Elijah stepped out into the room. "I'll be pretty busy helpin' your uncle William while your daddy's makin' sure James is gettin' better. You stick close to home for a while." He nodded to Clarissa. "James is sleepin'."

William's already churning attitude had turned stormy at hearing Frank explain he would be unavailable for a few days. Every overheard exchange of words between them had set Clarissa on edge, waiting for a slip-up. But the brothers had finally compromised on a lighter work schedule if Elijah would pitch in, starting this afternoon.

"All right, young man?" Elijah poked at Morgan's arm.

"Yes, sir." Morgan slid off the chair and slogged to the back door.

"Where are you going?" Clarissa stood, hands on her hips.

"Pull some weeds in the garden." He pushed the screen door open and tromped down the steps.

Elijah chuckled. Clarissa wanted to, but her whole body spun with nerves and morning sickness. She dropped her arms and smiled at Elijah. "Can you work some of that magic on me, Elijah?"

He tipped his head to the side. "No magic. Jus' the joy of the Lord." He captured her gaze in his. "But I can see you're troubled, and I know you have some mountains to climb. Jus' remember what you already come through to get this far."

"It doesn't feel like I can climb it today."

"Don't need to feel it. Jus' believe it. Then give it time."

Talking to Elijah always felt like a warm bath, soothing and cleansing. Her shoulders relaxed as she let his sentiment stick like honey to her heart. She knew the truth when she heard it. If only it would help her to open old wounds with Frank. Perhaps news of the baby would soften the blow. Anyway, she would get her chance. Frank's footsteps neared the back porch.

Elijah turned his ear in that direction, his eyes still on Clarissa. "I'll be goin' now."

"Thank you, Elijah. Always, thank you."

He hesitated but headed for the back door, meeting Frank on the threshold.

"Elijah. Thanks for pinch-hitting for me. William is waiting for you in the southeast corner."

"Yes, sir." Elijah bounded down the stairs and trotted across the yard.

Clarissa wondered how a man his age could manage such feats, let alone working the hours it would take to cover for Frank. Yet she had no idea how old Elijah was. Sometimes he seemed as old as Moses.

Frank reached Clarissa, and her face filled with heat.

He kissed her cheek, then felt it with the back of his hand. "You still look tired and flushed. Why don't you sit down, and I'll clean up the lunch dishes. Deal?"

"I had something else in mind." She had to commit to the inevitable conversation. "Can we sit out on the porch so we won't disturb James?"

Frank stretched out his arm. "Lead the way."

Clarissa placed her hand on her abdomen, her breakfast threatening at her throat. Just as they stepped onto the porch, the sun broke free from the morning clouds. Bright rays streamed through the lattice above them, making squares of light and shade on the concrete. Frank sat on the padded wicker and tapped the seat next to him. Impossible to sit at a time like this. "Honey, I have some news, and I'd like to stay standing to tell you."

Frank seemed to look right through her, one side of his lips curling up. Breaking the first part of the news wouldn't be difficult. They had given up on more children, and she knew Frank would be overjoyed. The following conversation that would send their world into a tailspin.

"I can't be one hundred percent sure, but I'm almost positive that we're going to have a baby." She raised her brows, feeling sick to her stomach. She was sure all right.

Frank burst into laughter and jumped up to wrap his arms around her. He squeezed her tight, laughing and kissing her neck. Then he pushed her back and stared at her tummy.

"I sort of knew about it, but hearing you say it—well, I'm so happy, Clary."

Wait. He knew? How could he, except that Elijah told him. Elijah would never do that. Still, her blood boiled to think her secret had gotten out.

"How did you sort of know? I barely knew myself. I didn't want anyone to know."

Frank laughed again. "Then you shouldn't tell loose-lipped nurses you want an appointment with a baby doctor."

The nurse? Great. What else had she revealed?

Frank returned to the sofa. His wide grin dissipated into a frown. "You don't even seem happy about this. Are you worried we'll lose another one?"

"A little. Aren't you?"

"Nope. Not even a little."

She sat next to him, willing her shaking to stop. Her worry about losing a baby couldn't compare with her concern over Frank's reaction to her next bombshell. She pulled in a deep breath and let it escape slowly.

Frank jumped up. "Okay, now that it's out in the open, let's celebrate with some of that iced tea you made."

"Frank, sit down. I have more to talk to you about. It's concerning the accident." She closed her eyes. "And more."

Frank returned to the sofa. "I was going to ask you what happened when things settled down. If you want to talk about it now, that's good with me. I want to make sure it doesn't happen again."

The moments drug on, slugging away at her confidence. The sun disappeared behind an enormous cloud. Any joy over talking about a baby would also disappear in a moment. Frank waited silently while Clarissa's heart thumped in her ears. She had rehearsed her speech a hundred times in the last several hours.

"James fell off the ridge where they weren't supposed to be playing, and a sharp rock sliced his thigh, puncturing an artery. He lost a lot of blood on the way to the hospital. William drove as fast as he dared." She paused and swallowed down tears.

Frank just stared at the floor. "So thankful. We owe him a lot."

She had to keep going or she would run from the cottage.

"The doctor came out and told us James had lost so much blood that he needed a transfusion by a close relative, preferably a parent. They don't have blood stored at the hospital yet. I couldn't give because I'm pregnant and too thin evidently. You couldn't have given either, since you're not his birth father. As the doctor said, the safest bet was for a birth parent to donate. There wasn't even time to test for blood type."

She hung her head for a few seconds. When she glanced at Frank, his knit brows told her the questions in his head were rolling fast. She had to hurry and finish before she lost her nerve.

"William was the only one who could donate blood." She

could no longer steady her voice or hold back the tears.

"Why could William donate and not me? That doesn't add up. What was it about his blood that made it okay?" The vessels on Frank's temples pulsed.

"Frank." She couldn't say it. The words stuck in her throat like thick glue.

"Clary. I don't understand. Unless—"

"William is—William is James' blood father."

Frank jerked as if he'd been hit by lightning. He stood so abruptly, Clarissa nearly bounced out of the sofa. His face faded to snow white. She saw the expression she dreaded. He hated her. He despised her. She had asked too much of him all their lives, and this could be the final blow to his love.

"Frank, I knew William before I married you. We were serious. I thought I loved him, that we'd be married. I didn't know he was your brother. He never said… I didn't know."

She stood and reached for him. He backed away from her touch, his fists clenched by his side. The silence ripped at her heart, but it kept beating. So loud that she thought it echoed through the air.

Her voice finally broke through the tears. "I'm so sorry. I didn't know until we arrived who William was. I didn't know what to do."

"So—William knows he's the boy's father. Has he always? Why did everyone keep it from me?" He took another step away from her, then another.

Clarissa shook her head. He wouldn't hear anything she had to say in her defense. She stood still and watched in horror as Frank looked at her like she was a stranger. Painful as it was, she deserved it, but William was innocent. At least in the fact that he didn't know James was his.

Thunder rolled in the distance. Rain would be upon them soon—one thing the crops didn't need right now. William would be upset.

Frank turned and shuffled down the steps and toward the barn. She knew him well enough to know he had to be alone. Rain would be the least of their worries today. The flood of emotion just might drown them all.

He knew exactly where William would be. The thunderstorm would have already passed over that area by the looks of the wind direction. Frank had kept his eye on the black clouds as he marched his way down the road. It reminded him of how he scanned the skies back home for signs of billowing brown clouds—the kind that would bury a man in dirt.

Part of him wished lightning would strike him dead right there on the road. Then the pain of Clarissa's confession would stop. Everything would stop. But he hadn't come this far through drought, poverty, and sorrow to give in now. At this moment in time, William was in his way and had to be dealt with.

"Then we'll leave this place, just like Clary wanted," he shouted into the clearing sky. Now he knew why she had suggested they move into town. It wasn't just the sky that was opening up. His unanswered questions had shifted into focus, as a gun sight aimed straight at his chest. This test of his strength reached to his soul.

The thunder rumbled far away as he rounded the last bend in the rain-pocked road. He spied William at the end of the best row of trees in the orchard. Small applets clustered on the branches, waiting for the sun and warm air to ripen. All they had to do was to keep the birds from eating them and avoid any freak frosts.

No. He wouldn't be here to worry about such things. This was William's problem—and his landlords'. The fact that Frank had come to love the place was inconsequential. The only thing he needed to do now was to deliver a message to William.

Frank saw William in the distance and picked up his pace. The charged air between them wasn't because of the thunderstorm. Only the storm in Frank's mind and William's obvious concern at Frank's demeanor electrified the area.

Frank felt his fingernails dig into the palm of his right hand. Then it was over. William lay on his back in a muddy puddle, shaking his head. He bled from a small cut on his cheek just below his eye.

"Get up." Frank ground out the words through gritted teeth. Hitting William felt good—a release he had never known.

William wiped his face and rested his elbows on the dirt. "She told you."

"Good guess. Get up. I want to finish what I came to do."

William curled to a sitting position. Frank's adrenaline faded a bit, partially due to the throbbing pain in his knuckles. He remembered the same pain from the day he'd punched a hole in the plaster wall of his bedroom after an argument with his father. He didn't feel any better after that explosion than he did at this moment. Nothing could make him feel better. Except maybe the truth about what really happened all those years ago between William and Clarissa.

"Mr. Wilding?" Elijah's voice rang from out of nowhere. "Everything all right here?"

William huffed and pulled a handkerchief from his pocket. "Gonna let your boy finish the job for you, Frank? Or shall we figure this out on our own?"

Frank turned to Elijah. "It's all right, Elijah. I think I'm done making a fool of myself. This is between my brother and me. Thanks though."

The nod from Elijah was like the final bell rung in the prizefighter ring. No use going on. No one was going to win this fight. Who could he blame for the pain he felt deep down?

He had lost two babies to the drought. Now he'd had lost a son to another man. Up until now, it was a phantom stranger who'd fathered James, someone far away and disconnected. The phantom had just become real—a brother.

William pushed himself up from the ground and took a few steps back. "What now?"

Frank shook his head. "I don't know. I just found out I'm to be a father again, only to also find out I've lost my oldest boy to my brother. How am I supposed to deal with that?"

William slapped his hat on his thighs. Dust plumed upward. The dryness had already soaked up the short rain.

"How do you think I feel? I come back to town to find my girl had run off with someone else. Now I know it was my brother. Clarissa should be *my* wife!" William's shouts pierced the humid air, backdropped by more rumbling from the distant sky. "I suppose you were after her behind my back all that time."

Frank unlocked his jaw and rubbed his aching knuckles.

"Don't be absurd. She was someone else's girl. I didn't know who."

Hitting and yelling wasn't going to solve anything, but he wanted so much to hit William again. He had come to Clarissa's rescue back then knowing full well the child she'd carried wasn't his. He thought she had grown to love him as much as he loved her. Perhaps he was wrong. She must have loved William. Did she still?

"Well, she's *my* wife, and she'll have to be in on how to deal with this mess." Frank took a step toward William. "Let me make one thing clear. You are not to say a word about this to anyone, especially James. That is for me and Clarissa to take care of. You stay out of our way."

He turned to walk away. William followed behind him.

"I'm not sure this working arrangement is going to happen after all, brother. You always had it easy growing up and got whatever you wanted. You even got more of Dad's inheritance. And now I find out you got my girl and my son. Don't think I'm going to give him up so easily. I need some time to decide what I'm going to do, but I don't think I'll like playing second fiddle to you again."

So that was it. William's hardness had a foundation built long ago on jealousy and envy. Now he had an upper hand knowing James was his son. It was entirely possible he still loved Clarissa and that she still had feelings for him. The unknown tie that secretly bound them was exposed. A tie that could easily strengthen or unravel. Frank felt the impact of the new realities weighting him down. The phantom image of the two of them together twisted like a knife in his gut.

Frank whirled around, his fists poised. He stuffed them in his pockets for safe keeping. "You didn't deserve her. You took what you wanted of her and then left town without a word. I was there for her. No special favors for her or for me. I loved her. She needed me. You'll have to live with it, brother. She's had to all these years."

Frank willed his feet to move, walking faster and faster away from the man who could tear apart his world. William let him go, but Frank knew there would be more coming. This was only beginning, this picking up shattered pieces of their lives.

He increased his pace until he hit a sprint speed. By the time he reached the cottage, out of breath and aching, Clarissa had left the porch. The hot sun emerged from the passing storm, lifting steam from the wet ground. The shade of the porch cooled the sticky sweat on his back. He held the doorknob in his hand for several breaths, then pulled open the screen and stopped. Clarissa sat at the table with her face to the window. She didn't flinch when he let the door slam behind him.

She was far away, and they were far apart. James had been their bridge, and now they each had a hand at burning it. His life had only started when he'd fallen in love with her. He would wait as long as it took to reach her again, no matter how he hurt and regardless of William's involvement. He would keep fighting through it all.

He was never one for competition. Until now.

Chapter 8

*J*ames had called to her when Frank stomped off the porch to find William. She had turned the corner of the doorway so fast a sharp pain shot through her abdomen. She didn't stop but limped all the way into James' room and sat on the edge of his bed.

James thrashed under the sheet, sweat beading on his brow. "It hurts bad."

She pulled back the sheet to check his bandage. No blood seeping through.

"James, I'm going to give you some of the laudanum the doctor gave us. It will help the pain. Lie still and I'll be right back."

James winced and nodded.

Clarissa met Morgan in the hall by the bathroom. She nearly gasped at the mud-caked, soaking wet little boy in front of her. His eyes widened, as if he'd been caught stealing from the cookie jar. His familiar sheepish grin made him suspect.

"Morgan. What have you been up to? You are a mess." She led him by the shoulder to the back door. "Take off your wet clothes and leave them outside. I'm going to run bath water for you."

"It's too hot for a bath." Morgan slapped his muddy hands on this thighs.

"No arguments. Wait in the bathroom while I give James his medicine."

Her mind buzzed with frustration at Morgan's repeated disappearing acts whenever it rained. Each time he came in the house soaking wet would send him into a wheezing fit. Inevitably he'd cough for a few days afterward. With everything going on in this family, the issue was low on the list to deal with.

She wished Frank would come back. His state of mind when he'd stormed away worried her. He wasn't a fighting man, but the news she gave him would push any man to the brink of rage. Surely he wouldn't start a fistfight with William?

She hurried back to James' room. He had settled some, but his pale face gave away his fight with the pain. He swallowed down the laudanum. The effects were quick. She watched his body relax and his eyelids close. She cracked the window to let the gentle breeze drift in.

Morgan!

She tiptoed out of the room and shuffled down the hall. The stitch in her side stung again, this time making her stop in her tracks. "Slow down, Clary."

"Mama. Are you coming?"

"Yes, Morgan."

She ran the warm water into the claw-foot tub, remembering how only a few months ago they were hauling water from the well on the homestead to share baths. Gratitude abounded for running water and a real bathtub, especially now that she would have a little one to bathe soon.

"You soak for a while, and wash behind your ears. Then dry off and get into clean clothes. Your dad should be back soon. He can help you wash the mud out of your dirty clothes."

Frank should be back by now.

She turned to see Morgan slip into the water. He was growing up—like James. If only she could keep them sheltered. But what good had it done her? The smothering shelter her father had made for her hadn't kept her from making a mess of her life.

She found a sunny place by the kitchen window and relaxed into the only chair with a padded seat. The pain in her side had subsided by the time Frank walked in the door. He stood by the door, waiting for her to acknowledge him. She didn't. Even when she felt him standing next to her. Even now when she felt his hand on her shoulder.

Her face heated from the sun streaming through the window. She wanted to move but would rather burn up than have to turn and look into the pain she knew would be written on Frank's face.

"How's James?" he said just over a whisper.

She turned from the window but busied her hands folding the napkin in front of her. "He's sleeping. I gave him some laudanum."

"Where's Morgan?"

"In the tub. He went out in the rainstorm again and got soaking wet and muddy." She reached across the table for the other two napkins and folded them, then refolded them.

Frank left her side and sat across from her. "Clary. Look at me."

Her chest felt as though she had been holding her breath too long. She forced her head up and met his gaze. Her pulse raced as she tried to read his expression. His sad eyes and slumped shoulders could mean many different things. It usually meant he was about to apologize.

"I'm sorry I stormed off."

There it was. She knew him well but wasn't sure he knew her well enough to understand her guilt and regret. And did he see her fear of what William could do now that he knew the truth about James? Did they see each other?

"Frank, I don't know what to say. If I had known Will was your brother—"

"Half brother."

126

"Well, if I had known, I would not have consented to come here. All of this would have been avoided." She blinked back tears. No falling apart now.

"Evidently, that's not what God had in mind. It would have been too easy for you to keep your secret if we had gone somewhere else. Easy is not always best." He squeezed his hand together until his knuckles turned white.

Which of his emotions should she trust? They seemed to change every hour. If only she could lessen his turmoil. She couldn't even ease her own wild ride of anger and shame.

Morgan called from the hallway. "I'm almost dressed. Can I go play in the barn?"

Clarissa raised her brows to Frank, who shrugged.

She stood and walked to the hallway, not willing to shout and wake James. "Don't be gone long." She knew it was futile to say it. His brain didn't run on the same timeline as a mother's. Still, she needed a while to talk to Frank.

"Okay." Morgan tied the last shoestring and bounded out the door.

Clarissa caught it before it slammed. "Stay out of the puddles!" she hollered.

Frank was right where she'd left him. She sucked in a quick breath to hide another stitch in her side. It didn't help that her pants had tightened from her swelling belly. A welcome problem to have, considering nearly starving in Kansas.

Frank leaned back in his chair as she slid into hers.

He cleared his throat. "So what are we going to do about all this?"

She looked away.

"Before you answer, I suppose I should tell you I don't think William wants us here anymore. You may get your wish about moving off the farm." He grabbed one of her folded napkins and wiped his face.

The heat from the window penetrated her cotton blouse, making her woozy. She reached up and pulled the shade down before responding. "I'm not surprised he reacted that way. My worry is that he will want to be a father to James."

She glanced in the direction of James' room. Nothing stirring. The last thing they needed was James to overhear this discussion.

"Clary, *I'm* James' father—the only one he's ever known."

"But he doesn't know you're not his blood father. How's he going to react to that news? I think we should wait till we're away from here before we tell him, and pray Will doesn't say anything to him."

Frank closed his eyes and sighed hard. "Please stop calling him Will. It just reminds me of the past. A past I wasn't a part of."

Clarissa rubbed her temples to lighten the tightness stretching over the top of her head. "Sorry. Can we take some time to think about this? I'm feeling sick and—"

Frank jumped to his feet. "Of course. You need to rest. I'll fix you some tea and bring it to you in our room. No objections." He held out his hand and pulled her up. "Scoot."

Clarissa shuffled to the bedroom and stood at the window. Frank was too good to her. After all he'd learned today, he still treated her like she was an innocent princess. She was anything but innocent, and at the moment she felt more like an old hag than royalty. She would never understand what it was in Frank that made him so understanding and forgiving. He was her hero, her example, and her friend. All that in just a few short months since leaving Kansas. She didn't deserve him.

Morgan crossed her vision through the window. He ran from the back of William's house with something tucked under his arm. She pressed closer to the glass and squinted to make out the object.

"A mason jar."

Her mouth hung open. Morgan was the culprit William had complained about. What on earth did he need with mason jars? The image of the jar under his arm jarred her memory to the day she and Elijah discovered the jars of water hidden behind the vine on the pump house. Morgan was hoarding jars of rainwater.

But why?

Frank stared into the small pot of water until it finally bubbled, contemplating how long he could pretend to Clarissa that he was handling the news well. It would be a long time before he could look at her the same way, even though they were going to share a new baby, a child besides Morgan he could be a *real* father to.

He watched the bubbles erupting from the bottom of the pot, about to come to a full boil. He would have to keep his emotions from doing the same. So would James. Poor boy would soon be forced to grow up before he should, facing the consequences only the adults in his life should face.

Clarissa stood at the bedroom door. "Frank, did Morgan come inside?"

"Nope."

He reached for a teacup from the cupboard and filled a tea strainer with Clarissa's favorite mint tea. He turned off the burner and poured the water into the cup, spilling some of the hot liquid onto the stovetop. Clarissa should have a real teapot. He would get her one on his next trip to town. He had seen one in the window of one of the many secondhand stores. With dozens of families selling their belongings, those shop owners had a plentiful inventory.

The water turned colors as he swirled the strainer in the cup.

The smell of mint drifted to his nose. His stomach growled. Or was it just the pain of the day churning it? It was likely Clarissa hadn't eaten all day, knowing what she had to tell him and worrying about James. Tears welled behind his closed eyelids.

Please, God. Don't let her lose another child.

He grabbed an oatmeal cookie from the bowl on the counter as he cradled the cup and saucer in one hand. More conversation with his wife loomed, but she needed to rest and get her mind off the issue for a while. He'd check in on James, find Morgan, and prepare some dinner. What would he cook? He wasn't good at that sort of thing, but the boys would be hungry in a few hours, or at least Morgan would.

The teacup rattled on the saucer as he shuffled his way to the bedroom. Clarissa stood at the window, her arms wrapped around her chest. Her hair dangled on her shoulders, loose from their pins. The curtain-filtered sun glowed around her head. Getting away from the terrible dirt and drought had brought color back to her cheeks, and the sun had kissed her nose with freckles once again. She looked tired but still the beauty he'd fallen in love with.

He pushed back the twist in his gut and set the teacup and cookie on the bed table. "Drink it while it's hot."

She moved her arms to her hips. "Did I tell you about the jars of water Elijah and I found behind the vines on the pump house?"

Frank relaxed at the change of subject. He let his shoulders go limp and motioned for her to come sit with him on the edge of the bed. "No. Why would someone put jars of water there, or anywhere?"

Clarissa picked up the cup and blew on the tea before taking a sip. She sighed. "William approached me a week or so ago and asked me if I had been taking jars from his porch. I told him I wouldn't do that. He seemed upset, but he let it go. Then

Elijah found the jars, and I realized they could be the ones missing from William's porch." She took another sip.

Frank blinked to keep focused on what she was saying, his thoughts still winding back to his fight with William. He didn't even like Clarissa talking about a conversation with William, no matter what it was about. *Breathe and listen.*

"So who did it?" Frank wondered where all this was going.

"Well, while you were making my tea, I saw Morgan out the window. He was coming from the direction of William's house. He had an empty mason jar tucked under his arm. He disappeared behind the cottage somewhere."

Frank tried to imagine Morgan stealing anything, if that was indeed what Clarissa implied. His sweet boy would never stoop to such deceit. Why on earth would anyone want to steal jars and fill them with water?

"Okay, I'll take a look at the jars and maybe talk to Morgan when things settle down. I don't think William will be watching his stash of jars for a while. He has other things on his mind."

Clarissa set the cup on the saucer, her fingers shaking. He reached for her hand and squeezed it. It was all he could manage in the way of comfort.

"You need to rest for a while. Don't worry about dinner. I'll rustle up something."

She stared at the floor for a moment, then lay back on the bed, a tear dripping from her face onto the pillow. He hated that she was starting this pregnancy with so much emotional drama, but if she had been honest with him earlier, things would have been different.

No. He'd still be as torn up as she.

Frank closed the door behind him. As long as the bedroom window was open, the breeze should keep her cool. He pushed the door to James' room open a crack. The boy was awake and had pushed himself to sit up against the brass headboard. His tousled hair lay low on his forehead. Frank would have to get out the scissors and cut both the boys' long mops.

James turned to see Frank. He rubbed his eyes and then smiled.

"You're awake finally," Frank teased as he stepped into the room and bounced the mattress with his fist. "How's the leg?"

James brushed the hair from his moist brow. "Hurts sometimes." He pushed back the covers. "It's hot in here."

Frank opened the door to let the same breeze flow that he hoped Clarissa was enjoying. The temperatures had risen this afternoon. He wondered how it would affect the crop hanging in the vineyard and orchard. William hadn't told Frank what happened in the case of extreme heat.

"I heard you and Mother talking." James stared into Frank's eyes.

Frank's heart slammed against his chest. He and Clarissa should have been more careful. If James had heard too much it would be the worst timing. He casually slid onto the edge of the bed, trying to read James' face.

"Sorry if we woke you."

James shifted in the bed and winced. "I couldn't tell what you were talking about, just that you sounded upset. Is anything wrong? If it's about the hospital bills, I'll work to help pay for them. It was my fault that I got hurt. I shouldn't have been by the ridge. I'm sorry."

Frank almost sighed with relief. He paused to decide what to say to James' confession. For Frank it was the least of the turmoil about to hit this young man he had loved since birth. Love wouldn't be enough to wipe away the agony of what was to come.

"Well, son, I'm glad you know you did wrong, but let's not worry about it now. And you're not to be concerned with the hospital bills. You let your dad worry about that, which I won't, 'cause there's no need to worry." He had to change the subject and get back on track for the evening soon to come.

James nodded. Frank thought he saw a tear form before James turned his head to the window.

"Tell you what." Frank patted the mattress. "If you're feeling up to it and your leg isn't too sore, we'll get you out to the living room after dinner. You can keep your brother company for a while before bed."

James cleared his throat. "Sure."

Frank winked and hurried out of the room. He stopped and reached for the napkin to wipe his face. The cottage air was stifling. He had to open more windows and the front door. He took one step to the door, when he heard a faint knock. Through the glass in the door, he saw Elijah standing on the porch.

He swung the door open, wondering why Elijah wasn't working with William. Elijah's set jaw told the story.

"Elijah?"

"Sorry to bother you, Mr. Wilding. Mr. William told me to quit for the day on account of the heat. Told me he didn't know if he wanted me back tomorrow. I believe Mr. William is in a bad way. Very angry."

It was just what Frank expected. Soon they would all be off the farm. Elijah deserved an explanation, even if he already knew the situation.

"Have a seat, Elijah. Let's talk for a minute. Then you can help me fix this family some dinner."

Elijah smiled wide. "Be glad to, Mr. Wilding. I can do the cookin' outside so we don't heat up this cottage anymore. There's some fine meat hangin' in the smoker out back. Mr. William said to help ourself." Elijah rubbed his chin and frowned. "Then again, that was before—"

Frank waved his hand. "Before Mr. William got mad."

He didn't care. They would eat well tonight. It could be their last good meal for a while.

Elijah and Frank had fixed a fine meal, surprising Clarissa with their culinary talents and teamwork, and delighting her with the aromas of sweet barbeque smoke. The boys had laughed and enjoyed a picnic in the living room, with Morgan on the floor and James propped up on the sofa. Frank insisted she sit and watch the magic happen without lifting a finger to help. She was grateful for the chance to be still and nurse her aching side. Bending and twisting only made the pain worse, and now that dinner was over she longed to go to bed with a hot water bottle.

"Morgan, you can help dry the rest of the dishes. Then James will have to get back to his bed." Frank shook a finger at Clarissa. "And I think your mother needs to be in bed early tonight."

Elijah knocked on the door, having been on outdoor grilling clean-up duty. Clarissa giggled at his persistent formality. When would he feel comfortable just walking in like one of the family? Perhaps it was too much to ask of his ingrained segregation habits.

Frank answered the gesture. "Come in, Elijah."

Elijah shyly made his way to the kitchen. "Jus' have one more plate to be washed, Mr. Wilding."

Clarissa put her palms together, elbows resting on the table. "Thank you, Elijah, for the wonderful smoked ribs. It's been a long time since we've had such a feast."

Elijah set the dish on the counter and bobbed his head to Clarissa. "My pleasure, ma'am. It was my dear mother's recipe. It was a blessin' you had all the ingredients right here in your kitchen. I appreciate you all lettin' me join you." He slid his hands into his overalls pockets. "I sure hope tomorrow brings good things for this family. I'll be sayin' good night."

Clarissa held her breath. Elijah knew just enough of everything that had transpired over the last two days to stumble and say too much. But he left quickly, inciting no questions from the boys. She indeed agreed with his wish for a better day tomorrow, but it was more likely the sky would fall once William had a chance to plan his revenge.

The pang in her abdomen made her gasp. She reached for her right side and glanced sideways to see if Frank noticed. He had. In a quiet moment he was at her side.

"What's wrong, Clary?"

Her mind raced with options. She could lie and say she was fine, risking that nothing was wrong with the baby, or confess that she had been in pain for some time, causing a fuss she dreaded dealing with. Neither option suited her, and the fact that now all eyes were on her added pressure to her already heavy chest.

"I'm not sure. I've been having these strange pains all afternoon. I don't want to worry everyone. I probably just need to go to bed like you suggested." She lightened her tone and forced a smile. The last thing she wanted was to scare the boys. She wasn't ready to tell them.

Frank's scowl penetrated her heart. He would never take a risk with the baby. She knew what he would say.

"Yes to bed. And we're taking a trip to town to see a doctor in the morning."

Morgan appeared by her side. "Are you okay, Mama?" She could barely feel his little hand on her shoulder. She longed to share the news about a new brother or sister, but considering this pain, it was premature. A visit to the obstetrician would be needed now, if only to confirm the pregnancy. She couldn't be very far along, even though she showed a little. She needed to know when the baby was due.

"Yes, dear. I'll be all right with some rest. You help your

daddy get James settled, and I'll go straight to my room. Deal?"

His whisper made her smile, despite her mind spinning with all the things that could go wrong. None of her other pregnancies had been difficult, yet she had still not escaped the loss of two children. A few pains shouldn't be confirmation of anything serious. The morning would tell. All she wanted now was to crawl beneath crisp sheets and pray the mountain of troubles weighing on her and Frank would disappear.

As she undressed, she listened to the clanging of dishes and pots and pans as Frank cleaned up. He had been so attentive and understanding today, even after the bombshell she'd dropped. It was almost too good to be true that he had not been angrier, or at least in a very bad mood.

She turned the switch on the bed table light. Before slipping on her nightgown, she stood in front of the mirror and examined her swelling belly. The tired young woman in the mirror looked almost too old to be pregnant. Yet many 31-year-old women had babies. Since they were away from the drought and dust, perhaps the timing was right. The soft cotton gown felt cool against her skin. The breeze through the window had chased away the stale heat of the day. She settled into the chair by the window to breathe in the smell of the vines and ripening fruit from the orchard.

"Smells good, doesn't it?"

Frank had slipped into the room without her noticing. He had long ago kicked off his boots, but now he peeled off his shirt, as if he were in a hurry. The sun had burned a crescent where his collar left his skin exposed. His arms and face were touched by the sunshine of the last week. It had been so long since she had seen his skin bronzed.

"I'm gonna go outside and hose off with nice cool water before I come to bed. Okay?"

Clarissa giggled. "Sure. Too bad the pond is so far away. You could skinny-dip."

Frank frowned. "With the luck I've had today, I'd probably drown."

His words stung. Kidding or not, she hated that he suffered because of her. It would be up to her to pry out of him any lingering doubts or resentment he had inside. She closed her eyes.

Frank touched her shoulder. "I'm sorry. I didn't mean that the way it sounded."

Without opening her eyes, she reached up and patted his hand. "It's okay. Go take your cold shower."

He grabbed his slippers and backed out of the room. Frank had been going a hundred miles an hour since their talk this morning. What would happen when he stopped long enough to consider their predicament?

She opened her eyes and turned to look out the window into the darkness. So many things had to align in the coming days. A confrontation with William was inevitable, whether it be her or Frank, possibly both. James would have to be told. Elijah could lose his job on the farm. Her pregnancy needed tending, and then little Morgan with his fixation on hoarding water.

She tucked her legs under the sheets. The temperatures had dropped enough to need a blanket, and Frank would be grateful she'd warmed the bed before he crawled in. His cold shower in the dark might be just what he needed to bring on a peaceful sleep. For her, it would take a miracle to calm the rushing uncertainty in her mind.

The door creaked as Frank scooted in, shivering. "Checked on the boys. Both asleep."

He hurried to get his legs in pajama bottoms and slide beneath the covers next to her.

"Your hair is still wet. You'll be cold."

"Don't care. Not sleepy anyway."

"The pillow will get soaked." She threw back the sheet. "I'll get you a—"

"Don't. It's fine. Stop fussing." He turned over with his back to her.

Clarissa slid down and covered herself. It shouldn't have surprised her. He hated her now. She had messed up everything.

Chapter 9

*F*rank woke with a jolt and opened one eye a slit. A golden light glowed through a window. Where was he? Nothing felt familiar. He felt for Clarissa next to him, but his hand met with the back of the living room sofa.

He groaned, remembering that he'd snuck out of the bedroom after Clarissa had drifted off to sleep. He had been awake most of the night, sitting up, lying down, or walking. He must have nodded off only a few hours ago—finding none of the answers he craved. It seemed God had closed His mouth, leaving Frank alone to muddle through all that had happened yesterday.

His head hurt to think of how he had treated Clarissa when he went to bed. His harsh words were a surprise even to him, revealing the darkness that sucked the life from his good intentions. He would control his feelings from now on. Exposing them would make others aware of his turmoil. Once he sorted through the issues, he could handle them better. He had to get the shattered pieces of this family glued back together. Starting with making sure Clarissa was healthy.

"Frank?" Clarissa called through a moan from the bedroom door.

He bolted off the sofa. He knew well the urgency in her voice.

"I'm here." He stepped closer and reached out his hand. "What's wrong?"

She grasped his hand so tight, he felt her fingernails digging in. "It's the pain again."

Together they crept to the sofa. "Sit down. I'll get your robe."

He could feel her arm shivering as he helped her down. He ran his hands along the footboard of the bed until he felt her robe. By the time he returned, Clarissa had stretched out on the sofa, whimpering softly. His chest ached to see her in pain.

"I'm going to get some clothes on and bring William's car around. I'll tell Elijah to come in here and sit with the boys. You're going to the hospital." He bundled her in her robe like a chenille cocoon. "Better?"

She nodded. "But I don't want to go to the hospital. Maybe it will go away."

"Nope. We're going. Sit tight while I get dressed." He kissed the top of her head. When she closed her eyes, he crept to the kitchen and opened the cupboard above the icebox. Clarissa couldn't reach it, so he had hidden the stash of ten dollar bills he had saved from Kansas there. He kept one eye on Clarissa as he lifted money from the jar and put it back nearly empty. He pulled on pants and a shirt in record time and buried the cash deep in his pocket.

Elijah was already awake when Frank reached the tack room of the barn. Frank smiled to hear him singing softly—a hymn Frank hadn't heard for years. He hated to interrupt him, but after explaining about Clarissa, Elijah was eager to help.

"She'll be fine, Mr. Wilding. I know it."

William's car sat between the big house and the barn. Frank put it in neutral, and he and Elijah rolled it toward the cottage. Just as they reached the flat area beside the back door, Frank heard a door slam from the direction of the big house, then footsteps stomping the hard ground. Elijah peered wide eyed over the top of the car. Frank stood up straight and braced for an explosion.

William stopped short and folded his arms across his chest. "What do you think you're doing with my car?"

"Borrowing it for a while." Frank faced him with legs apart and fists clamped at his side.

William smirked. "I don't think so. You're not running off in the night with my possessions. I'll call the sheriff."

Frank snickered. "It's not night—the sun is coming up. Look, William. Clarissa is in a great deal of pain. I'm taking her to the hospital in your car. I don't want to fight you over it, but I will."

William glanced at Elijah, who moved closer. "Your boy going with you? Or is he just helping you steal?"

"William, I don't have time to argue about this. I'm going in to get Clarissa, and Elijah is staying with the boys. We'll be back as soon as the doctor has examined her."

Frank's heart beat hard against his chest. He had no patience for an uncooperative brother making a scene. James' bedroom window was open. Suppose her heard?

William stepped closer to Frank. His breath smelled of liquor, but Frank could see he was steady as a rock. The silence lingered on for several moments. Just when Frank opened his mouth to break the filibuster, William dropped his arms to his side.

"If you're not back by this afternoon, I'm calling the sheriff." He turned and marched toward the house, then stopped and looked over his shoulder. "We need to talk soon, brother. I have things to say to you."

"Fine." Frank concentrated on a civil tone. He patted Elijah's shoulder as he scooted by him and into the house. "Wait here, Elijah. I might need your help with Mrs. Wilding."

"Yes, sir."

Clarissa groaned as he slipped his arm under her shoulders to help her sit. She was wide awake now and let him pick her up in his arms. He was shocked to feel how light she was. He hadn't lifted her since the day they'd crossed the threshold of the farm-house on the homestead. She'd been shapely and strong then.

Frank glanced to the backseat each time Clarissa groaned. He squeezed the steering wheel so tight, his knuckles ached. The image of the little graveyard behind the farmhouse flashed before him, reminding him of the day not so long ago they had buried Sarah Margaret next to her baby brother. Clarissa had wanted a girl so badly. To lose another child now would be like blowing out her barely flickering candle of hope.

"Almost there, Clary."

"Mmm-hmm."

The sun was up but covered by clouds. Frank stopped the car at the curb as two nurses, one rolling a wheelchair, ran from the entrance doors, as if they were waiting for them. Frank pulled Clarissa from the backseat with care, making sure she didn't stumble from the curb to the chair.

Once inside, a nurse whisked Clarissa away.

"Have a seat over there, sir, and we'll take care of her."

"Can't I go with her?"

Another nurse strolled up next to him with her hands on her hips. Her bushy brows wiggled up and down. "Now, what kind of hospital would this be if we let everyone go back there while we try to care for patients, hmm?"

It seemed all hospitals felt the need to employ a cranky nurse. Then again, if he had taken Clarissa to a hospital to give birth, maybe all their children would have survived. After surveying the nurse's broad shoulders and steely eyes, he took a seat in the half-full waiting room.

Elderly folks in wheelchairs and mothers with coughing children lined the walls. Only a few months ago he and Clarissa had sat in such a room, praying that Morgan would recover from dust pneumonia. He and his wife had shared more than their measure of anxious times.

The nurse at the desk waved him over. Maybe she would let him sneak in to see Clarissa. Instead, she slid a clipboard across the counter and whispered, "I need you to fill out these forms. Do you have means of payment?"

He reached into his jeans pocket and pulled out the small wad of savings. "This is all I have at the moment. Can you bill me for the rest?" His face heated as he imagined everyone in the waiting room staring at this poor farmer, begging for his wife's care. It didn't matter. This was better than taking her to the public hospital, wondering if she would get the attention she needed. Shivers ran up his arms as he envisioned her lying in a cold hallway waiting for someone to see her. If he had to work off the bill for years, it was better to be here.

She rolled her eyes as she unfolded the bills. "Of course. We won't know how much the bill will be, but I'll let the office know. Just be sure you list your current address."

The cranky nurse was suddenly by his side. "Mr. Wilder?"

"Wilding."

"Your wife is next to see the doctor. We're making her as comfortable as possible. Poor thing must have had a terrible night." She patted Frank's shoulder before scurrying off to the desk near the door.

He had misjudged the woman, a skill he had been sharpening the last few days. The knot in his stomach was familiar. As a boy, his mother supplemented his conscience, but as a grown man he had to be more careful to extend the grace he had been shown. If Clary would get well, he would do his best to refrain from judging her—and William.

For all their sakes.

The room temperature made Clarissa's arms shiver. People dressed in white fussed over her on both sides. She didn't care about the prodding and poking. It was the bright light overhead blaring in her face that caused her to flinch and squirm. Her stomach rolled at the smells of rubbing alcohol and disinfectant, so she breathed shallow to minimize the effects.

"Why don't they hurry up with whatever they're doing to me?"

"What's that, Mrs. Wilding?" A man's voice broke through her kaleidoscope of confusion.

Had she spoken aloud, or was someone reading her thoughts? She tried to decipher the chatter in the background, but each poke interrupted her concentration. She opened one eye, squinting it against the light. A nurse stood on one side of her, and a short balding man on the other side. He leaned in close to her face.

"Mrs. Wilding? Did you ask a question?" His voice was resonate and loud.

"I'm not deaf."

The man smiled. "No, I don't suppose you are. I'm sorry."

Did he just wink at the nurse?

"Don't make fun of me."

She winced. Why was her tongue so loose? She felt as though she could say anything she wanted—anything that came to her mind might slither its way out of her mouth. She held back the urge to giggle once she realized how much the pain had subsided. She closed her eyes and felt for her tummy. The bump still there. It felt like a girl bump. After four pregnancies, she should know.

"We've given you a little something to help you relax so we could examine you. We're almost done," the nurse chimed in with a singsong tone.

Someone removed Clarissa's hand from her abdomen and then ran theirs along her right side. A jab of discomfort made her jump. Someone covered her with the sheet again and patted her shoulder. Clarissa realized it was the doctor when he leaned in close to her face again, stethoscope around his neck.

"Mrs. Wilding, I'll have the nurse bring your husband in, and then I'll explain to you both what I have determined. Fair enough?"

Clarissa smiled at hearing that Frank could come in. "Oh, thank you so much. You're a nice man."

Her eyelids felt weighted. She kept them shut and wondered if she could stay awake until Frank came. She covered her face with her arm to shield her eyes from the bright light, but suddenly it shut off.

"Well, that's better."

"You're welcome," called the nurse to Clarissa before she shut the door.

The doctor pressed his fingers to her wrist, then pumped the cuff still wrapped around her arm. He kept it up until she thought her arm would go numb.

She moaned. "Do you have to squeeze so hard?"

"Sorry."

She opened one eye again to see the doctor's frowning face.

"What's wrong?" She mimicked his low voice. Her giggle wouldn't be contained this time. It felt good to feel so well.

He smiled and pulled the cuff from her arm. His silence reminded her of her father's demeanor each time he'd scolded her. The familiar knot settled in her stomach even now. The urge to giggle was gone, as if someone had pulled the plug on her levity.

The door opened, and Frank stepped in the room. She lifted her head to focus on his deep and pitiful worry lines. She smiled to try and ease his pain. Now if only the doctor had good news for them, they could be on their way—home to deal with the unpleasant issues she had imposed upon her little family. Home to reckon with William.

"Please, sit down, Mr. Wilding." The doctor motioned to the chair next to her bed. "I have determined the cause of your wife's discomfort."

Frank grabbed Clarissa's hand out from under the sheet and squeezed it. He shifted to sit on the edge of the chair. The doctor turned the crank on the end of her bed and sat her up.

"Better?"

"Yes, thank you, Doctor." She could feel the effects of whatever they had given her start to diminish. It was time to be serious.

Frank tapped his foot on the floor, his favorite nervous habit.

"I believe, Mrs. Wilding, that one of the ligaments in your abdomen that usually stretches over the duration of a pregnancy has been stressed. In my opinion, you are too thin, and that has aggravated the situation. Plus your blood pressure is too high."

He paused to clear his throat. "In addition, and I hope you won't take offense, you're a bit frail to continue bearing children. I understand from your interview before we sedated you that you have had a rough time of it for several years." He glanced at Frank.

"That's true, Doctor. The drought took its toll on her, I'm afraid." Frank's voice cracked.

Clarissa couldn't speak. The past raked over her again as if it were yesterday. The missed meals, rationed drinking water, lack of vegetables, and only dust-filled air to breathe had been a returning enemy. Now a lingering dark cloud threatened to take another child.

The doctor raised his brows at Clarissa. "Let me tell you that despite all the damage to your health, the baby seems to be fine. You are only at the beginning of your fourth month and not out of danger yet for a miscarriage. So I'm going to recommend some things to ensure health improves for you and the baby."

Frank broke in. "I'll make sure she does whatever it takes."

"Good." The doctor nodded to Frank. "I want an advanced nursing student to come to your place a few times a week to take your wife's blood pressure. She should be getting more rest and more food." He turned to Clarissa and shook his finger. "When I see you again, I want to see some meat on those bones, young lady. No heavy lifting, more sleep, and more leisure time."

Clarissa wanted to cry and laugh at the same time. It had been so long since she was a woman of leisure, she wouldn't know where to begin. Her sister, Treena, had bragged about the good old days of lounging in the estate gardens or sitting on the front porch reading a book. Perhaps Clarissa would need some lessons from her.

"If you say so," was all she could muster for a response. "I'll do my best."

Frank nudged her. "Don't worry. I'll see to it, but will a student know what to do?"

"This one will. She's top of her class and just about finished with her practical training. I'd send a regular RN, but we're short of them at the moment. A growing problem in these difficult times. Happening all over the US. We just can't afford to hire new ones in this state of economy." The doctor paused and took off his spectacles to rub his eyes.

Clarissa took note of his tired posture. Not enough nurses, and now she was going to be cared for by a student.

"Anyway. Miss Watkins will report to me regularly on your wife's condition, and I'll give her instructions accordingly. This will save you some expenses and give the student some valuable experience." His spectacles back on his nose, he smiled.

Frank stood and let go of Clarissa's hand. "I need to be clear though on something, Doctor. Would you be opposed to Clarissa going through a move at this time? You see, we have a situation that may—"

"I suggest you find any other way to deal with that situation other than moving."

"Yes." Frank sat again. "We'll find a way."

The doctor picked up a clipboard and scratched something on it. "I'll make arrangements for the visiting nurse. It so happens she lives not far from you. She's a good nurse and very likable. She'll monitor your condition, and then I'll expect you in my office when she feels the time is right."

He slid the clipboard onto the counter and removed his spectacles. "I'll have the charge nurse release you to go home now. Call us if you have any questions or concerns. All right?"

Frank stepped up and shook the doctor's hand. "Thank you, sir."

Clarissa's voice trembled. "Yes, thank you."

The happy medicine was out of her system. She closed her eyes to try and think of anything to be happy about. She would practice smiling on the way home.

She might have to summon Elijah to spread his good cheer. Poor Frank would have to deal with William on his own. Just the thought of seeing him again was enough to do just what the doctor didn't want—raise her blood pressure and dampen her mood. The rest of their problems could wait.

Riding down the hall in a wheelchair, with Frank at her side, she let out a deep breath. Releasing all the troubles pricking her heart would require skills she didn't have. She would learn. It was simple, really. The baby was priority. She was determined to make it so.

No more little graveyard markers for this family. Now or ever.

Clarissa dozed with her head against the window all the way back to the farm, her face still and peaceful at last. She didn't stir when the afternoon sun flashed past her eyes, so Frank let her rest. He took the opportunity to rearrange the puzzle pieces in his head of what he had thought his life was. The broken Wilding family picture would be hard to put back together as long as his emotions were frazzled.

The boys waited on the porch as Frank turned the car around and stopped as close to the cottage as possible. At least he had kept his promise to William to return the car before afternoon. The angry look on William's face this morning had haunted Frank all day.

Frank nudged Clarissa awake. She jumped and grasped his arm.

"We're home. I'll come around and help you out of the car."

He opened the door after telling the boys to give their mama some space. Clarissa slung her arm around Frank's waist for support but seemed to be steady on her feet.

Morgan grinned wide when his mother looked up at him.

Frank patted Morgan's head as he wiggled around him to reach for his mother. "Now don't go hugging her too tight."

Clarissa glanced at James sitting on one of the porch chairs. Elijah stood on the ground by the corner of the porch, a watchful eye on James.

"James, should you be out of bed?" Clarissa called to him, her voice shaky.

"I'm all right. Doesn't hurt much today."

Frank swallowed down the dread of inflicting more pain on the boy. They wouldn't be able to hold off telling him about his real father for long.

"Welcome home, ma'am," Elijah said as he stepped closer. He turned to James. "He's a stubborn one. Tried to make him stay in bed, but he wanted to be out here when you got home. I didn't let him strain—carried him through the door."

"I'm fine. Don't talk about me like I'm an invalid."

Frank smiled. He was a strong boy. Maybe he would take the news better than Frank feared.

Clarissa leaned into him as she took the steps one by one. Morgan took her hand and wrapped it around his shoulders. "You can lean on me too, Mama."

Just before they reached the top step, Frank saw movement out of the corner of his eye. He tilted his head to see William standing near the old oak tree by his house. Even from a distance, Frank could see the intensity in his staring eyes. William's chin tipped up, and his arms crossed his chest.

Frank eased Clarissa into Morgan's vacated porch chair next to James. He leaned in to whisper his intentions. "I need to get the car over to William. He's waiting. Don't look over, but he's watching us from the yard."

Clarissa's mouth opened as if to protest, but when he put his finger to her lips, she formed it into a gentle smile. She reverted her attention to Morgan and James, asking questions about James' leg and how Morgan had gotten along without them this morning.

Frank backed down the first step, aware that James watched him, his eyes squinting. Frank turned and strode to the driver's side of the car. He started the engine and backed the vehicle all the way to William's house. He stomped on the brakes just as he pulled up close to his brother.

William walked around the front of the car and approached Frank as he slammed the door. "Did you leave any gasoline in the tank?" was all William said.

Frank caught William's glance to the porch. He stuffed his shaking hand in his left jeans pocket and pulled out several $1 bills. He separated two bills and held them out to William. "This should take care of it. Thanks for the use of the car. I appreciate it."

The sun filtered through the leaves high above, creating

shapely shadows across William's face, distorting his expression into a reflection of the meanness inside. For an instant, Frank pitied his brother. William grabbed the bills and crumpled them in his fist. He took one step back, eyes darting to the porch again.

"Is—is she all right?"

"She'll be fine with some rest and three meals a day." Frank stepped around William and moved in the direction of the cottage. He could see James staring at them.

Frank stopped and spun around. "Just so you know, there will be a nurse stopping by here once in a while to check up on Clary. Also, we haven't said anything to the boys about the baby, so I'd appreciate the rest of the day to take care of family matters."

"Family matters? I guess that would include me."

Frank's fingers twitched, ready to slap the smile off his brother's face. "Don't, William."

William stuffed the bills in his shirt pocket. "Take today." His voice dropped to a whisper. "But soon we'll have to come to an understanding about James. And your job here."

Of course they would. Not today. Frank turned and continued moving toward the cottage. For the hundredth time, they needed a miracle.

He hoisted his foot up on the edge of the porch step. Elijah was telling a tall tale about his childhood escapades but managed to throw a concerned glance at Frank. A reassuring wink Elijah's way might ward off suspicion, but it didn't do anything for his churning stomach. Only Clarissa's giggles lifted his mood. He loved to hear her laugh. He wanted to be happy about the baby like she was. He wanted to love her like he should, despite what he now knew. He would have to spread himself thin to meet all the needs of his little family. James would need him to be strong soon, as would Clarissa. Morgan would need a firm hand about stealing the mason jars, and William... What would William need from Frank? His oldest son? His absence?

Clarissa pushed herself up from the chair. "I think I'll lie down."

Frank jumped to take her arm. "But you haven't had lunch. I can fix you something."

"I'm not hungry."

Frank stood his ground. "Now didn't you hear what the doctor said?"

"Frank, I'm too tired to argue. I promise to eat a big dinner." She took a step and then stopped to gaze at each one on the porch. "Do you think there is enough cold meat and bread to make sandwiches for everyone for dinner?"

"Sure, Mama. I can help." Morgan clutched her waist.

James scooted to the front of his seat. "I'm not much help today, but tomorrow maybe Elijah and I can go rabbit hunting for some rabbit stew. That's easy enough."

Frank tugged on her arm. "We'll all figure it out. Just rest for a while, and we men will get organized." He nodded to the boys and Elijah. "Right, men?"

A unanimous answer rang out. "Right."

Elijah opened the screen door. "Remember how the good Lord provided on the homestead? He'll do the same here. Don't you worry 'bout a thing."

"Yes, I remember, Elijah."

Frank shuffled alongside of her to the unmade bed. The window was still open, letting the warming afternoon air stream through. After lifting her feet and removing her shoes, he shut the window and pulled the tattered blind down to the sill.

"I'll leave the door open a crack so the air flows. I promise to keep the boys quiet."

She nodded and laid her head on the pillow.

Frank leaned over and kissed her forehead. She slipped her hand into his and closed her eyes as a tear wet her cheek.

"Frank. We have to tell the boys about the baby tonight."

"Sure." He stroked her thin arm, thinking of how he was going to fatten her up.

"And tomorrow, James needs to hear the rest of the news. Agreed?"

Frank stood up straight and let go of her arm. "We'll see, Clary. We'll see."

In a moment, her chest rose and fell slowly. As she rested, he needed to think. Frank pulled the bedroom door almost shut. Elijah extended his arm to help James to the sofa, and Morgan was nowhere in sight.

"Mr. Wilding, I need to speak with you for a moment if you don't mind."

Frank wondered if Elijah had been reading his mind. Then again, surely he had questions about what was going on, having been stuck in the middle for three days now. Frank wouldn't blame the man one bit for saying goodbye to this mess. Only a few months ago Elijah called himself a drifter with no place to call home. He should know they considered him part of their family now—if he wanted to be.

"That's fine, Elijah." He stooped to look James in the eyes. "You stay off that leg for the rest of the day. We'll check your bandages tonight. Anything you need before I go outside with Elijah?"

James shifted back against the sofa cushion. "No. I'm good. You go on, and I'll listen for Mother. Morgan's out in the barn looking for that hawk again." He shook his head.

Frank followed Elijah to the door.

"Dad?"

He hadn't heard James call him that for a while. "Yes, son?"

"Is Uncle William mad about something? He's keeping his distance lately."

Frank's neck twitched. The boy was catching on to innuendos and body language.

"Don't know, son."

But he did know, and Clarissa was right. It was time to have that talk.

Chapter 10

"*I* want you to tell me what happened with William before we were married."

Frank sat on the edge of the bed, his head bowed and hands folded. His silhouette in the twilight of the rising sun revealed a posture matching his tone of voice. The strong breeze through the open bedroom window played with a lock of hair on his forehead.

Clarissa pushed herself up against the headboard and leaned her head back. Sleep had just come when she had felt the nudging on her arm. Her first reaction had been that something was wrong with James, but it was soon clear that Frank was at the end of his patience. Of course he should have the facts about her past relationship with Will, but her words would cut deep and possibly leave permanent scars.

"I know it's early," he whispered. "But I can't take it anymore. I have to know about the past before I can deal with the future."

"I know."

"I need to have a conversation with William today, and I don't want to go into it blind. I know it's hard for you, and I'm not going to like what I hear. But knowing the truth is better than my imagination running wild."

Clarissa forced out a slow breath. He would get the truth, but not details. That she could not bear and would not do. Frank would know only what he needed to know—that a very young and foolish girl made a mistake and paid dearly for it. She was still paying for it. Perhaps when she shared the facts with Frank, it would abate everyone's suffering.

She grabbed up a wad of the white sheet in her hand. "Okay, I'll start at the beginning. I don't want you to look at me while I talk."

Frank nodded and slid next to her on the bed, his back also against the headboard. "Can I just sit here? Can't see you in the dark anyway."

"Yes."

The words she had to say caught in her throat. She turned her face to the window. The lace curtains blowing on either side reminded her of the day her mother died. Clarissa had stood at her mother's window, staring out at the garden they both loved. The silence in the room that day was the silence of death. She hoped nothing between her and Frank would die from what she was about to say.

"I met Will Larson through a mutual friend. Jonathan Hill."

Frank sighed. "I knew him, but not well. He was William's friend."

"Frank, please don't interrupt. This is hard enough."

"Okay."

"Anyway, Jonathan introduced us at an event downtown. I don't even remember what the event was. Maybe a concert in the park. We spent most of the evening talking, and I guess I was pretty taken by him. He was handsome, like you, and very charming. Too charming. He asked me to meet him the next day. Well, to make this story shorter, just know that we met many times over that summer. We had to be very careful because Father didn't approve of me seeing young men at that time. He said I wasn't old enough. He said a lot of things."

She paused to take a drink from the glass of water on her bed table. Her hand shook as she drank. How would she make this tale palatable? She couldn't.

"I met you that summer too, remember? At the church picnic. Your last name was Wilding, and you never mentioned a brother. I had no idea you and Will were related. I liked you very much, but William had captured my heart, and I wanted so much to get away from Father, especially after Mother died in July. Will asked me to be his girl about the time I met you. He gave me the affection I never got from my father. I guess I craved the attention. Anyway, he said we would get married, but he wanted to get a job. He neglected to tell me he was leaving town to find one."

Frank cleared his throat and shifted in the bed. She could smell the perspiration forming on his temples. Pity ate at her stomach like a deep hunger. What a horrible place for him to be—caught between his wife and his brother—and his son too.

"We were only—*together*—that one time. He took me to the overlook on Miles Gulch in Jonathan's new auto. We talked about getting married that night—and he said he loved me. I believed him. Then a few weeks after that, he disappeared. By then you and I had become good friends, and even though I was devastated that Will had dropped me, I pretended to be fine. Remember?"

"Yes, I remember. You made me promise not to ask questions."

"And remember I told you I had a beau. I just never told you his name."

Clarissa's tense muscles relaxed. "I found out I was pregnant when Will had been gone for over a month. Ginny Jones had taken me to her doctor on the other side of town, and there was no doubt. I lived in constant fear that Father would find out, but yet I knew he would eventually. Especially when I heard that Ginny had told her mother my secret. That's when I came to you. The rest you know." She slid her hand over to touch his. "I'm forever grateful you rescued me. That you loved me."

Frank didn't move for a long time. Clarissa started to pull

her hand away, but he wrapped his fingers through hers and held them tight.

"So you never heard from William, never saw him until we stepped off that train? I can't imagine how you must have felt to see him standing there. If I had known, I would never have brought you here."

She sighed. "We've both been dwelling on a lot of *if onlys*. I wish we could accept what is and move on."

The sun had reached the edge of the sky. Any other day the warming breeze from the window would have been an invitation to be lazy and free, but only the words she had kept locked inside were free now. Clarissa's relief was like medicine to her soul, but she had to be mindful of how her story would affect Frank. His grip on her hand was comforting, but it didn't reveal Frank's feelings about what he had just heard.

"I thought there would be more to it. I thought you would tell me something I hadn't already guessed. I always knew you loved the father of your baby—it's just the fact that it was my own brother has been eating away at me. It made it too personal, the jealousy more intense."

"Can you live with it, Frank?"

He let go of her hand and slid his legs off the bed. He threw back his head and groaned. "I don't know yet. I had a good talk with Elijah last night. I can see why you and the boys depended on him so much while I was gone from the homestead."

Clarissa rolled onto her side. She wanted to stroke his back, but resisted. "What did he say?"

"That God knew all our stories long ago, that He had a plan. We make our choices and He's not surprised by them. We are failing humans, and God is God. Elijah's words are helping me put things in perspective."

He rubbed the back of his neck. "I found a way to think of what is happening to us… or to me at least. When William first showed me around the vineyard, he gave me a lesson on pruning the vines. At the time I thought I could use the philosophy of the task as a way to reach William. But I think the lesson was for me. I've been pruned—we've been pruned as a family. But it's necessary to prune off the old wood, the unproductive part of us, so that we can produce the right kind of fruit in our lives."

He huffed with a smile. "I shared my theory with Elijah, and he said I was pretty smart to learn all that."

Clarissa smiled and now felt free to stroke Frank's back. "He's a good man."

"Or a good angel."

"Maybe both." She laughed, then bit her lower lip. "Do you hate me? I never meant to hurt you. And you must know I love you now." She touched his arm. "Loving you happened faster than I dreamed at the time. I wish things would have been different. I guess you're right—I've been pruned too. I hope it's not too late to fix the mess I made."

Frank stood. "It wasn't your fault. William is responsible, but he can't have James." He crossed his arms over his chest. "Can I get you anything for breakfast?"

Clarissa threw her shawl over her shoulders. "No, but you can help me to the bathroom."

Frank held her around the waist as they shuffled to the bedroom door that was already slightly ajar. Clarissa swung it open. James sat on the floor, leaning against the wall outside the bedroom. Clarissa's heart dropped to her toes. Her arm pulled Frank in tight to her side.

"James—are you—"

James' face was tear stained, his expression flat. He looked up at Frank and opened his mouth. Nothing came out.

Frank let Clarissa ease to the floor. She reached for James, but he leaned away from her. She glanced up at Frank, pleading with her eyes for him to do something. They should have made sure the door was shut, that the boys were still sleeping.

Frank knelt next to James. "Son?"

"Don't call me that. I heard everything you said." He sat bobbing his head, tears rolling.

Clarissa cringed. It wasn't supposed to happen this way. If one more person in this family fell wounded by her sin, she wouldn't survive. To hurt James like this tore at her soul.

She reached to pull his chin toward her, but he slid away. He cowered like a wounded animal, waiting for a predator to pounce. She wanted to crumple, or to run. To stay and make him understand, or disappear and hide. She was trapped in a small conflicted world with no escape. James must have felt the same.

Frank sighed hard. "James. Let your mother and I explain."

James' head lifted slowly. The tears stopped, replaced with a blank stare toward Frank. She expected to see hatred, but instead his glassy eyes reflected pity. He seemed sorry for Frank, sorry for himself, leaving her as the only enemy.

She looked away, not wanting to see what emotion his eyes held for her. Reaching up to hang onto the doorjamb, she stood on numbing legs and shuffled along the wall to the bathroom. Once inside, Frank's muffled voice floated under the shut door.

"Don't blame your mother, James."

Frank had scooped James up in his arms and carried him to the porch, leaving Clarissa in the bathroom. He imagined her in a heap on the floor, but he couldn't rescue her this time. His efforts had to be directed at James, the boy he had raised as his own, never dreaming he was an uncle.

James stared out above the row of cottonwood trees across the driveway. The fluffy snow-like cotton from the trees still lay on the ground. Soon a wind would come along to blow it all away. Time would likely blow away James' sorrow, but for now, Frank had to conjure an explanation that would make sense to a young boy whose life had just been swept under an ocean wave. He let the silence work its magic to calm them both. Fatigue settled in his aching bones, and he suddenly felt old and very tired. He hadn't slept most of the night, and the whirlwind of events this morning muddled his thinking. James shouldn't suffer because of it. But he had.

"I'm sorry, James. Your mother and I should have been more careful about our conversation. We had no idea you were even out of bed. Why were you at our door?"

James kept his eyes ahead. "I wanted to show Mother my bandage. No new blood. I heard you talking, and I thought I'd come in and tell her. I thought she'd be happy."

"It was a long conversation. You didn't interrupt us. Instead you eavesdropped."

James jerked his head to face Frank, a tear falling. His breath quickened. "I—I…"

Frank rested his hand on James' shoulder. "It's okay. It's not your fault. I'm not scolding you. I just want to know how long you were there." He leaned back in his chair, wishing he didn't have to cover this territory with James. He checked the sun in the sky. It had to be close to 8:00 a.m. William would be out in the orchard already, expecting Frank to join him. His brother hadn't fired him yet, but if he didn't show up soon, it would be a sure thing. Besides, he needed to have a serious discussion with him as well.

"James, I don't want you to jump to any conclusions about what you heard. Your mother and I will explain it all to you. There's only one thing you need to believe right here, right now. We both love you very much."

James' tears dried up. He looked into Frank's eyes with a cold stare. "I know Mother does." His chin dropped to his chest. "Or maybe she hates me for being a mistake."

Frank stood and faced James. "I see how you might feel that way, but you're wrong about that—and about how I might feel. I think I've proved through the years that I've loved you as my own. I chose you, James. You didn't happen to me by accident or surprise. I chose to be your father. I do love you, even if you don't believe it now."

James' shoulders shook.

"Please give your mother and me a chance to work through things. A lot has happened in the last two days. We need time to sort everything out. I know it doesn't seem fair, but we need your patience and understanding. Your mother especially because—"

James frowned. "Why especially her? Is she still sick? Is it something serious and you're not telling me?" He raised his posture as if he would bolt from the chair. Fire flickered in his eyes.

Frank put both hands out. "No. Nothing serious." The news about the baby could be just what James needed to hear. "Your mother is going to have a baby."

James fell against the back of the chair. His face paled. "A baby?"

"Yes, and the doctor said we need to fatten her up and not let her do anything too strenuous for a while. Can you help me with that?"

Another tear fell down James' cheek and past his quivering chin. "Yes. But what if it happens again? What if the baby dies like the others?" His sight drifted off to the trees again. "She'd be so sad again."

"Things are different now, James. We aren't living in a drought, breathing sand, and fighting to survive each day. I don't want you to worry. I just need your help."

Frank heard pots clanging and dishes rattling in the kitchen. Then Morgan's voice floated through the screen. "Where's James?"

Frank knelt by James. "Morgan must not know anything yet. This is between you, me, and Mother. Right?"

James glanced at the door, wiping his nose with his nightshirt sleeve. He pushed himself off the chair and held on to the arm of it. Frank didn't assist. He hoped James would agree to his plea.

Morgan's bare footsteps came closer. James looked at Frank. "I won't say anything, for Morgan's sake. Not yours or Mother's."

James met Morgan at the door. "I'm right here." He held on to Morgan's shoulder. "Let's go help Mom with some pancakes."

Frank surveyed his clothes. He hadn't undressed last night. His trousers were wrinkled and his shirt unbuttoned. He would have to grab his boots and make his way to the orchard before William came looking for him.

He leaned over the porch railing and peered around the cottage. It was too late. William's truck rounded the side of the barn. The showdown was about to begin, but Frank would insist they go elsewhere.

Frank waved at William and held up a finger. He just needed a minute to get his boots. As he spun around to go into the house, a car crept up the drive. It was unfamiliar—driven by a young woman. She steered the car in front of the cottage just as William strolled around the corner of the porch, looking mad enough to punch someone.

The young woman stepped out of the driver's side and shut the door.

"I hope I'm not lost. Am I at the Wilding residence?"

Before Frank could answer, William stepped close to her. "It is. I'm William Wilding. Can I help you?"

The young woman shook his hand. "I'm Martha Watkins, the nursing student. I'm here to check on your wife."

Frank wanted to jump out of his skin at the assumption that William was Clarissa's husband. The nerve it struck brought back all the angst he had just calmed. He descended the steps and stuck out his hand. "Hello. I'm Frank Wilding, Clarissa's husband." He held out his arm in William's direction. "This is my brother."

Martha's face flushed. "Oh, I'm sorry. Dr. Stimson says I'm to come by a few times a week and check on your wife. I was on my way to the hospital this morning and thought I would stop by just to introduce myself. I know it's early. If she's not up, I can stop by on my way home later today."

Frank relaxed. He took discreet inventory of her stature and features. Her tall, slender frame seemed adequate to help Clarissa up and down if needed. Her black hair curled around her ears, neat and tidy. Her white uniform was crisp and clean, but her sensible white shoes concerned him. They wouldn't stay white around here for long. Her handshake had been strong and her tone upbeat, and more importantly, she was friendly.

William disappeared around the corner. Martha leaned back, as if to see where he went.

Frank had to overcome William's rudeness with some hospitality. "Won't you come in and meet her? I know for a fact she is up fixing our boys breakfast." He opened the screen door and hollered inside. "You decent, honey? We have a visitor."

Clarissa sat at the table. James teetered atop a stack of pillows on a kitchen chair, flipping pancakes. Frank couldn't see his face—was he all right? Morgan handed his mother a steaming plate and looked up at the young woman.

Clarissa stood and pulled her robe tight across her chest. "I'm not dressed proper for visitors, but come in."

Martha strolled over and stretched out her hand over the table. "Martha Watkins, your nurse."

Clarissa glanced at Frank, who shrugged. He had a feeling

Martha would take over the conversation and, quite possibly, the flipping of the pancakes.

"I'll leave you two to get acquainted. I have business to attend to." He snatched his hat off a chair seat and motioned for Martha to sit. "Nice to meet you, Miss Watkins."

"Call me Martha."

He turned to Clarissa. "I'll check on you later." Her eyes were moist, and when he patted her shoulder, she grabbed his hand tight.

"Be careful out there," she whispered.

The nurse had shown up just in time. He could leave Clarissa in Martha's hands and go find William. Frank searched his tired mind to think of what he would say to his angry brother. Playing it by ear could be dangerous, considering how fatigue had left him feeling short tempered. The last thing he wanted was to explode with the rage that had been simmering deep inside, like a pot responding to the flame underneath. He had feigned a calm exterior for Clarissa and James' sake, and he would have to contain the overflow of emotion in front of William.

For one fleeting moment Frank wished for the refuge of their homestead. Life there had been hard, but at least they could live in ignorance and be free of internal conflict. Fighting the dust storms and drought took less of a toll on him than the tempest about to rise between him and William. If only Clary had been honest from the beginning about the name of the father, Frank could have reconciled everything by now.

"Good mornin', Mr. Wildin'." Elijah's voice sang out from the middle of a row of vines. "How's Mrs. Wildin' feelin' today?"

Frank detoured from his mission and approached him. "Hello, Elijah. Clarissa's better today. The nurse came by to introduce herself. She seems real nice. It will be good to have someone take care of Clary until the baby comes." Frank stretched out his hand. "I want to thank you for being there for my family. I'd say it was a good idea I had, bringing you here."

Elijah chuckled. "Oh, I'd say maybe the Lord put that idea in your head. He sure does watch over us all. We jus' have to let Him do His work without gettin' in the way. I'm happy to be of some help. You've been mighty kind to me."

Elijah's deep humility intrigued Frank. He squatted to watch him examine the plump grapes. The man's thick-knuckled fingers were as gentle as if he were caressing a baby. Such a contrary picture of bridled strength. It occurred to Frank that the same touch might be what he needed to deal with William.

He stood and patted Elijah's shoulder. "Gotta go. I'll be back to help, if my brother doesn't fire me." Frank managed a smile, but Elijah kept his eyes on the vines.

"I'll pray for you, and even more for Mr. William."

All this trouble was his brother's fault. Why should Elijah pray more for him? He stopped midstride. Elijah wasn't the brunt of William and Clarissa's sin, so he could pray all he wanted. *It's time to do whatever I need to do in the here and now.*

He plodded his way back to the path and down the rocky hill to the orchard, the sun heating the top of his hat. He could see the bend of the river down the gulch to his right. Frank imagined stripping down to his underwear to jump in, like he'd done as a child in the deep creek that ran by their house. On hot days he and William had run straight after school to a tree-shrouded cove and cooled off in the clear water. William had shinnied up one of the trees and tied a piece of rope to a high branch. Frank knotted the end. The hours spent on the bank of that creek were some of his only fond childhood memories with William. Most were of him and their father fighting or William getting whupped with a belt. Frank would hide behind the kitchen door and wince at each blow. He looked to the blue sky. There would be no whupping today—by anyone. He knew that now.

The wind kicked up the dirt under his boots and whipped it into a swirl of reddish-brown haze. William's truck was parked at the end of the first row of apple trees. It would be over a month before the sweet fruit could be harvested, an impossible task without Elijah and him to help.

Frank wove through the trees, stopping to fix a wooden prop that had slipped away from a low-hanging branch. When he finished, William stood to his left, pruning shears in his hand. For a moment, Frank's heart skipped. The scene could be laughable if not so close to possible. William must be angry, but he was a distant player in this saga. Frank had to bear his own burden of pain, but he was determined that there would not be another violent showdown. They might have had a few physical brawls as kids, but the delicate circumstances between them had to be settled with words, however painful.

Frank released pent-up breath when William tucked the shears under his arm and spoke.

"What are you doing here?" William's gruff tone split the air.

Frank licked his dry lips. "I thought I should be, unless you're going to fire me. And then what? Kick us off your place, I suppose." He could remind William his landlords might have something to say about it.

William stood his ground, his eyes twitching. "Does Clarissa really need a nurse? I don't much like strangers coming around here. I'd give you time off to look after her—for a while."

Frank toed the dirt under his boot. He didn't like the condescending words. If William thought he could call the shots about Clary, there would have to be some discussion about that too. He didn't own Clary, and he couldn't tell Frank what to do about her—or James. He supposed that would come next.

"I could have James come out and help me in the orchard in your place."

Yes, there it was. The suggestion made Frank's temples pulse. He pulled in a quick breath and held it to find calm.

"James isn't well enough to be working in the orchard. Besides, Clary plans on getting him caught up on his schooling before fall. And I don't think you understand Clary's condition. If you did, you wouldn't begrudge her a nurse." He paused and slowed his breathing. "William, I know you must be hurt, and I'm sorry, but Clary is my wife, and until James chooses otherwise, I am his father. I'll make the decisions regarding my family."

William grabbed the shears again and let his arms drop to his side. Frank kept a close eye on his movements. One twitch of William's hand on those shears and Frank would either grab him or run. Running seemed the safer course, although cowardly.

William pressed his lips together. His grip on his weapon had whitened his knuckles. Frank's chest tightened as if in a vice. William lifted his foot to move forward. Just as Frank tensed to defend himself, a voice sounded between them.

"Mr. William? I'm done in the vineyard. What would you like me to do now?"

Elijah. Frank wasn't sure if he should be relieved or frightened for his friend.

William jerked his head in Elijah's direction. Elijah stood staring at him, a figure of quiet strength. Once the air cleared of tyranny, William barked his orders.

"There's some broken branches on the end of the rows from the wind last night. Take these shears and go lop them off. Then you can do what you want with the rest of the day." He turned to Frank. "You go take care of your wife. I'll decide tomorrow what I'm going to do." He reached out the shears to Elijah.

Frank nodded to William and turned to walk away.

"Mr. Wildin'?" Elijah called after him. "Tell little Morgan we'll search for that hawk when I'm done."

Frank's tension lifted. He gave Elijah a half grin. "Will do."

Turning his back on William sent a mixture of emotion through Frank's mind. The nurse would be gone by the time he got back to the cottage. He and Clary had some talking to do. And once Elijah came to entertain Morgan, James would likely want to talk about William.

It would be hard on Clary, but it had to be today. Before William made his move. He mulled over the image of William's face and voice, both contorted into an unrecognizable figure, not the brother of their youth.

Frank agreed with Elijah now. William needed prayer.

Chapter 11

Clarissa lowered onto the sofa next to James' bed. The nurse had stayed an extra few minutes to check his wound and change his bandages. Martha's gentle touch and skillful movements were a thing to behold. She had distracted James with her quiet voice, telling him a tale about how when she was four she had snuck under the fence of a corral where her folks kept their prize bull. Both the boys' eyes had opened wide when she said she was charged by the bull and her uncle had to jump in and rescue her. By the time her story ended, she had finished with the dressing and James was smiling.

Clarissa sensed the chemistry between them. James didn't give away his affection easily, but he seemed taken with Martha. Especially when she offered to show him her favorite fishing spot. But James needed a nurse, not a big sister. Or another mother figure.

"How's the leg after Nurse Martha fixed you up?" She reached to take his hand, but he pulled it away.

James' reaction was what she dreaded after seeing him outside their bedroom this morning. His eavesdropping had put them all in strained place. Clarissa wasn't prepared for rejection, but now it hit her like a gut punch.

"It's fine," was all he replied. He picked up the textbook lying next to him and opened it. "I need to do some studying."

She blinked back tears. "Sure. You go ahead. I'm going to

take a short walk. Maybe down the drive to check the mailbox. Martha said if I didn't overdo…"

James kept his eyes on the pages, his lips moving as he read. She pushed herself up off the sofa and looked down at him. His straight posture and tight jaw made him look so grown up. It was as if he'd aged several years from yesterday, losing his childhood innocence.

She descended the porch steps with care, pulling her sunbonnet on. She tucked her straggling hair behind her ears. She should have glanced in the mirror before venturing out, in case she looked as disheveled as she felt. While waiting at the hospital when James was hurt, she had flipped through a magazine, something she hadn't done in years. All the women sported modern hairstyles of soft waves with flat-brimmed hats tilted to one side. As she walked, she imagined herself with a new style. For now she would settle for some moderate grooming.

When Frank returned from seeing William, she would have him help her into the tub. Some lavender soap would be just what she needed to wash away the perspiration. She glanced at her fingernails. Chipped and ragged. She thought back to the day her sister arrived at the homestead unannounced. She had envied Treena's manicured red nails and silky skin, but a few short months of hard work and storms had also robbed Treena of her pristine look.

Several yards ahead of her, the sun reflected off the galvanized mailbox. She had made it this far without pain, but now she had to get home. She pulled a small bundle of envelopes wrapped in a rubber band from the box and flipped through them. Treena had promised the inheritance would come soon.

"Now would be a good time, Lord."

On top of a small bundle of mail sat an official-looking envelope with her name on it. The return address was that of the attorney Treena had been working with. Clarissa turned and leaned on the mailbox post. Her shaking fingers slipped under the flap. A check lay tucked between the folds of a single piece of paper. Clarissa squeezed her eyes shut tight.

I can't look. What if it's not much? She envisioned a typed-out sum of five dollars, which would be in line with her kind of good fortune.

She turned the bank check over, her hands shaking, and held it up to read. *Pay to the order of Clarissa Wilding, $5,290.* The note at the bottom left-hand corner said, *Remainder of Marcus J. Tate estate/final.*

Her elbows refused to bend and lower her arms. The amount was less than she'd hoped for but more than she'd expected. It was enough to move off the farm and put a down payment on a new place of their own.

Her muscles finally released her arm, and she stuffed the check into the middle of the rest of the mail. She gripped the bundle in both hands and padded in the direction of the cottage. As soon as Frank returned from the orchard, she would surprise him with a well-deserved bit of good news. It was her money, but whatever she had, he was welcome to.

"You've been through enough, Frank Wilding. Maybe this will help." She stopped in the middle of the road to look to the heavens. "And thank you, Lord, for your provision."

She smiled. *Something Elijah would say.* If it weren't for the looming tough conversations in her near future, today would be the perfect day for a celebration. A baby on the way, a nice inheritance sum, and James on the mend. But all the blessings had their dark sides. Her physical health could endanger the child, the money could soon be gone to pay the bills, and James could end up hating her.

When she reached the porch, she heard voices coming from the living room. Frank and James were arguing. Her heart sank to hear harsh words from her son. She glided onto the step.

It was her turn to eavesdrop. Besides, Frank and James had to work toward an understanding.

"It's not fair. Why did she have to do it? I thought she was a good person."

James' words seared through Clarissa's heart like a knife with ragged edges, twisting to give maximum damage. She couldn't fault him. He was right—just like her father was right.

"Your mother *is* a good person. She's kind and loving and caring. You can't judge a person by one impetuous act. God forgave her, and so should you. The part about William being your father is something we will have to work on over time."

James spoke up louder. "So—have *you* forgiven her?"

Clarissa strained to hear, and didn't know how to interpret the silence. Her muscles twitched to step up. She tossed the envelopes on the ground and covered her ears. She couldn't bear to hear Frank's answer. He had been gentle and kind since she'd told him, but that was his way. He could hide his emotions as well as she. Maybe better.

Frank's muffled voice spoke only a few words. Then more silence.

She dropped her hands to her lap, waiting for more painful conversation. Instead, the clamor of a slammed back door and shoes running on the hardwood floors took her attention.

"Hey, Daddy. Come see the snake I found in the garden. It's..." Morgan's voice faded.

Clarissa took advantage of the interruption to go inside. Her fluttering stomach and weak knees called for small, deliberate steps. When she swung open the screen door, all eyes darted her way—James' red with tears. Frank's cheeks were also crimson. Morgan pulled his gaze from them, brows scrunched together and bottom lip quivering.

"Mama, James is crying. What's wrong?" He ran to her side. "And I think Daddy's mad," he whispered.

Frank jumped to his feet. "No. I'm not mad. James and I were just having a man-to-man talk. Right, James?"

James wiped his face with a quick swoop from his shirtsleeve. "Yeah. That's all." He gave Clarissa a cold glance. "Help me up, Morgan, and I'll go see the snake with you."

Frank walked toward Clarissa, his eyes full of pain. "James said you went for a walk. Do you think that's wise?"

Clarissa's throat tightened. She couldn't answer him. Her attention went to James hobbling beside Morgan. How would she live without his forgiveness?

Frank touched her arm. "Clary?"

"I'm fine. I'd like to sit for a while. And may I have a glass of water?"

"Sure." Frank took her elbow and guided her to the sofa.

She gasped to think she had left the mail on the ground outside.

"What is it? Another pain?"

She had missed her chance to give Frank a reprieve from some of his worry. The money lying out on the dirt could be the beginning of brighter days for them.

She opened her mouth to tell Frank to fetch the envelopes, but a knock on the door stopped her. William was on the other side of the screen, holding the mail. Her brighter day turned dark at his peculiar expression.

Frank squeezed her hand. "You stay inside."

You bet she would. Exhaustion set in like a shock wave as Frank shut the door behind him. His surprise would have to wait till this evening. She had a feeling she wouldn't see him before then.

William shoved the dusty envelopes in Frank's chest. "These were on the ground."

"Oh. Clary must have picked up the mail on her walk. Thanks." His attempt at gratitude stuck in his throat. William's tall frame towered over him—more so today than most days. Frank's anticipation of an argument made William loom like a formidable enemy.

"I'm not sure what you're thinking about staying on the place," William blurted out, "but this all has to be settled. You and your happy family includes me—especially now."

Frank glanced behind him and tossed the mail onto the porch chair. "Let's go somewhere to talk. I don't want Clary or the boys to hear. I thought you were going to give me your decision tomorrow."

William shook his head. "Let's go to my house." He wagged his thumb in that direction.

Frank had never been inside the big place. He had expected to be invited before now and was tempted to follow the landlords in when they had come. What a pity his first visit had to be under a black cloud. A cloud about to erupt with a storm.

William walked ahead of Frank, his stride long, pounding the ground with each step. He reached the screen door and held it open for Frank to go in ahead of him. The minute he stepped inside, Frank sensed the emptiness of a house that had no life in it. There was no sign that anyone lived there—no human touch, even on the nice belongings around the rooms.

Frank followed William into the kitchen. The stale air weighed the atmosphere down even more. William opened a window above the kitchen sink, then pulled out a chair for Frank and plopped into one on the other side of the table. Frank searched the uncluttered counters and near-empty shelves on wallpapered walls. Just two of plates, bowls, and cups sat on one shelf, and a set of china teacups on the other. Everything else needed in the kitchen must have been tucked behind cupboard doors.

Frank felt William's eyes boring into him.

"I'd like to settle things," William announced.

"William, I wish you would let it all go for a while. Clary isn't well, and James is—"

"Yes, I know. James is hurt. He wasn't that bad off. Should be up and around in a day or so. If I had raised him, he'd be a lot tougher than he is now."

Frank's blood boiled. William had no idea what James had been through in Kansas. Any boy who'd lived through that was tough enough for Frank and tougher than William.

He leaned in, his hands on the edge of the table. "You don't even know the boy."

William glared back. "Don't have to. He's my blood, not yours. That gives me the right to judge what's good for him. I intend to make sure he doesn't grow up a spoiled brat like you did. Always Mom's favorite. You never had to endure our father's drunkenness and meanness. Mom made sure of that. You turned out soft."

Frank stood, ready to bolt out the door as soon as he spoke his piece.

"Then why did you ask me to come to the farm?" His voice raised before he could stop it.

"Because I needed cheap help, and I knew you had a son who was old enough to work. Better than hiring a bunch of drifters to do a job I could get you to do for less wages. Planned to make your wife our cook until I saw who she was. You ruined her too, I see."

Frank's hands rolled into shaking fists. "You're a sorry excuse for a brother." His voice spewed out even louder now, but he couldn't hold back. "You're not getting James. I raised him and love him like my own. We'll get out of here as soon as he and Clary can travel."

William took a defensive upright stance. His voice bellowed

176

through the old house. "We'll just see about James. Maybe I should have a talk with him instead of you."

Frank's fists ached to hit his brother. Rage rumbled up inside him with a strength he had never known before. It was the wrong kind of strength—he knew it from the still voice in his mind.

Stand back.

He willed himself to move one of his feet back, but the glower coming from William's face kept him on guard. Frank stilled, but William took one step forward, his fists also clenched.

Like a thunder clap, the back door slammed. James hobbled into the kitchen, his face red and his shoulders stiff.

Frank and William turned at the same time to face him. Shame washed over Frank. The suspense thickened the air as silence ruled for several ticks of the clock.

"I could hear you both shouting clear across the yard. Mother was about to rush over here, but I told her this was between the three of us men."

Frank had never heard such rigidity in James' voice before, such command. He unclenched his fists. It was time for James to speak.

William chuckled. "Men?"

James stared straight at William. "I guess I have to be now, don't I? Thanks to what you did to my mother."

William held up his hand. "Listen, James—"

"No, you listen. Both of you sit down and listen."

Frank sat first. William scooted to the edge of his chair and laid one arm on the table. Frank positioned his feet, ready to jump up if William made a move.

James sighed and relaxed his shoulders. He seemed so much taller and older than yesterday. Frank knew pain would either bring a man down or grow him up. James was about to prove one or the other was true for himself.

"Right now I hate you both. You're fighting over me like I have no say in anything. I *do* have a say, and I'll be the one to decide about my life. You two have messed things up but good. Mother too. Her part in this ended a long time ago. Now I'm stuck in your mess. It's not fair, but I'll get over it. Both of you just leave me alone."

Frank looked at William. His lips were pursed, and the disgust in his eyes angered Frank.

James stuffed his hands in his trouser pockets. "Understand?" His glare darted from Frank to William.

Frank jumped in before his brother could pounce on the question.

"Sure, son. I get it. I'm proud of you for speaking up."

William didn't get a chance to say yay or nay. James turned on his good leg and half hobbled, half stomped out of the room. The door slammed again. Pity took over as other emotions faded—pity for William, and maybe for himself too. He couldn't look at William or he would lose this moment of grace.

He marched out of the room and bounded down the steps and stopped to watch James march up the cottage porch stairs one at a time. Clarissa waited at the top with the screen door open. She glanced at Frank as James wiggled past her and into the cottage. Frank gave her a nod and headed toward the barn. He hoped Elijah would be there. Only another man could understand his predicament, and Elijah should stay informed about William's attitude. Just in case.

When Frank reached the barn door, Elijah turned from his perch on top of a ladder to the loft. He didn't smile as he usually did, but took each rung in slow steps to the ground. He stood watching Frank.

"You heard, Elijah?"

"Yes, sir. Couldn't help."

Frank leaned against the barn door. "What am I going to do?"

Emotion clogged his throat. How could Elijah understand what it was like to lose a child?

"Pray first, then listen."

Frank let out a laugh. "Just got orders from my son to listen. I must be a bit rusty at it. It can't be that simple. This is a complicated problem. I don't think you understand." Frank pushed away from the door and turned his back on Elijah.

"You're wrong, Mr. Wildin'. I do."

Elijah's statement had grabbed Frank's attention, so much so that he waved Elijah into the back room, where they could have privacy. Elijah sat on his cot, and Frank pulled in a bucket to sit on.

Frank looked him square in the eyes, ready to read whatever they illuminated. "What did you mean by what you said?"

"Well, sir. You think I don't know what it's like to lose a son. I suppose since I've been a drifter and never talked about any kin, y'all thought I was always alone. It ain't so."

Frank's curiosity stirred. "Can you tell me about it?"

Elijah looked away for a moment, his lower lip quivering.

"I need to hear your story, Elijah. I need some wisdom."

Elijah turned back to Frank and tipped his head. "I had a wife and son. They're gone. You see, my parents were young slaves before Mr. Lincoln set all slaves free. When they came of age to leave home, they made their own way, got married, and had a family. I was born last of five. I left home at 17 and met my beautiful wife. We married a few years later. Didn't have much money, but we made out. Our first child came early, and Chloe, that's my wife, had a hard time givin' birth. Right after our son was born, Chloe died."

Frank's heart skipped. "Elijah. I'm so sorry."

"Was a long time ago, and too close to the slave days for

some people to be acceptin' of a black man raisin' his son alone."

"Even then? I had no idea."

Elijah hung his head. "The town we lived in had some old laws about that, and some of the elderly women in town took it upon themselves to get into other folks' business. They came and told me I couldn't have my baby. They said he would go to a better home and that I was nowhere near able to take care of him or give him a proper education. I had to work to live, and there was no one to watch over him. I was still so upset about my wife, I didn't have the strength to fight. So they took him."

A tear escaped Elijah's dark round eyes and trickled to his chin.

Frank choked out a question he was afraid to ask. "Did you ever see him again?"

"No, sir. But I keep thinkin' someday I might run into him if I keep travelin' around."

Frank stood and lay his hand on the man's shoulder. He would never be able to endure such grief. Losing two babies had been hard, but giving up a grown child he loved would be inconceivable torture. For him and Clary.

Frank stood near his friend, ashamed for all the terrible atrocities Elijah had been through. There were no words he could say, no way to make up for such a loss.

"What was your boy's name?"

A smile spread over Elijah's face. "Emmanuel." He met Frank's gaze. "Every time I think of him, I remember, *God is with us*. That's what his name means. So I know wherever he is that God is with *him*."

Sobs echoed from inside the barn. Frank peeked around the doorway to see Clarissa standing not far away. Her face in her hands, her shoulders shook as she cried openly.

Frank scooted to her side. "You heard?"

She nodded with her hands still covering her face. Frank

pulled them away and wrapped his arms around her. She sobbed into his chest. He knew she would never let James go. The implications of that knowledge were unthinkable. Yet he had to consider it. If James chose to go with William, he could lose them all.

Clarissa calmed her cries. "Poor Elijah. I would never dream he had experienced such heartache. He's always so happy and thinking of others."

Elijah stepped out of his room. "I learned somethin' a long time ago, ma'am. You have to do what's good to do and let the Lord take care of the rest. Can't let sorrow get in the way."

Clarissa slid from Frank's arms and approached Elijah. "That's what we should do, then? It sounds so easy."

"No, ma'am. Not easy. Jus' necessary. If you want to have peace, that is."

Frank let Elijah's words settle into the turmoil swirling around his family. He couldn't change William, and he couldn't mend James' broken heart. He would leave that to the One who knew how.

Clarissa held her head high and strolled past Frank and out into the yard. He nodded to Elijah and followed her. She had to know their mission now. If they weren't together on the journey that faced them in the coming weeks, they would be torn apart by the opposition.

Clarissa stopped in the middle of the yard and turned to look at William standing on his back steps. Frank's stomach flipped. Then Elijah's words echoed in his ears. Clarissa whirled around and marched to the cottage just as Morgan appeared from the bushes in back of the garden.

"Look, Daddy! Another garden snake!"

A wiry, wiggling reptile dangled from Morgan's hand. The smile on his son's face sparked Frank to chuckle. Such simplicity of joy from the child who knew nothing of his parents' trials.

Frank sprinted to him and grabbed him up, snake and all, and spun him around. By the time he set him firmly on the ground, they both doubled over with breathless laughter.

"You… better… put that snake back," Frank panted.

Morgan nodded and scampered into the bushes, still laughing.

Frank stood straight and looked to the sky. "Is this how it is when we chase peace, Lord?"

No answer came to him as he walked through the back door to the cottage and down the hall to James' room. He poked his head through the bedroom door left ajar. James' eyes stayed on the pages of the book in his hands.

Frank had only one thing to say. "I love you, son."

James remained still. Frank closed the door. He would give James the space he needed, but Clarissa was another story. He found her at the kitchen table, gazing out the window.

"Penny."

"What?"

"For your thoughts."

"Not sure they're worth a penny."

Frank wanted to extend the same compassion for her as he did for Elijah—even more. Blame was a trap, and he hated being caught in it. The only way out was to forgive and understand. It could just as easily have been him that made a mistake such as this.

He sat across from her and leaned to the side to make sure James' door was shut. No more overheard conversations were needed. He kept his voice low.

"Before Morgan bursts in here waving another snake—"

"Snake?" Clarissa jumped, eyes wide.

"It's okay. I told him to set it free in the garden. He's a real outdoors boy, that one."

Clarissa sighed through a half smile. Her eyes then fixed on the window. "What did you want to say?"

Frank reached a hand across the tabletop. Clarissa turned but took her time easing her hand into his palm. He grasped it tight and hesitated, making sure he chose the right words.

"I want to say—we'll make it through this—together. What's done is done. I forgive you. Actually, I have nothing to forgive. You were honest with me from the beginning, except for William. That you didn't know yourself. Do you think we can join up to put this family back together? We need a strong front against a force that wants to separate us. William is being used to do that."

She met his gaze. "But he is James' father. Doesn't he have rights?"

Frank released her hand and leaned back. "Not unless he chooses to exercise them. We need to pray for God to change William. God is in control—not you or me. Or even James. Not if God is in it."

"But what if James wants to have a relationship with William?" She wiped a tear from her cheek. "What will we do then?"

Frank paused. "Whatever God says to do. Agreed?"

Clarissa returned her gaze to the window, then back at Frank. Her eyes and voice steadied. "Agreed."

Chapter 12

The sunset was barely visible from the front porch, but the soft, cool breeze felt so nice that Clarissa didn't want to move from her rocker. Fragrance from the row of lilac bushes down the driveway drifted under the porch roof, and crickets had already started their night songs. The forgotten envelopes from this morning were now safely inside, and the check from the law office was tucked in her pocket. The excitement over the inheritance had dwindled in the drama of the last eight hours.

"Been a long day, hasn't it?" Frank stepped out of the cottage and stood next to her, dish towel over his shoulder.

She laughed when she noticed her apron tied around his waist. "Aren't you the perfect image of a dishwasher? And yes, it's been a long day. But it's over now." She reached for his hand. "Thanks for cleaning up the kitchen. Are the boys getting ready for bed?"

"Yep." Frank pulled off the apron and tossed it through the open door.

He sat beside her in the bigger rocker. His droopy eyes and stubbled face made him look as though he had been up for days. Maybe he hadn't been sleeping at all since the sad story of her life broke open. She didn't deserve his understanding, although he had seemed eager to give it this afternoon. So many men would have given up love after what she'd put him through.

"Why don't you go to bed, Frank? You need some sleep if you're going to work tomorrow."

Frank huffed. "Funny. I don't even know if I have a job here. William has been evasive about that. I think he's afraid that if we leave, he'll have to hire some of *those* people to help with harvest. The crops are about ready."

"Who are *those* people?"

Frank sat up straight. "Migrant workers. Mostly folks out of work, some not from around here. He doesn't hold a high opinion of them. Too bad for him. I hope it doesn't come to that. I would hate to see William treat them poorly. He warned me not to make it common knowledge in town that we're so fond of Elijah. Afraid of offending people. I don't think all those poor folks care about things like that while times are so hard."

Clarissa reached into her pocket and opened her mouth to tell Frank about the money, but turned at the sound of boots stomping toward them. Her heart sank to see William bounding around the corner of the cottage, his face contorted like a bull about to charge. Frank wasted no time in jumping to his feet and stood in front of her.

William bellowed before he reached them. "Where's my ledger?"

"What ledger?" Frank moved to the steps and stood tall.

William stopped just short of the porch steps. "My bookkeeping ledger. It was in my office and now it's gone." He leaned to look around Frank at Clarissa. "You were in my house. You said so. You must have taken it."

Frank stood his ground but craned his neck to glare at her. She should have told him she had been in the big house. Now on top of all the dissension, she had to defend herself while being caught at the same time.

She stood and faced William. "I didn't take your ledger. I

only looked around, saw my mother's painting, and left. What would I want with your bookkeeping records?"

Frank squinted at her. "You were in his house? And what's this about your mother's painting?" He looked back and forth between her and William. "What's going on here?"

She looked into Frank's eyes. "I snuck into the big house one day while you were all in town. I just wanted to see inside. I didn't touch anything. I noticed a framed picture hanging on the wall that looked like something Mother would have painted. I moved in closer." She turned her attention to William. "It was one of Mother's signed paintings. I'd like to know how he got it and why, but I've not pressed the issue."

Frank shot a glare to William. "What about it, William? It's rather strange you would have one of Mrs. Tate's masterpieces."

William waved his hand. "None of your business. Don't change the subject. I want my ledger. Now." His voice raised to a fever pitch as he pointed to her. "You took it out of spite."

Frank moved to the step below. She wanted to grab him by the belt and pull him back before William took a swing at him. She glanced to the doorway. The boys were likely to hear the commotion. She pushed herself up and scooted to the screen door. Reaching in, she felt the twinge return. She grabbed the knob to the big door and pulled it shut, breathing through the pain.

"She doesn't have your stupid ledger. I know who does."

Clarissa sat on the edge of the rocker, shocked by Frank's confession. What did he have to do with this?

William snapped at Frank. "Tell me who has it."

Frank stuffed his hands in his jeans pocket. "With all the things going on around here, I forgot to mention to you that your landlords came by a while back. They took it."

William's mouth fell open. He leaned in, feet still planted

firm, but his hands shook. "You gave it to my landlords? Why? You had no right to do that. Who do you think you are?"

As William's face reddened, Frank pulled his hands out of his pockets. Clarissa's heart raced. She took some deep breaths.

"Hold on, William. I didn't give it to them. They went in the house and came out with it. They told me you worked for them and that you often shared the bookkeeping with them. I had no reason to doubt them. Why don't you ask them about it?"

William's shoulders slumped. "You should have stopped them or waited till I came."

Frank's tone softened. "You were in town, and they seemed in a hurry. I should have told you about it, but it got crazy around here." He paused to watch William for a moment. "What's so important about that ledger that you don't want them to have it?"

After taking a few steps back, William trudged toward his house. Frank backed his way into the rocker and sat on the edge, shaking.

Clarissa's questions stuck in her throat. What had they just witnessed? The image of a young, happy William flashed in her mind. Back then she had been enchanted with his energy and outlook on life. The man walking away from them now was contrary and bitter.

She slumped in her chair. "What in the world?"

Frank grabbed her hand. "I've never seen him like this. Something is very wrong, but I don't think he's going to tell us about it."

The sun had completely disappeared, and only the full moon and porch light lit the area. Clarissa shivered. She hated having to live so close to this angry brother. She could only thank God the boys hadn't heard. No matter what she wanted for James, this display of emotion would only serve to confuse him more.

Frank still stared at William's house. "I'm worried about

him, Clary. What sort of trouble do you think he's in? I don't know what to do. Just stay out of it, I guess. He's right. I should have stopped them."

"Mama, are you coming in to say good night?" She could hear Morgan holler through the open window.

She had forgotten about the boys. "I'll be inside in just a minute, Morgan. Stay in bed."

Frank looked far away, as if mentally going over the events of the day. She knew him well enough to guess his thoughts. She touched his chin. "It's not your fault. You didn't know. We need to think about leaving here, Frank. I don't want the boys to be around this volatile atmosphere. We can use my inheritance."

He leaned back and closed his eyes. "If you ever get it."

She stood and opened the screen door, then whispered, "I got it today."

Frank's eyes popped open. "What?"

She closed the screen door, letting him stew in the realization. The stitch in her side poked her again, but not as bad as before. She heard Frank mumble something as she headed down the hall to Morgan's room. James' door was shut, but a dim light crept under it. She would tuck Morgan in and then see to James.

He may not like her right now, but she was still his mother. He needed her whether he thought so or not.

The week had brought not only turmoil but hot days, and Frank could see the fruit ripen before his eyes. He hadn't seen William at all yesterday, and it was already 11 o'clock with no sign of stirring from the big house. Late last night he had heard the clanking of glass outside, and when he investigated after the sun came up, he could see empty alcohol bottles in the trash barrel by the barn. The only drinker on the place was William, and it was likely the reason for his absence.

It was fortunate that Clarissa had declared today catch-up time for schoolwork for Morgan and James. They would be in the cottage most of the day, until it got too hot to stay cooped up inside. A breeze through open windows was the best they could hope for when the sun hovered high over their small abode.

"Gonna be hot today, Mr. Wildin'." Elijah emerged from the orchard, shovel in hand, his overalls sweat stained. "The apples are turnin' quick."

Frank glanced at the big house one more time before joining Elijah at the end of the last row of ripening grapes. He didn't know enough about grapes yet, even though he had soaked up all the information he could. Anyone could tell harvest was fast approaching.

"Elijah, do you know anything about harvesting grapes?"

Elijah pulled a handkerchief from his overalls pocket and wiped his dripping forehead. "No, sir. Don't know much. What does Mr. William say about when we're gonna start?"

Frank shielded his eyes from the sun to search down the rows of vines, hoping to see William's form roaming the fruit-laden plants. "He hasn't said a word about it. We aren't exactly on speaking terms, and I don't even know if we'll all be here for long." He dropped his arm and shook his head. "I keep saying that. I wish I knew William's thinking. We have a real mess for God to get us out of, my friend."

Elijah laughed and leaned on the shovel handle. "He's all right with that. It's not the Lord's first mess you know."

Leave it to Elijah to find the positive aspect of a poor situation, like a candle in the dark. Frank closed his eyes. So much to worry about—the ripening fruit, Clary's condition, James' anger, and his own dashed dreams.

William's back door slammed. Elijah looked up, his smile vanishing. Frank hesitated to turn around, for fear of seeing

William drunk and ready for a fight. He moved with slow precision to view William walking toward them. No wavering. William's steady gate surprised Frank. He did have a scruffy stubble on his face, and his shirt looked as though it had been slept in. A pitiful sight.

"Good mornin', Mr. William." Elijah tipped his hat and then moved on in the direction of the barn.

Clarissa would be out soon with lunch for the two of them. He hoped William would be civil, or at least go about his business in the orchard. Despite the conflicts in the family, William needed to tend to the business of the farm.

Frank stepped forward. "I'm ready for work, if you are."

No one had a chance to do anything before the rumble of a car bouncing up the drive took their attention. Frank and William turned in unison to see a familiar vehicle roll into the yard and stop next to William's house.

William glared at Frank. "Now see what you've done. You go in the barn and let me handle this." He removed his hat and smoothed his hair back before marching to greet his landlords, tucking his shirt in as he walked.

Frank's back stiffened, but he did as he was told. He would help Elijah replace some boards in the loft to keep busy.

He took one step into the barn, when he heard someone call after him.

"Frank Wilding, may we see you for a moment?"

It was the voice of the man Frank believed to be the owner, George Tanner. The sister, Felicity, stepped out of the passenger side of the same fancy car they had been in the last time they'd visited. If he could only turn back the clock and do that day over.

George waved him over. Frank nodded, wondering if William would protest. By the time Frank reached the group, William was arguing with George, his voice strained and cold.

"You don't have any proof except the word of an unhappy migrant worker. You going to believe one of them instead of me? I've made you lots of money, George, and you accuse me of stealing?"

George stood his ground. He had at least 50 pounds on William and maybe two or three inches of height. George's face didn't show the slightest inflection. Felicity, however, spouted off, her grinding voice howling like a cat with its tail caught. She cursed at William and called him names. George stepped in front of her and murmured something. She huffed and leaned against the car again, tossing her hair off her face.

Frank had never seen a woman get so mad. He stood still, waiting for the shouting match to stop. George finally saw him and held out his hand. "Hello, Frank. Nice to see you again."

Frank glanced at William before shaking George's hand, ignoring the tug of war between two strong men on opposite sides. What did George want from him—to accuse his own brother?

William pointed his finger at George. "Frank can tell you I'm an honest man. He shouldn't have given you the ledger. I was still working on it."

"I bet you were," Felicity chimed in.

Frank wanted to crawl under a rock until the fight was over. He glanced back at the cottage. *Stay in there, Clary.*

William cleared his throat. "Frank doesn't need to be involved in this."

George looked at Frank but directed his words at William. "I want him here. First as a witness and then to ask him an important question. I got the distinct impression when I met Frank that he was a straight shooter. When he let me take the ledger, I knew he had nothing to hide and was probably ignorant of your antics."

Frank realized he had been holding his breath as George spoke. He let it go in a quiet sigh.

William took off his hat and slapped it against his trousers, shaking his head at Frank. "I think my brother knew exactly what he was doing. He framed me."

George wiped his brow, taking his time to speak. "I don't think so. We have all the information we need to make our decision. In fact, we've made up our minds." He paused. "We want you off the place, William. You're no longer trustworthy, and we want you gone."

Frank thought his heart would stop. Was this a joke? What had William done?

"Mr. Tanner, you must be mistaken about whatever you think William did. I know I've only been here a few months, but he's a hard worker."

Felicity laughed. "Yeah, hard at working the books in his favor."

So that was it. Frank studied William's face. He remembered that same look of guilt when they were kids. William would lie his way out of just about everything their father confronted him with. Frank always took William's side. Maybe he shouldn't today.

While George hushed Felicity, Frank stole another look at the cottage. Clarissa stood on the porch, discretely watching and listening. *Stay there.*

George addressed Frank. "It's settled. Your brother is finished here. My question to you, Frank, is will you stay on to harvest our crops? We'll pay you well."

The legs on which Frank stood wobbled under him. How could he answer? William might be in the wrong, but he was still his brother. Yet this brother had caused so much pain, and if he was indeed a thief, his influence on James should be terminated.

George's voice came into focus. "…difficult position. I'm sorry."

He pulled in a breath and scanned past William's defiant stance to the vineyard in the distance. The afternoon sun beat down on the grapes. The crops could all be lost if someone didn't do the job. If he said yes, he could always make up with William and give him part of his portion of the pay. Where would William go? How would he live? His temples throbbed with the pressure of his decision.

George's voice again interrupted his thoughts. "I realize I'm putting you on the spot, but you have to understand our problem. We have proof that your brother altered the books to give himself more than he should. We're confident we're making the right decision. Please say you will stay on. I don't have anyone else."

Frank stilled, waiting for inner assurance his instinct was correct. He was 99 percent sure he knew his answer. He had to talk to Clary first. He saw William out of the corner of his eye, frozen in a defensive posture. There was only one thing to do.

"Mr. Tanner, before I answer, I'd like for you and your sister to meet my wife."

Clarissa scurried from her perch on the porch into the cottage and told James to take Morgan out the back door. "Stay in the barn until someone comes to get you."

"What's going on?" James craned his neck to the window.

"Some people visiting William are on their way over here right now. I'm not sure who they are, but I'm sure everything is fine." She wasn't sure at all, but James didn't need to know that.

James shrugged as Morgan clapped his hands at the reprieve from schoolwork. He ran out before James could hobble down the hall. Clarissa glanced in the mirror by the front door just in time to hear footsteps on the porch. She wet her lips and pinched her cheeks, then opened the screen door.

Frank's stare and pursed lips were so intense, she faltered as she stepped out of his way. He took her hand and held it tight while the strangers filed in behind him. She plastered a smile on her face and gave them a nod.

Frank let go of her hand. "This is my wife, Clarissa." He turned to her. "Honey, this is George Tanner and his sister, Felicity. They are the owners of the vineyard, William's landlords."

George reached out his hand, and she extended hers, feeling his strong grip pinch her fingers. "It's very nice to meet you, Mrs. Wilding."

Felicity stepped forward and added her handshake to a gracious smile. "Hello, Clarissa." She stole a glance at Clarissa's waistline.

Frank gave her no clues about what to do next, but the awkward silence had to be broken. She pointed to the sofa. "Please, won't you sit down?"

Frank pulled a chair from the kitchen, letting Felicity have the overstuffed chair next to George.

Felicity cleared her throat, then leaned ahead of George. "Don't you have children?"

Frank turned to look at James' bedroom door.

Clarissa answered before Frank tried to call for the boys. "Oh yes. Two boys. They're out in the barn playing at the moment." She heard Frank let out a quick breath. She put her hand on her belly. "And we're expecting another."

Felicity nodded. "How nice." She brushed back a lock of hair and continued to look Clarissa up and down.

George leaned back and surveyed the room. "You've fixed up the cottage. It's very nice. I hope you enjoy living here, Mrs. Wilding."

Clarissa gathered it wasn't the best time to be totally honest about her desire to leave. "Oh—"

Frank patted her back. "She's good at homemaking. We've been very comfortable here. We just appreciate the change from the drought and dust storms of Kansas. Right, honey?"

"It's a lovely cottage. I like it very much." That was the truth, and it seemed to satisfy.

She hardly finished before George leaned forward and clasped his hands together. "Frank, can we talk about our proposition? I assume that's why you wanted to bring us to meet your wife."

The kitchen chair legs squeaked across the floor as Frank turned it to face Clarissa. "Mr. Tanner has decided to let William go and has asked me to stay on at least until after harvest. I want to know what you would think about that before I answer."

Shivers ran up her arms. She had discerned from the intense conversation in front of William's house earlier that something had gone wrong. She couldn't have dreamed this would happen. Her tongue seemed too thick for her to speak. She swallowed hard, hoping she wouldn't stutter.

"William is leaving? I'm not sure what all this means." She stared at Frank. "So you would be running the entire farm? Can you do that?"

"He can hire help if he needs it," George interrupted.

"It would be a lot of hard work, but I would be earning more money. I have Elijah to help me too."

Felicity sat up. "Who's Elijah?"

Frank's face flushed. "I'm sorry. I supposed you knew. William said it was all right for our friend Elijah to come here to work for room and board. He was with us in Kansas—a kind and gentle man. A hard worker who never complains."

George rubbed his chin. "I see. William never told us, but I see no harm in it. However, room and board hardly seems enough compensation if he's that valuable. If he would also agree to stay on, I would pay him."

Clarissa smiled at the prospect, but doubts still lingered. Why had William been fired? Even though relief spread through her, she had to know about William before she voiced her opinion.

She tucked her hands into her lap to hide that they were shaking. "Mr. Tanner, are you confident about your decision to fire William and give Frank that much responsibility? I know Frank could do it, but I would like your assurance this would be a sure thing."

George looked at the floor for a moment, then at Felicity, who nodded.

"Yes. I feel good about Frank taking over. And for reasons your husband understands, William is definitely finished here for good."

She turned her face to search Frank's eyes. "Is this what you want? Can you support your brother being thrown off the place?"

His eyes stayed locked on hers. "I think it's the right thing to do, but only if you agree. Remember what we talked about? We're in this together and must lean on what He says is right. I agree that William is untrustworthy. He's going whether I stay or not." He turned to George. "Right, Mr. Tanner?"

"Yes. The sooner the better."

Clarissa closed her eyes, willing her head to stop spinning. William gone. Frank in charge. It seemed too good to be true, but Frank's steady words and her inner calm gave her courage to speak her answer.

"Then I'm with you. I'll do what I can to help as well."

Frank took her hand once more and faced George. "I guess we're on board then, Mr. Tanner, but may I ask how you will handle my brother?"

George and Felicity stood. "I'll not expect you to be a part of this unpleasant business. I don't think William will give me any trouble. Not with what I have over him. He's lucky he's not going to jail, and I'll make sure he knows that's still on the bargaining table if he resists."

Clarissa shuddered. *Jail?*

Frank took to his feet, pulling her up with him. "I'll wait to hear from you that everything is in order. In the meantime, Elijah and I will get to work. We can ask around in town for harvest help if that suits you. Someone with experience with a vineyard and orchard."

"I agree. Take a day to stay out of William's way, and you'll hear from me when everything is settled. I'll have some papers drawn up to make sure we are in agreement about wages and duties. Is that all right?"

Frank stuck out his hand. George shook it with three hard pumps. He bowed to Clarissa. "Thank you, Mrs. Wilding, for your support."

She searched for impressive words, something intelligent, but could only smile and squeak out a goodbye.

Felicity took her by the hand. "Good luck with the new baby."

"Thank you, Felicity."

Frank left her standing there to follow their new landlords out to the yard. Her stomach fluttered to think William might cause trouble. She ran to the window. Frank, George, and Felicity were alone by the fancy car. She scanned the yard and whispered into the window.

"Get back here, Frank. I want to know what happened."

George and Felicity got in the car and sped down the driveway. Frank looked to his right at William's back door. No movement.

His attention turned to the barn. He hesitated, shading his eyes with his hand, as if searching the area. She strained to see what he might be staring at, but the Hawthorne tree at the corner of the cottage blocked her view from this window. She turned to run to Morgan's room, but stopped at the return of the stabbing pain that had plagued her.

She heard the doctor's words about taking it easy, eliminating anxiety. Deep breathing all the way to the sofa eased the discomfort. She settled in to wait for Frank.

There was so much to figure out about her feelings over William's firing.

So many plans to make.

Seeing William in the distance set Frank's nerves on edge. Through the sunlight and shadows past the barn door, his brother stood next to James, his hand on the boy's shoulder. No other picture could have riled Frank more, considering everything between them now. His feet moved before he could command them, and he marched to confront whatever William was up to.

He could hear William coaxing James about something, but James said nothing, just staring at his would-be father ignoring James' command to leave him alone. Two more steps and Frank made out a few words from William.

"Just you and me, boy... go away... anywhere you say..."

Frank's blood iced, but he had to play this right. Another showdown would be disastrous for James. He stopped short at the barn entrance. James jerked his head to lock glaring eyes with Frank. William dropped his hold on James and rested his hands on his hips.

"Well, well. Are you and George done building a case against me?" He leaned down to James' ear. "You dad has been conspiring with my landlord to kick me off the place. He wanted it for himself, and now he made it happen."

Frank took another step. "James, that's not true. Your uncle made his own trouble long before we got here." He looked around the barn for Morgan or Elijah. "Where's your brother?"

James folded his arms across his chest. "With Elijah, checking for dropped fruit in the orchard."

Frank toed the ground. "I think you should go back to the cottage and see if your mother needs anything."

James looked at William, then at Frank. "I'll go check on her, but not because you said so." He limped past Frank and out the barn door.

William called after him. "Think about what I said."

James kept walking. "Not for long."

Frank forced back a smile and took another step toward William. "I understand you're leaving first thing in the morning. Until then, you are to leave James alone. Don't ever corner him again like this, or—"

"Or what? It's a little late to play the big protective daddy, don't you think?"

William stalked away. Frank held his breath, resisting the urge to follow him and finish the argument once and for all. He flinched when Morgan skipped into the other side of the barn, his pockets and shirt bulging.

His smudged face broke into a shining smile when he spied Frank. "I found lots of apples on the ground. Mama can make applesauce."

Frank knelt down to see Morgan's stash. "Not bad. She might need your help though. Can you peel an apple?"

"Sure." He puckered his face. "I mean, I think so."

Frank had a compulsion to grab him and squeeze him tight. Instead he patted his head. "Where's Elijah?"

Morgan took a bite of one of his treasures. "He's comin'. I run faster than he does."

Elijah appeared behind Morgan. "He sure does."

Frank winked at Elijah and poked Morgan's nose. "Why don't you go show your mama what you gathered? I need to talk to Elijah for a minute."

Morgan waved his half-eaten apple in the air. "Bye, Elijah." He wobbled out of the barn, juggling the bundle wrapped in his shirt. One dropped to the ground, but Morgan kept walking.

Elijah wiped his brow and laughed at the sight. "He's a good boy, Mr. Wildin'."

Frank watched Morgan until he reached the back steps of the cottage. "He is, and he loves it here." He turned to Elijah. "And he loves you."

Elijah teared up. "He's a lovin' child. His special gift."

Frank rubbed the back of his neck. "I have some things to tell you, Elijah. Some bad, and some could be good."

"Yes, sir. Would you like to sit in my room?"

"No. I'd like to be able to see the yard." Elijah tipped his head. "I need to keep an eye out for William. You see, he's been fired by the landlords and asked to leave by tomorrow morning. Mr. Tanner, the owner of the place, has asked me to stay on and take care of harvest." He waited for Elijah's surprised expression, but he only nodded.

"So I will need all the help I can get. Experienced help, you know? Will you stay on and be my right-hand man? Mr. Tanner said he will pay you wages."

Elijah stuffed his handkerchief in his pocket and stared at the ground. "Well, that's some news."

Elijah's response wasn't as revealing as Frank had hoped. If Elijah said no, there would be no way for anyone to stay. It hadn't occurred to him that the man might prefer to move on. The silence pushed and pulled between them while the heat of the day prickled at Frank's already frayed nerves.

Finally Elijah looked up. "Is Mr. William in trouble? If you don't mind me askin'."

"Yes, he is. William is a troubled man, and if he weren't leaving, I would have to take my family elsewhere. I don't like staying under these circumstances, but with Clarissa's condition,

I don't think it's wise to move. She has agreed to stay as long as William is not here."

Elijah removed his hat to brush off the dust. Frank shifted from one foot to the other, impatient with Elijah's slow interaction.

"My place is here with you. Until the Lord tells me to go, I'm at your service."

Frank tipped his head back and sighed. "Thank you."

"Mr. Wildin', you and me don't know much about harvestin' grapes. But I know some people who do. Fine folks too."

The words were music to Frank, but what people? "Elijah, where did you meet such folks around here?"

"Well, when I was waitin' for Mrs. Wildin' and Mr. William at the hospital the day James was hurt, a family came by. We got to talkin'—"

Frank held up his hand. "Say no more. As long as you know where to find them, we can go see if they need work."

"I'm sure they do. We can talk to them most anytime. Folks out of work have little else to do but stay close to family. They live in tents outside town. Most come from some city far away called Seattle. It's a shame times are so hard."

Frank knew their need. He had been there, and his spirits lifted just to think he might be able to lend a helping hand. "I'll be in touch with Mr. Tanner soon, and then we can make plans. We have a lot of work to do and a lot to learn."

Morgan hollered from the back porch. "Mama says dinner is cooking. You comin', Daddy?"

Frank waved. "Yeah."

He turned to walk away. "I'll have the boys bring something out to you. Unless you want to join us in the cottage."

Elijah smiled. "No, thank you. I have some prayin' to do."

Clarissa set aside the skillet of beef, carrots, and potatoes simmering on the stove. The meeting with Mr. Tanner had taken her meal preparation time, so leftover hash was her only choice. She was too tired to come up with something new anyway.

She glanced at the clock to affirm it was time for dinner, but she had no one to serve dinner to. Frank must have gone to the barn to tell Elijah the news, and James and Morgan were nowhere to be seen. Usually the aroma of food cooking instigated the sound of pounding footsteps racing up the porch stairs.

As she wiped her hands on her apron, the back door squeak signaled someone had been hungry enough to eat. She recognized the steps as James' limp. By the time she reached the hallway, he had already holed up in his room with the door shut. She shared his agony. The pain she felt must be magnified for James, with the kind of turmoil he had experienced.

She leaned against the wall by his door, uncertain if she should leave him alone or go in to encourage him to get on with life. She couldn't let James hold everything inside. Her hand grasped the doorknob. She tapped three quick knocks. "James?"

"What."

The hairs on her neck bristled. Not an acceptable answer. Despite his feelings, she wouldn't tolerate bad manners. She turned the knob and pushed the door open with her shoulder. James sat on the edge of the bed, facing his open window. The curtains hung straight for lack of a breeze. With the door shut, the air had stilled with stifling heat. She ambled up to James.

"*Yes, Mother,* is the better response." She sat next to him. "James, I know you're hurting. You've had a shock and only a few days to deal with it, but you need to face it and learn to deal with it better than staying in your room and not speaking to any of us."

"I don't feel like talking. Besides, you and Dad have other things to talk about. Or so I hear from Uncle… William." He picked at the bandage around his leg.

She reached over and pulled his hand off the wrapping, hoping her demeanor fared well. "What did William say to you?"

James stood and moved to the window and sat on the wide sill. "I don't want to talk about it."

"If this family is going to hold together and move on, we have to start communicating. It's important you let us know what William said. If you don't want to tell me, then tell your father."

James' eyes narrowed. "You mean Uncle Frank?"

Clarissa bolted from the bed and lifted a hand to slap him. His tears stopped her. She dropped her arm, not only to keep from hitting James but to ease the sudden pain in her side. She too cried and bent over, rocking on the edge of the bed.

James knelt beside her. "I'm sorry, Mother." His tears flowed harder. "I'm so confused. I don't know what to do." He wiped his nose with the bedspread. "Are you all right?"

"What's wrong with Mama?" Morgan stood in the doorway, his bottom lip quivering. In his shirt he held what looked to be a bushel of apples.

James jumped up and swiped the back of his hand across his tear-stained cheeks. He sat back on the windowsill, biting his lip and leaving Clarissa to soothe Morgan's worry.

"I just had a little stitch in my side, and James was helping me. I'm all right now." She raised up off the bed, tipping her head toward Morgan. "What in the world do you have there, young man?"

Morgan's composure returned, and he wiggled his bundle. "They're apples. Can we make applesauce?"

She moved with caution, patting James on the shoulder as

she passed him. "I think we can manage that. Why don't you dump them in the sink and run some water to clean them. Then holler at your father to come in for dinner."

Morgan glanced down at his offering. "Yep. Can James help?"

James turned to stare out the window. She wanted one more try at convincing him to talk.

"I need James for just a few more minutes. I think you're big enough to handle the job, right?"

Morgan smiled wide. "You bet." He cradled his bundle and marched out to the kitchen.

Clarissa held on to the brass footboard. "James, please just tell me what William said to you, and then we can talk more about it later. There's a lot going on—some things you don't know. Your father and I have some decisions to make, and anything William said might be helpful."

James fidgeted with the curtain, then folded his hands in his lap. "He said Frank—Father—had talked the landlords in to kicking him off the place. He asked me to go with him and live somewhere else, just the two of us. He said he had lots of money saved up and he would buy me whatever I wanted." James' face reddened. "He said I needed to get away from you."

Clarissa's chest deflated to think of William inflicting such hatred onto his own flesh and blood. A real father would never do such a thing. James must know that deep inside.

Morgan's voice rang out from the back porch. He had done just what she asked, and Frank would be here any minute. They needed a normal, peaceful dinner tonight. Tomorrow would be soon enough to arrange for their new life—the second new start in four months.

"Thank you, James. We'll get this straightened out with the truth soon. For now, let's just have a nice dinner in the kitchen. Deal?"

James hesitated but then nodded.

Clarissa had just reached the doorway when James spoke. "He seems nice. Why does he have to go?"

"James, do you really think a man who would try and take you from your mother is a nice person?"

She stood still. He needed to believe his father was good, but to let him believe another lie would hurt him in the long run. She turned her head enough to whisper, "We'll talk later."

Frank met her in the hallway from the back of the cottage. He stopped short and studied her face. "What's wrong?"

He had changed over the last few months. She could tell by the way he noticed every detail of her countenance, asked to know about her feelings, and worked hard to make thoughtful decisions. His new awareness would be needed in the coming days and months, and she would need to follow suit.

"Let's have dinner, and then we can talk things out later. Is that okay?" She tilted her head toward James' room. It seemed all they did lately was discuss issues or put off talking altogether.

Frank glanced at James' door and then nodded. "Sure. What's cooking? I'll set the table. You sit down. You've been on your feet too much today."

Morgan stood on a chair at the sink munching on one of his apples. "Mama, you don't want that nurse to yell at you when she comes tomorrow. She said to rest."

Oh no. Martha would stop by tomorrow and see what a mess this family was in. Clarissa and Frank exchanged frantic glances. It would be quite a trick to put on an air of normalcy. Especially with so much unsaid between them and James and with William packing his bags to leave.

Frank bent to see Morgan face to face. "Well, we'll just have to make sure Mama rests tonight. You can do the dishes." He pretended to punch Morgan's stomach.

They played back and forth while Clarissa moved to the table to sit. She pulled out a chair and grabbed her belly.

Frank rushed over. "Pain again?"

Clarissa stood as still as she could and reached into her blouse.

"Wait," she whispered.

Morgan's mouth hung open. She winked at him to relieve his mind.

"There. I felt something flutter."

Frank let out a breath and smiled. "You mean *someone*."

She recalled the last time she'd had this feeling. The joyous realization that a child grew inside her never got old. She closed her eyes, waiting for another tapping against her skin. *Life.*

"I wish you could feel it, but it's too early."

Morgan crept closer. "Too early for what?"

She looked up to see James standing nearby, his lip curled into a half smile. He put his hands on Morgan's shoulders. "I think Mama's going to have a baby."

It was a strange way to reveal her secret, but they all needed a moment set apart from trials. New life had a way of making troubles seem far away, of gathering loved ones and igniting new plans. She had seen it with her other pregnancies, and with all the excited faces around her now, she knew this child would bring them together.

If it could hold on to the life it was given.

Frank closed the closet door in the upstairs bedroom of William's house. It was definite. William had left either in the night or early this morning. When Clarissa had woken Frank at 5:00 a.m., she had been up and noticed the car was gone and the back door to the big house was wide open.

"Go see what's going on," she'd said, shaking Frank out of his sleep.

It didn't make sense that William would leave so abruptly. If anything, Frank had expected resistance this morning, another confrontation about James or William getting fired. How strange William had given up and actually left when no one would see. The better scenario would be that William had come to his senses and seen the error of his ways. Frank scratched his head. It seemed unlikely, considering the man's displays of rage.

Frank wandered through the rest of the rooms, each bedroom adorned with fine furniture and décor. Whoever had designed and decorated the house aimed for elegance. Frank surveyed every bedroom. Not a thing out of the ordinary, at least upstairs. He half expected something to be out of place or missing altogether. With all the valuables in the house, William might have been tempted to help himself. Perhaps he'd left in the dark because he had taken something that didn't belong to him.

"The painting."

He clambered down the stairs and into the parlor, where Clarissa had said the artwork hung on the wall. Only a square of faded wallpaper remained in its place. William certainly knew how to hit back. Clarissa hadn't found out how he came to have the painting in the first place, and now she would likely never see it again.

Frank stepped outside and pulled the door shut. Clarissa stood on the cottage porch, waiting for him. He shrugged, holding out his arms, and walked across the yard in the first light of the morning sun. Feeling the warmth on his face told him they were in for another scorcher. With Elijah's help, he would keep a close eye on the fruit.

His stomach tensed to realize he was really alone in this

now. The ultimate test was only a few weeks away. William's teaching would be all he had to go on—and instinct.

"He's gone," he told Clarissa when he got to the porch. "He must have put the car in neutral and rolled it out of earshot. Otherwise we would have heard him leave."

Clarissa pulled her shawl around her neck. "Why would he do that? What was the point of sneaking out?"

Frank rubbed his face and yawned. "Don't know. It doesn't make any sense. Sometimes I wonder if he really is the kind of man everyone accuses him of being." He yawned again. "I know in my mind he is."

"But not in your heart." She shook her head.

He pulled her through the open door. "I need coffee, woman." He kissed her cheek, noting that she was still mulling over the situation. Any minute she would ask about the painting.

"Frank, did he leave everything in the house? I mean, all that stuff belongs to the landlords, right?" Her finger rested on her chin, a sure sign another question was coming.

"I suppose. I understood that the only things he owned were his personal belongings, not the furniture or collectibles."

She shuffled to the kitchen and filled the coffeepot with water. Frank sat at the table, waiting for her to ask about the painting. She seemed more relaxed this morning. Maybe the pains had lessened, or at least her concern over William's parting had.

She spun around, coffee can in hand. "Did you see Mother's painting?"

He knew her well, and it didn't make it easier to tell her.

"It's not there, Clary. I'm sorry. He must have taken it with him. Out of spite, I'm sure."

She stared out the window, tapping the can with her fingernails. He waited for her to digest the news, expecting tears or a rant. Instead, she stared outside. When she did speak, it was in such a soft tone, Frank strained to hear her.

"It's going to be a hot day. We need to make sure the boys wear hats outside."

Frank's heart fractured at her pathetic rambling. Had she heard what he said?

She spooned the coffee into the strainer and started the burner. Her slippers flapped against the floor as she walked to the bedroom. The bed squeaked, signaling that she had crawled back into it.

James emerged from his room, rubbing his eyes. He frowned at Frank. "Why is everyone up so early? I heard you out in the yard. Is something wrong?"

Frank patted the seat of the chair next to him. "Sit with me, James. I'd like to talk to you. There are some things you need to know."

James rolled his eyes but took the chair Frank pulled out for him. His eyes stayed focused on the table as he mumbled. "Seems like there's always something to talk over these days."

"William is gone. He must have left before dawn or in the night. Your mother said he had a talk with you yesterday. I understand he blamed me for getting fired. Is that right?"

"That's what he told me."

"Do you believe him?"

He held his breath for the answer. If William had convinced James he was innocent of George's charges, the tension between them would be unbearable.

James rubbed his eyes again. "I don't know. There are so many secrets around here, it's hard to know what to think. Why would he lie to me?" Now he looked at Frank, his eyes pleading for truth.

Frank cleared his throat. "I'll tell you what I know, James. William is my brother, and I never wanted this to happen to him. I love him, but his attitude changed after—your accident, and the increasing hostility made me wonder if we could stay here. The landlords have solid proof he was dishonest when doing the bookkeeping. William is a troubled man, and our situation didn't help matters any. But neither your mother nor I did anything against him. I hope you know us well enough to believe that."

James' pursed lips could have meant anything at this point. The silence convinced Frank that James still had some thinking to do on everything that had blindsided him. No boy should have to fret about such things.

Frank groaned inside. He had brought his family to this farm to rescue them, not bring down the wrath of past secrets. James bore the brunt of it. Frank was old enough to weather grown-up issues, but he wasn't certain James could get through this without wounds that might never heal.

He nudged James. "You okay?"

"Yeah. Just need to decide about a few things." James stood and glanced out the window at the reflection of the bright predawn sky.

James' words spun in Frank's head. They struck fear in him, wondering what the meaning was, what would James decide, and about what? He was old enough to choose which father he wanted. The only choice they had as his parents was to support and love him.

"I understand, James. I'd still like to talk about everything in more detail. Your mother and I want to know how you're feeling. This is a time for open, honest discussion. No more secrets, right?"

James sighed. "Right." He shuffled in the direction of his room, but turned to look at Frank over his shoulder. "You'll need my help for harvest then, won't you?"

"Absolutely."

At the sound of James' door closing, Frank covered his face

with his hands. At last a small sign of assurance from James that his heart was still open.

If James planned to help with harvest, he must also plan to stay with his family. At least the hope was worth clinging to.

Chapter 14

*F*rank shouldn't have let her fall back asleep. Martha would be here any minute, and Clarissa barely had time to get a bath. She combed through her wet hair, thinking it had been too long since she'd cut it. With a baby coming, she didn't need long hair for her little one to pull. *Her.* She had to stop thinking about the baby being a girl. Another boy would be fine, just as long as he was healthy and stayed that way.

She reached to hang her towel over the rack on the bathroom wall and felt the familiar twinge. All the rushing around not only made her dizzy, but now the pain had returned. Martha was only a student nurse, but she was intelligent enough to know what was going on. Worry was the worst thing for this pregnancy, but it couldn't be helped. Now that William was gone, she would improve.

"Need help?" Frank called from the hall.

Clarissa opened the bathroom door with a fake smile on her face. "Nope. I just need to get dressed. Are the boys up and dressed?"

Frank nodded. "And breakfast eaten. They're in their rooms working on the homework you gave them yesterday." He headed for the kitchen. "They sure are glad it's Friday."

She pulled on her only calico print housedress and wrapped it around to tie on the side. Martha would want to examine her tummy. A splash of much-needed rouge would make her more presentable. Despite getting some sun in the last few weeks, her skin still paled as if she had been hiding away in the dark. If she could just find her slippers, she would be ready.

Morgan hovered just outside the bedroom when she opened the door. Each of his hands were covered with one of her slippers. He grinned as if he had just invented the world's best prank. She raised her brows at Frank.

He smiled, then shrugged. "He escaped."

She played along. "Morgan, have you seen Mama's slippers?"

His grin fell. He jiggled his hands, leaning toward her.

"Oh, you've been wearing them this morning." She poked his stomach and laughed.

He doubled over and dropped the slippers before running back to the kitchen.

She stooped to pick them up, and the room spun. Grabbing the wall, she snatched up the slippers with her eyes closed, hoping no one saw her.

Breathe.

When she could open them again, it was clear her episode had gone undetected. Skipping breakfast had been a bad idea. She backed into the bedroom to take more slow breaths. Fainting spells weren't on the agenda today. Once composed, she made a second entrance into the hallway, bright eyed and smiling.

No one there to notice her attempt at cheerfulness. Frank and James were at the back porch pulling on work boots. James grimaced, struggling to balance on his healing leg. She didn't like him out tromping around so soon. It had only been four days, yet he was able to do more of what he wanted to now, which was be outside in the sunshine. At least he hadn't run off with William in the night—the thought had crossed her mind when she'd seen that the car was gone. Frank didn't know that she had snuck a peek in James' room to make sure he was there.

"I'm taking James out to inspect the fruit trees with Elijah. We'll be back soon. You ready for Martha?"

"Yes. Be careful, James."

James stood up straight and frowned at her. "I think I've learned my lesson about falling off cliffs, Mother. I'm not a baby." He stomped his boot to squeeze his foot in. Frank shot her a half-shrug.

Morgan opened the front screen door from outside. Clarissa guessed he had been waiting for a certain nurse to come up the drive. The boys had taken to her right off, and she to them, it seemed. Clarissa recalled Martha talking about her two brothers. She was used to boys.

"She's coming up the drive."

Clarissa fluffed her drying hair and smoothed her dress. "Good."

She sat on the sofa and picked up a magazine. Looking relaxed might save her a lecture. Frank and James tromped into the living room, no doubt not wanting to miss a chance to see the pretty young lady again. James hobbled out the front door and met her when the car stopped. Frank held the screen door open and greeted Martha, her admirers close behind.

Martha wasn't in her uniform. Instead she wore a plaid shirt with the sleeves rolled up to her elbows. Her wide-legged pants stopped at the top of brown saddle shoes. Her curly black hair hung loose without the constraints of a nurse's cap. Clarissa was taken aback at her tomboyish appearance.

"I know, I know. I don't look much like a nurse today. Sorry. I've been helping Mom and Pop clean out their house. It seems they may have to move in a few months."

Martha explained the whole dilemma while the boys and Frank looked on. James' demeanor went from bothered to cheerful just being around their new friend. Her way of telling stories captivated his troubled mind, a welcome distraction.

"Don't you men have work to do?" Clarissa stared at Frank.

"Oh, yes. Nice to see you again, Miss Watkins. James and I need to get out to the orchard."

"You said you'd call me Martha, and I understand. My parents always wanted to have a vineyard or orchard. They would love it out here in the peace and quiet."

Clarissa shooed Frank on with a wave of her hand, then turned to Morgan. He looked back at her with a hopeful rise of his brows.

"Morgan, the nurse needs to take a look at Mama. I'd like you to go out and pull some weeds in the garden. We'll be picking the rest of the beans and tomatoes later."

Morgan hung his head and sulked all the way out of the room.

Martha called after him. "When I'm done here, can I come see your garden?"

It was as if someone offered him the world. "You bet." With a wave he bounded out the door.

"Get it cleaned up pretty."

She pulled up a kitchen chair close to Clarissa, opened her bag, and pulled out a stethoscope, blood pressure cuff, and thermometer. Next she lay a notebook in her lap and folded her hands over it.

"Now, suppose you tell me why you're so pale, your breaths are coming too fast, and your right hand is always at your side."

Clarissa's mouth fell open. Martha Watkins was not one to be fooled, despite Clarissa's best efforts at looking and acting healthy. She leaned against the arm of the sofa and grunted. A friend would be a relief, if Martha was willing to extend beyond her nursing duties. If it would help bring a healthy baby to this family, Clarissa would do anything.

"While you think about your answer, I'll take your pulse and blood pressure. If you're a good girl and tell me what's been going on, I'll see if we can't hear the baby's heartbeat."

As Martha pressed on her wrist and then wrapped the cuff around her arm, Clarissa debated on just where to start telling the story of the Wilding family. She might as well spill it all. Then Martha could understand why she wasn't always in the best of moods.

Clarissa settled into the back of the sofa. "Can we talk after the heartbeat thing?"

"Sure. Just so you know, you're pulse is jumping, your blood pressure is too low, and you're too skinny, which is why you're showing so early, I suspect. Unwrap your dress and let's take a listen."

She warmed the end of the scope with her palm before placing it on Clarissa exposed tummy bump. She put her finger to her lips and closed her eyes. Clarissa lay as still as possible. After two minutes of silence, Martha took off the earpieces.

"Can't get a heartbeat, but it's probably too early. I say we give it another couple weeks, fatten you up, and try again." She rested her hand on Clarissa's arm. "No need to worry. It's normal."

Clarissa let out the breath she had been holding and tried to calm her panic. "Are you sure the baby is okay?"

"No reason to think otherwise." She closed her bag. "Now can we talk about what might be stressing you? I know you don't know me well, but I think we could be friends."

Clarissa smiled as tears pooled in her eyes. "I don't know where to start. There's so much to say."

"Start where you want. I know by the looks of you that you're going through something hard. Confide whatever you want to. The rest is none of my business."

The words came spewing out like rapids from a raging river. A river that still flowed under the surface of this place. If Martha was to see her through this pregnancy, she deserved to know all the facts, even about James' father.

217

Maybe especially about that.

Frank slowed his pace so James could keep up. Today could be an important day of restoration if all went well. James might like farming so much he would choose to work alongside him and see that he belonged to the parents who raised him. Blood or no blood, James was his son.

"Sure your leg is up to this?"

"Yep, I'm fine. Just a little stiff where the stiches are." James rubbed the area but kept moving toward the barn.

They stepped into the barn to see Elijah coming through the opposite door with a shovel in his hand. His chin went to his chest for a moment when he saw James.

Frank stopped. Something about Elijah wasn't right—not his usual happy self. He glanced at James, who must have sensed it too. The boy walked over close to Elijah.

"What's wrong, Elijah? You look sad."

Elijah locked eyes with Frank, as if to beckon him. Frank moved up beside James. Elijah tossed the shovel on the ground away from them. He put his hand on James.

"I'm afraid the hawk is dead, James. I jus' buried him out back. I found him this mornin', over there." He pointed to a pile of old hay under the rafter where the hawk always perched.

James moved away from Elijah's hand. He shook his head. "What happened? Did an animal kill him?"

Elijah raised his brows at Frank. He hesitated, then tucked his hands in the top of his overalls. "No."

Frank was done with the guessing game. "Elijah, what happened? A healthy hawk doesn't just die."

Elijah cleared his throat. "No, sir. I heard noise here in the barn, oh, way before sunrise. Woke me up. Sounded like someone diggin', so I got up and peeked through the knothole in the wall of my room. I saw a lantern on the ground in the other corner of the barn and a pile of dirt next to it."

Frank had a feeling this story meant more than a dead hawk. "Go on."

"Well, then I saw Mr. William. He was pullin' something out of the ground. He pushed the dirt back in the hole and picked up the lantern and whatever he dug up and started for the door. Then I heard a rustlin' noise. Mr. William must have heard it too. He stopped and set everythin' down, then looked around the ground and found a big rock."

"No." James wrapped his arms around his chest.

Elijah paused and then directed the rest of the story to Frank.

"He threw the rock above the loft. I didn't think about the hawk. I figured he was after a coon or somethin'. Anyway, I didn't think he hit anythin', so I stayed still. I waited till Mr. William was gone and then looked up in the loft to see if I could see a dead animal. Weren't nothin' there."

Frank rubbed his chin. "So how did you find the hawk?"

Elijah shot a glance at James. "Well, early this mornin' I got to thinkin' I hadn't seen the hawk yesterday. Went lookin' and found the bird layin' in dirt by the wall. It was dead. So I waited till sunrise to bury it. That's how it happened. I swear."

Frank studied James' face. The blank stare to the ground gave him no hint of how Elijah's story affected him. He would have to let James tell him. In his time.

Frank addressed Elijah's need to swear to his story. "It's all right, my friend. You did the right thing. There was nothing you could have done. William was angry and must have taken it out on the bird. It's a shame."

James jerked his head to Frank. "A shame? It was a terrible thing to do. I hate him. I thought I liked him, but I hate him. I'm glad he's gone."

James tried to run from the barn, but his leg wouldn't

cooperate. He stumbled and fell in the dirt. Elijah darted toward him, but Frank grabbed his arm. Together they watched James pick himself up and walk away.

"He'll be all right. It was good to get out some of his pent-up feelings. He doesn't hate William for the killing. He'll come to realize that someday. He's mourning for more than the hawk." He turned to Elijah. "Did you know the boys named that hawk after you?"

Elijah took a step back. "No, sir." His eyes teared. "I never knew that. I'm honored." He pulled out his handkerchief and wiped his face.

Frank waited for Elijah to compose himself. He picked up the shovel and leaned it against the wall. "Where did you say the hole was?"

Elijah pointed in to the far corner. Frank crept over to the spot and moved dirt around with his toe. Nothing caught his eye. William must have taken all of what he was after. He took a long look at Elijah.

"Let's get to work. Lots to do. It'll be good for James."

Elijah held out his arm through the barn door opening. "You lead the way, Boss."

Frank shook his head and grinned. "Don't call me *boss*." He patted Elijah on the back. "Clarissa is the boss around here, didn't you know?"

Outside the barn, James leaned on the old tractor wheel. Frank was surprised he had waited—a good sign.

"Ready to work, son?"

His nod was good enough for Frank.

Frank shut the door to Morgan's room and shuffled down the hall. Clarissa wrapped her robe around her and followed him into the living room. The long summer days made it hard to get Morgan to bed, and having to tell him about the hawk hadn't helped tonight. James had come home from his day's work with Frank and Elijah and announced he wasn't hungry for dinner. When she tried to protest, Frank had waved his hand at her. James had gone to his room and stayed there all evening.

Clarissa snuggled in next to Frank on the sofa. "How's Morgan taking it?"

Frank groaned and leaned back. "Not good." He tipped his head at her. "How can a kid get so attached to a hawk he only saw a few times? He's so sensitive."

"That's not a bad thing. It's better than the reaction we're getting from James. I don't know what to do about him. I feel bad, but how do we work through this if he won't talk to us?"

She wanted him to give her the perfect answer, anything to make it all go away. William was gone, and she didn't have the strength to pick up the pieces for James. Her son had obviously decided to stay with them, or he would have snuck off with William.

James' door creaked. Clarissa leaned forward to see him shuffling into the living room. His black-and-gray striped pajama bottom hem was halfway to his knees. She put her hand to her lips to keep from giggling. She hadn't been shopping for new clothes for the boys since they'd arrived. She knew James had grown, but his pajamas showed just how much.

She patted the arm of the sofa. "Having trouble sleeping? I should think you'd be pretty tired after a busy day."

James hung back, one hand behind him. Clarissa and Frank glanced at each other. She knew that look—James had something to say. She pulled in a quick breath. *Brace yourself.*

Frank filled in the silence. "Does your leg hurt? Maybe I worked you too hard."

Yes, that was it. He was having pain.

"It hurts a little, and I had to change the bandage 'cause it had some blood on it. It's okay. I wanted to give you something." He pulled out his hidden hand and moved closer to Frank. He opened his palm to reveal a gold coin.

Clarissa's heart jumped, her mind whirling to think of where he could have acquired it.

Frank took the coin and reached behind him to turn on the floor lamp. He held it up to the light and turned it in his fingers. He handed the coin to Clarissa and asked the question hanging in the air.

"James, where did this come from?"

James stared at the floor. "Unc—William gave it to me yesterday when you saw us in the barn. Like I told you, he asked me to go with him since he was fired and couldn't stay here, and he said he had lots of money. He gave me that coin as proof. Told me to keep it."

Clarissa held out the coin to him. If William gave it to him, he should have it, no matter how much the idea of it sent shivers up her neck.

James shook his head. "I don't want it. You keep it, or spend it. I don't care."

Frank scratched his head and frowned. "I read something about gold coins a while back. What was it? Something about the government."

Clarissa looked closer at the coin. "We didn't keep up about government news much in Kansas. Only if it was farm related. Is it from a collection or something?"

Frank snapped his fingers. "That's it. The government decided after the crash that no one could hold any gold. It all went to the banks or some such thing. Can't remember all the details. Maybe this is a collector's coin, and I think they are okay to have."

James lowered onto the sofa arm. "I've been thinking. If

William ever comes back here for some reason, I'm gonna be nice to him. I just don't want him to give me anything." He looked square at Clarissa.

His cold eyes shot daggers at her, but she had to hear him out.

He moved his gaze between Frank and her as he continued. "I think you've made him out to be a monster, and when Elijah said he killed the hawk, I thought so too at first. He must have been awful mad after he got fired. If he's my—my father, then I think he deserves for me to give him the benefit of the doubt."

Tears stung in Clarissa's eyes. "James, I'm going to say this from my heart. I don't think William will live up to your hopeful expectations, but I think it's very grown up of you to extend grace."

Frank's jaw twitched. "He'll never come back here. You should accept that." He stood and pointed to the coin. "I'll keep it for you. You may need it someday."

James stood to face Frank. "I didn't want to hurt your feelings, Dad, but I thought I should tell you both how I feel. You've been telling me to share how I feel with you. Didn't you mean it?"

Clarissa could feel the energy from Frank's tense muscles. If he said the wrong thing now, they could lose James' trust. She held her breath.

"You don't need to worry about me, son. I'll love you no matter what you say or feel."

Clarissa's grip on the coin loosened. She looked down to see it had left a perfect round impression in her palm.

James gave one nod and returned to his room. Clarissa sniffled into her robe sleeve. She covered her face. None of their words were enough. If she couldn't express her pain and disappointment adequately, how could she expect James and Frank to do so?

"I'm sorry, Frank. I wish he hadn't been so blunt. I fear this will be a lifelong struggle."

Frank stared at the wall in front of them, the light dimming in the window. "I know you're tired of this whole thing. Believe me, so am I, but I can't blame James for being upset and unsettled about his future. I'm an adult, and I had my own difficulties sorting through my feelings about your past with William."

Heat flowed through her body, flooding her face. He was blaming her, and he was right. She had caused the whole painful rift between father, son, and William. If she had been stronger, if she had listened to her father. All the ifs tallied in her mind once again in a list of regrets. Saying she was sorry wouldn't make any difference. She had already said it so many times.

Frank finally looked at her. He swung around in the cushion and grasped her folded hands. "Hey, I didn't mean to get you upset too." He brushed the hair from her forehead. His fingers were rough against her skin. "What's done is done. We'll deal with it and move on with our lives. I'll concentrate on harvest. You concentrate on getting fat and sassy."

Her heartbeat slowed. He was too good to her, and she saw the wisdom in his words. But try as she might, worry still plagued her with palpitations and the overwhelming feeling all could be lost because of her failures. She had to keep her chin up for Frank and the boys.

"Fat and sassy it is."

He hugged her tight, not a conjured gesture, a hug that communicated his faith in her. She would have to find faith as well.

"We're going to start with getting you to bed. The boys will be fine, I'll be fine, and we just need you and the baby to be fine." He stood and held out his hand.

She let him pull her up and headed for bed. Her bones ached, and her eyelids grew heavy. By the time Frank finished closing up the house, she would be asleep. He was right. She had to concentrate on getting well. Her mind was already eased knowing they would likely never see William again. He had his money. There was no reason to come back here. At least that was her strongest hope.

Chapter 15

The August sun beat down early this morning. Frank poured his second cup of coffee and tiptoed out to the porch so he wouldn't disturb Clarissa's painting time. He had only agreed to let her work if she sat on the stool to stay off her feet. She had a little quiet time before Martha arrived.

Martha came more often than originally planned, but he was grateful for her attentive ways with Clarissa. James' healing had moved quickly, and the week since the accident had nearly lost his gimp. In time his mood would mend as well.

Frank stood at the porch rail, then turned to sit in the rocker. His eye caught a small piece of paper on the porch floor. It was folded and lay not far from the door. Someone must have left a note tucked in the door and it had fallen. Frank wondered how long it had been lying there.

He set his cup on the side table and picked it up. His eyes moved along the handwritten slip of paper. *This isn't over yet, brother. You won't get away with it.* Frank's hands shook. No need for a signature. William had left his mark in the words. The hair on Frank's arms bristled. William's attitude and actions over the last few weeks were all Frank needed to be convinced this note should be taken seriously. He sat in the rocker and stared out onto the shadows dancing on the ground. He shuddered at the shadow behind the words he just read.

Martha's car crept up the drive. He crumpled the note in his hand and stood to greet her. The coffee churned in his stomach. Just what he needed—a threat hanging over him. How could he protect his family? It would fit William's frame of mind for him to show up and take James.

Martha jumped out of the car, her uniform pressed and white. He dusted off the seat of the chair next to the rocker and met her at the steps. "Good morning."

"Hope I'm not too early. I had to get out of the house before Mom put me to work peeling apples. She's making her famous upchuck cake." She stood next to him on the porch.

Frank thought he hadn't heard her right. "Upchuck cake?"

"Yeah. One of my brothers saw the batter once before Mom baked it and he said it looked like someone upchucked in the pan. So we've called it that ever since."

Frank stood staring, trying hard to force a laugh. Martha's smile faded.

"Is something wrong? You look kind of piqued."

Frank motioned to the chairs. "Can we sit? Clary is painting, and I'd like to give her a few more minutes."

Martha frowned. "Sure. Is she okay?"

Frank held up a finger and reached in to shut the big door. He pulled the rocker away a bit and sat. "I need someone else to know about this besides me—in case something should happen."

"Know what?"

He handed her the note. She read it twice, mouth hanging open.

Frank answered the question on her face. "It's from my brother, the one you met the first day. There's been some family trouble, and William is very angry at me. He's not here anymore, but this note indicated he could be back. For reasons I can't share, I'm worried for James. It's a complicated issue. I don't know what to do."

Martha sighed hard. "How can I help?"

Frank leaned back and shook his head. "I don't know if you can. I just wanted someone besides me to read the note. He's probably harmless, but who knows."

Martha folded the paper. "I think you're right to be worried. I would be. Your wife has shared a little information with me, and I've sensed tension in the house. It's not good for Clarissa. I'll keep the note if you like."

"Good idea. I know it's not good for her, and I'll think of something. It's just that we have no family here, and you're our only friend besides Elijah. Keep this between us. I'll let you know if anything else comes up."

Martha stood and looked over at William's house. She looked deep in thought, but he didn't know her well enough to guess about what. He had to trust someone who had a handle on Clarissa's issues.

She leaned over and grabbed her black bag. "I'll go check on her."

He opened the door for her and followed her inside. Clarissa wasn't in her studio. She lay on the sofa, pale and pasty. His instinct was to jump to her side, but he let Martha approach her.

"Clarissa? How are you feeling?"

Clarissa tried to sit up, but Martha guided her back down.

"I'm just a little tired this morning. Been painting for a while."

Frank made his presence known. "I'm going to see if Elijah is up." He glanced down the hall to see both of the boys' doors open. "Where are the rascals?"

Clarissa shrugged. "They were gone when I came out of the studio. But I did notice the raisin bread package was open on the counter, with several slices gone, along with the last two bananas. No doubt they're with Elijah."

Martha nodded to Frank.

He took his cue to leave. "I'll be back." He kissed Clarissa on the forehead, feeling her cool, sticky skin.

He took his time walking to the barn. Halfway there he saw James and Morgan headed to the orchards with buckets in hand. There would be more grounded apples to cook up—with no one to cook them but him. Judging from the way Clarissa looked, Martha would put her foot down on any activities.

One more tug on the unraveling thread of his strength. He was in unfamiliar territory, trying to find his way in the dark, inching toward something he couldn't see. With no compass, he could fail, disappointing himself and Clary.

He stopped to scan the treetops in the distant orchard. He had dreamed of this place since the first time William wrote to him about it. Fresh air, productive acres, and a chance to feed his family stayed foremost in his mind when he took the risk to come. Had he known about William ahead of time, he wouldn't have made the move.

Or so he tried to convince himself. Truth be told, he might have.

When Frank left, Clarissa rattled on about all the good and bad times they'd lived through in Kansas while Martha fussed over her. Clarissa's strategy to sound energetic didn't appear to fool her nurse. She shut up when Martha leaned back in the chair and glowered down at her.

"No point in putting on a front. Your vitals tell me more than your attempt to act like you're on top of things. If you don't get some rest, I'm going to suggest to the doctor that he admit you into the hospital."

Clarissa shook her head.

"I mean it. You might be able to handle the tension, but

your baby can't." She patted Clarissa's hand. "I'm sorry, but I have to be truthful for your sake."

Clarissa deserved the scolding, but hearing Martha tell her the baby could be in danger from all the strain piled on the guilt. She squirmed in the chair as Martha buttoned up her little black bag. She didn't know Martha all that well, but she knew what deep concern looked like on anyone's face. Martha's tone and expression were all the reprimand Clarissa needed.

"I just had a bad night." That was the truth. Despite her efforts to remove her checklist of things to do, sleep had evaded her most of the night. "I promise to rest today. The boys can help."

Martha sat on the sofa and jotted notes in a notebook. Clarissa choked out the words she felt from the deepest part of her. "I can't lose this baby. I know you're right, and I'm so thankful to have you here."

Martha stopped writing and took Clarissa's hand. "Just doing my job."

"More than your job. You've supported me and my family in ways you didn't have to. You're not just my nurse. I count you as my friend. If you don't mind."

Martha let go of her hand and scribbled a few more lines. "I don't mind. I like being your friend, and I like taking care of you. So it works out well for us both, don't you think?" She dated the notes as Clarissa peeked to see what she had written about her.

Martha gave her the eye that said the notes weren't for her viewing. "You know, I need to remind you I'm not a full-fledged nurse yet. Almost done with my practical training, and then I'll be off up north to Spokane for obstetrics training before I graduate."

Clarissa snuggled back into the chair. "The doctor must think you're quite capable to take care of me."

Martha smiled. "Guess so. Did pretty well in school, and I love the practical training. Just can't wait to finish up and go do work somewhere, you know? I've wanted to be a nurse since my aunt Rachel inspired me when I was just a young girl. She was a doctor. I suppose you had someone inspire you to be a good mother, right?"

Clarissa could only nod. The clamor of footsteps from the back porch took her out of the emotion of the moment. Morgan and James stopped just inside the door. Clarissa noted the gasp from Martha and turned around in her chair. Both boys froze in their place, panic on their faces. Their dirt-caked hands and smudged faces would normally have sent shock waves through Clarissa. Had it not been for Martha's heavy hand on her shoulder, she might have burst into a tirade.

Martha spoke up before Clarissa could spew any words of chiding. "Have you boys been exploring the barn or wallowing in the mud?"

Morgan glanced up to James, who shrugged. "James thought we could help clean up outside. We made the garden beautiful. And then we dug up some rocks to—"

James nudged him. "I told him not to get so dirty."

Martha walked into the kitchen and pointed to them. "You best strip off those clothes and march right back out to the spigot and wash. I'll bring you a big bar of soap." She clapped her hands. "Scoot."

Clarissa giggled and moved from the chair to the sofa as Martha helped the boys. As long as things were under control, she would lie down. She settled in and reached behind her to fluff the pillow.

Her hand met Frank's. "You okay?"

She grabbed his arm and pulled him around to face her. "Yes." She slid over and patted the cushion on the edge of the sofa. She leaned her head back on the pillow and studied his face.

The new wrinkles around his eyes were telling. He needed rest as much as she did, but he had important duties to perform with William gone. If only she could spare him the drama.

She tugged on the front of his shirt. "How are you going to do all that needs to be done in the next few days? And harvesting is coming soon. I'm worried about you."

Martha waltzed into the living room, wiping her hands on a brown stained towel. "Did I hear someone say *worry?*" She tossed the towel on the kitchen table and put her hands on her hips. "I thought we had that settled? No worrying for you, Clarissa Wilding."

Frank stood.

The smile disappeared from Martha's face as she addressed Frank. "I'll be honest. I'm the one who's worried. Your wife will have to go to the hospital if she doesn't take better care of herself and the baby. I'd like to propose something to you that might help. May I?"

Frank and Clarissa exchanged glances. Clarissa's heartbeat sped up wondering if there could be any solution to what they faced in the immediate future. Taking over for William, the boys starting school, and finding workers for a looming harvest would require a miracle. She hoped Martha was as good a miracle worker as she was a nurse.

Frank motioned for Martha to sit, and he glanced down the hall.

Martha touched his arm. "It's all right. The boys are busy scrubbing out their clothes. I tossed some clean ones out to them to change into when they're done. I'm used to boys—have two brothers, remember?"

Frank helped Clarissa sit up and then sat on the floor by her knees. "We're open to suggestions. It feels like we've hit rock bottom."

Martha sat and glanced at her watch. "I have to get to school in a bit, but I think this is important to talk about now. You know I live with my parents close to town. My dad is a barber, and Mom stays at home. Our house is small, but there's an extra room. Your boys will start school in a week, and it's going to be tough for you to manage getting them back and forth from here with all the other things going on, especially Clarissa's health."

Clarissa perked up, her mind rolling with possible scenarios. If Martha were to offer Clarissa to stay with her, it would be out of the question. "I'm sure we can—"

Frank placed his hand on Clarissa's arm and squeezed. "Go ahead, Martha."

She looked squarely at Frank. "I'm proposing the boys come live with me and my parents. Just for a while. Until Clarissa is well rested and things are managed here. I can take them to school and help them with their studies. Mom will keep them busy with chores and eating her oatmeal cookies."

Frank's head was bowed, his hands folded close to his lips. She waited for him to speak, but he stayed still. Martha scooted to the edge of her chair. She looked straight at Clarissa, her tone softened.

"I would just hate to see you shipped off to the hospital."

Clarissa tensed. There must be a better solution than breaking up the family. Morgan wouldn't know what to do without her, and they needed time with James to settle all the turmoil about William. It wouldn't work. Frank would speak up any moment and tell her.

Martha stood. "Just think about it. I don't think you realize how hard things will be around here for a while. Mom and Pop would be more than happy to have the boys."

Frank pushed himself up from the floor and walked to the front door. A warm breeze brought the smell of the last of the lilac blooms into the room. She breathed it in as she waited.

Clarissa had expected him to protest by now, but he still

didn't speak. He wouldn't agree to such an arrangement. He was a strong man. *Go on. Tell her no.*

Silence hung in the air like a flowery aroma. Clarissa played with the loose button on the back of the sofa. Why didn't he answer?

Martha stood and picked up her bag. "I have to go. I'll stop by after I'm done with my rotation in surgery today. I hope you'll consider it—for the baby's sake."

She wagged a finger at Clarissa. "You know what to do, right?"

Clarissa forced back tears and nodded. Martha gave her a thumbs-up.

Frank opened the screen door and said goodbye. She listened for Martha's car to start and crunch the gravel as it traveled down the drive. They may only have a few minutes before the boys came in.

She talked over her shoulder to Frank. "That was sweet of her. But of course, we can't accept. God will provide for us."

He turned and smiled. "Yes, it was sweet of her. And I think God will provide—and just did."

Clarissa slid to the edge of the sofa. He was going to let it happen. He couldn't mean it.

She shook her head. "The boys belong here. They wouldn't go anyway. They barely know Martha, and we've never met her folks."

He came and knelt beside her. "You're thinking of this the wrong way. We need help, Clarissa. The boys fell in love with Martha the first time she was here. I think we've been offered the only viable answer to our problem."

She groaned. He wasn't listening. "We've always managed our own problems, and everything turned out fine." Her words stung. "For the most part."

He leaned in close to her. "Then why did you let Elijah stay on the farm to help you back in Kansas? Haven't you always said he was a godsend? I think Martha is our godsend this time. We have more at stake." He paused and looked away while she blinked back tears.

"I feel this is the right thing to do. Are you willing to risk the baby just so you can take care of the boys, the house, and me? I can't throw this opportunity back in God's face."

She had been throwing her issues in God's face for years. Obedience. Obedience was always the problem. Wanting her own way. Wanting to hide from her past. It was possible God had just issued her a challenge to rest and trust in Him. A test—hitting her at the weakest spot in her heart, her precious boys. Just this morning she had prayed for Frank to have strength and wisdom, but the same old question of trust again tapped her on her shoulder.

She waited for her throat to clear. "All right. If it's all right with the boys."

"That's accepting His will conditionally. Is that what you really want?"

Hadn't God held *her* to conditions? Frank should understand that she couldn't lose the boys, not even for a few weeks. She had already lost too much to give in that easily.

The back door slammed. Frank hollered to Morgan and James. "Boys, come in here please."

As the boys shuffled into the living room, she prayed they would be as opposed to the idea as she was. She had no doubt they wouldn't agree to Martha's plan.

Frank stood between them, an arm around each boy's shoulder. "Guys, you know your mother has not been feeling well. If she doesn't get better, she might have to go to the hospital to stay for a while."

Clarissa shifted in the chair, straightened her hair, and pinched her cheeks while they weren't looking.

Frank continued. "Martha suggested that you both come to stay at her house for a little while to give your mother a chance to rest. You start school next week, and she can take you there and bring you here to visit once in a while."

Morgan sniffled. Clarissa had to stop this now. "It's not *that* important. If you don't want to, I understand, and we—"

James broke in. "I think it's important. I'll go."

Morgan wiped his nose with his sleeve. "If James goes, I'll go. I don't want Mama to work so hard."

Clarissa thought her heart would stop beating. "Frank—"

His steady eyes seared into her. "It's settled then. I'll let Martha know, and we can get you boys packed up."

She couldn't think or even breathe. Frank had turned against her, and the boys didn't have a chance to say no. The heaviness of looming disaster lay on her chest. There had to be another reason Frank insisted on this. This time he was wrong.

She thought she knew him. His steady, consistent ways had been her rock of predictability, but he had changed. Her spirits sank to know she was the reason. If she stopped believing in him now, what would be left?

The clear choice for her would demand she relinquish control, and the clear reality was that she didn't have it in the first place.

At first she thought it was in her mind, but then realized it was the teakettle screaming on the stove. Clarissa folded the last pair of clean socks for each of the boys before shuffling into the kitchen to silence the steam. If only there was an off switch for her dread. She had prepared for this day by repeating Frank's words about how this decision would be the best for her and the baby and how easy it would be for the boys to stay with Martha. It would ease her worry to know she had sent them off well-packed.

She poured hot water into a cup through a strainer filled with peppermint tea leaves and breathed in the aroma. Clouds filled the view in the frame of the kitchen window. The crop needed a reprieve from the week's blazing sun. She moved close to the glass to see more of the gray skies. A sprinkle of rain tapped the window.

Frank eased up behind her. His rough, calloused hand rubbed her bare arm. "We need a rain, just not a pounding one." He stepped back and pulled a chair out for her. "I'll fix you some eggs and toast."

"I'm not hungry."

"I'll still fix you some eggs and toast. I'm sure the baby could use some breakfast." He opened the icebox and then rattled pans from the cupboard until he found the right one.

She scanned the kitchen. It needed a good scrubbing, but someone else would have to do it. Her orders to rest didn't include housekeeping. The bathroom also needed a go-over with bleach, and the dust under the beds must be the size of a small cat by now. She shuddered to think of how bad the house would look by the time she had the all clear from Martha to do some cleaning.

"What are you daydreaming about?" Frank spoke over his shoulder as he popped two slices of bread in the Toastmaster.

"Just wishing I could get my mop bucket and scrub brush out." She wrapped her hands around the warm smoothness of the teacup and closed her eyes. As soon as she ate enough bites to satisfy Frank, she would move to the sofa and finish her clean clothes pile for the boys. Martha would be here in an hour, and everything had to be ready. Frank broke her slide into self-pity by scooting a plate of scrambled eggs and overly toasted bread in front of her. "Want some jam?"

"No thanks."

The smell of the eggs rose to her nose, overpowering the sweet, soothing peppermint. Her stomach threatened to reject them even before she lifted the fork to her mouth. She had to try, or Frank would fix her something else. Maybe jam would help after all.

"On second thought, I'll take the marmalade in the cupboard."

Frank set the jar in front of her and twisted the top off. She and Morgan had made a day of cooking up the orange jam. It seemed so long ago. They would have to wait a long time to do things together again.

She smiled at Frank's expression as she smeared marmalade on the eggs. When his mouth fell open and it looked like he would protest, she spoke first. "I have to cover up the smell of the eggs or I'll throw up. Okay?"

He nodded, then shook his head. "I'll get Morgan and James up. They need to clean up before Martha gets here." He stopped halfway down the hall and picked up a dirty towel from the floor by the bathroom. He turned to Clarissa. "And don't worry about the mess in here. I'll get around to it."

Sure you will. He had so much on his list of duties now, she couldn't imagine how he would manage to stop and do housework. She would have to sneak it in while he wasn't looking. If Elijah could spare some time, she would have him at least mop the floors.

That's a dumb idea, she scolded herself. *Elijah isn't your slave.*

Morgan slipped up next to her and snuggled into her chest, yawning. His hair smelled of hay, and his cheeks felt rough. At least at Martha's house he would be free of barn smells and chapped skin. She hugged him tight. "Good morning, sleepyhead."

He pulled away from her. "Is Martha coming soon?"

"Yes. You better scoot and get into the bathtub. Daddy will help you."

His broad smile soothed her mind that he might resist leaving. It would be an adventure for him, but she feared James would only endure the time with the Watkins family. She would depend on Martha to keep his attitude in line and his manners polished.

Frank readied the boys while Clarissa dressed and combed her ever-growing locks. The tangled-hair image in the mirror made her homesick for health and energy. Her sunken eyes and dry lips put years on her appearance. Hard years without resolution.

A knock on the screen door startled her. "Anyone home?" It was Martha. And there was another unfamiliar voice.

Clarissa pulled in a deep breath and emerged from the bedroom with her posture as straight as she could muster. "Come in."

Martha swept through the door, a large bag in hand. Behind her was an older lady, shorter with graying hair and wrinkles around her eyes and mouth. She also carried something—a bulging satchel. Her sweet smile calmed Clarissa's shaking insides.

"I brought my mom," Martha announced as she set her bag on the kitchen table. "I know we're a little early, but we have some things to do before we gather up the boys. I hope you don't mind. And why are you still standing up?"

Clarissa tried to keep up with Martha's rapid monologue, but didn't catch on to the standing part until Martha had her by the arm, leading her to the sofa. Mrs. Watkins walked over and held out her hand. "I'm Ruth. How are you feeling today?"

Her voice was soft and sweet, like her smile. Clarissa grasped her hand. "I'm not too bad today, thank you, Ruth. It's nice to meet Martha's mother."

Martha headed for the front door. "I'll grab my medical bag."

Ruth set her satchel on the floor and took in the surroundings. "What a cute house." She sat on the sofa next to Clarissa. "And from what I saw of the grounds, this place looks like heaven."

Heaven. It was the last word Clarissa would choose to describe William's farm. Her experience here mocked heaven. Her greatest wish to be away from here had been dashed, but at least William wasn't around to plague her every day. Ruth was sweet to compliment, no matter what Clarissa thought.

"It is a pretty farm. The vineyard is especially picturesque. I hope to paint it someday when I'm feeling better."

Ruth tipped her head to the side. "Martha told me you paint. I'd love to see your work. My husband's sister, Rachel, paints too. She's a doctor in Indiana."

"I think Martha has mentioned her."

"Who did I mention?" Martha came through the door and sat in the chair on the other side of Clarissa.

"Your aunt Rachel." Ruth stood and took a few steps toward the kitchen. She stopped and turned to Clarissa. "Do you mind if I unload some things into your icebox?"

"Things?" Clarissa looked at Ruth and then Martha. "What things?"

Martha opened her bag and strapped a blood-pressure cuff on Clarissa. "Food. Mom and I whipped up a few meals last night. Don't want you trying to cook for a while." She put her finger to her lips and slid the end of the stethoscope under the cuff. "Just some pot roast and meatloaf. Oh, and oatmeal raisin cookies."

Clarissa winced as the cuff squeezed her arm. She nodded to Ruth.

Martha finished and then took the other vitals. "Better, but still not where you should be." She snapped her bag shut. "Are you eating?"

"Yes." She didn't dare tell her how little.

"Are you sleeping well?"

"No."

Frank strolled into the room, wiping his hands on a towel. "Because she worries too much. Hello, Martha."

"Hi, Frank. Meet my mom, Ruth."

Martha fluffed a pillow and motioned Clarissa to lie down. Soon all three of them were stuffing food in each cranny of the icebox and stacking boxes of bread and cookies on the counter. Clarissa nestled into the sofa to enjoy the spectacle. *This is what good neighbors do.* She had almost forgotten. Her face flushed to think how in her own desperate need, she'd stopped trying to be neighborly, or even let herself be around other folks.

After stocking the kitchen, the ladies went to work cleaning the kitchen and living room. Ruth pulled supplies from her satchel and hummed while she dusted. Martha busied herself sweeping and washing up the dishes in the sink. Frank dried them and put them away.

James and Morgan shuffled in, each dragging a gunny sack stuffed with clothes and belongings. Clarissa called them over and added a few last items from her laundry pile. Not even a suitcase to pack for them. She wished they didn't look so much like homeless children.

James stared at the crew, his mouth hanging open. Morgan ran to Martha and hugged her around the waist. He dropped his sack and skipped to the living room to stand in front of Ruth.

"Hello." He smiled and looked her over.

"Morgan, meet Martha's mama, Mrs. Watkins." Clarissa was sure how Morgan would react, but she kept an eye on James' reserved posture. "Mrs. Watkins, this is Morgan, and over there is James."

Morgan and James chimed together in greeting her. "Hi."

Frank grabbed Morgan's sack. "Boys, let's take your things and load them into Martha's car."

As the door slammed behind them, a melancholy fog snaked its way into the room. The boys were really leaving. No arguments, no fussing, no tantrums—even though she felt like throwing one herself. The emptiness came just as she had expected, only stronger.

While Martha and Ruth finished up in the house, Clarissa rehearsed her cheerful mood and parting goodbyes.

The final few minutes flew by, with hugs and a few tears, and some reminders to behave on both sides. Her brave smile didn't fool anyone. Martha held her in a hug for several moments while Ruth and Frank took the boys outside to the car. Now she was adrift in the empty cottage, forced to get accustomed to the silence.

It's only for a little while. They promised.

Until then she would be marooned here with no mothering to do. Except to the child within. That would be enough.

$\mathcal{L}$eaning against the doorjamb, Frank admired Clarissa's form against the morning light glowing from the window. The last few days without the boys had been good for her, and hard at the same time. She awoke the first morning and mixed a big batch of pancake batter. Her face turned bright pink when she realized the boys weren't there to eat them. He mourned with her in silence each day, waiting for her strength to return so they could have Morgan and James back home again.

This morning she had risen before him. He found her in the studio, her robe hanging loose on her rounding figure and her slippers off to her side. His barefoot painter had been stirred by something. He would never understand the artist's ways, but his chest filled with gratitude to see her at the easel.

He stepped back to leave her alone with her oils and brushes. Elijah was waiting in the barn, no doubt taking over the boys' job of picking up apples. When he sat on the edge of a kitchen chair, Clarissa appeared at the doorway, brush still in hand and blue smudges on her nightgown.

"You going out to work?" Her eyes seemed a little brighter today. Her cheeks rosy.

He pulled on the first boot. "Elijah and I have some preparations to do before harvest. I expect George to come by any day now. He promised to give me some guidance. Then I'll have to look for workers. I asked Martha to bring James with her tomorrow when she comes to check on you. I'll need his help for a few days."

Clarissa stared down at the brush in her hand. "Do you think Mr. Tanner would give us an advance? We still have my hospital bills to pay."

Frank stopped and turned his head to the window. The reminder he didn't need. "I know." His face scrunched.

She took a few steps toward him. "Frank, I have something to tell you about that. I don't want you to get mad."

Mad. It had to be something upsetting if she was afraid of his reaction. "What is it? I won't get mad."

She padded over to the sink, still barefoot, and lay the brush in the bottom. "I didn't tell you because, honestly, I forgot until this morning. William paid for James' expenses the day of the accident. He did it without asking me."

He felt her hovering behind him. His blood rushed to his face, but he had to control his temper. "That's why we never got a bill." He rubbed the stubble on his chin. "I wondered why they didn't say anything about it when I checked you in that day. I don't like it."

Clarissa moved around to stand in front of him. "There's nothing we can do about it."

Frank stood and backed away from her. "Yes there is. I'll pay him back. It might take me a while, but he's not paying for James."

"Frank—"

"No." He held up his hand to her. "It leaves me owing him, and I won't have that."

"You're being prideful about this."

His knees wobbled at her suggestion. "I don't care." He headed for the hallway and turned. "You should have told me."

He thought he heard her mumble something as he stepped onto the back porch. He would have turned back, but the familiar fancy car belonging to the landlord pulled up next to the big house.

Frank jogged over to greet him. No sister this time, thank goodness. He preferred dealing with George alone.

"Hello, Frank. Good to see you." George leaned on the car, holding a large envelope.

"George." Frank shook his hand. "Would you like to sit on the porch?" He didn't dare offer to go inside the cottage with Clarissa not dressed.

George glanced to the big house. "Let's just go in there and talk. All right?"

They stepped into the parlor. The smell of stale food and dust hit Frank as soon as they sat down. George stood again and opened up a few windows. "This place needs a good scrubbing. I doubt William did much of that."

Frank glanced up at the faded spot on the wallpaper where his mother-in-law's painting had hung.

George followed his gaze. "Something missing, I see."

Frank leaned back in the chair. "Yes. It was a painting by Clarissa's mother. We don't know why William had it, but he took it with him. Upset my wife."

George frowned. "That's too bad. Who knows what he was thinking."

"If it's meant to be, we'll get it back."

George folded his hands across the envelope in his lap. "I need to be straight with you, Frank. The farm is in financial trouble. I've been trying to build it up since this depression hit, and I might have succeeded if William hadn't embezzled a chunk of my profits."

Frank hadn't considered the term *embezzlement* before, but hearing it brought the issue into focus.

"Have you changed your mind about pressing charges?"

"Yes, I have, for the sake of keeping the place. If he can

be found. I've had a conversation with the sheriff. I seriously doubt I can recover the money. He's not stupid, and it looks like he had a plan all along. I need the best harvest possible, and even that won't be enough to cover the debt I'm in thanks to your brother."

The weight of his statement sank into Frank, heavy enough to bolt him to the chair. How incredulous that he hadn't seen what William was capable of. Fathering James was the least of his shortcomings. He might just have caused a good man to lose his farm and cost his own brother a way to make a living.

"I'm sorry. I didn't know the extent of my brother's crime. I suppose I'll need to be moving along then."

The man across from him couldn't possibly know what this outcome meant for him and Clarissa. The timing could not be worse.

George leaned in. "I wish I had better news. The banks just aren't too forgiving these days. I had hoped you and your family would stay on and take over for William permanently. I'd even thought you could move in here instead of the cottage. You still can if you like, but I fear after harvest, there won't be any money to keep you."

Frank fought the urge to swear. When would it all end? Poor George didn't know he had just piled on the last straw for this Kansas boy's back. At least there he knew his enemy, but the twists and turns of life the last few months had tested him to the brink of his sanity. He was a farmer without a farm, and right now, a God-fearing man without a miracle.

George held the envelope out to him. "I brought proof of William's scheme in case you needed it. I know it must be difficult for you to take my word that he stole money from me. You're free to look through what I've discovered."

Frank stared at the envelope. William's harsh words and attitude had shown Frank what kind of man his brother had become. The layers of family ties and brotherly love had peeled away before Frank's eyes, especially once they all knew about James' parentage.

"No need. I believe you, and again, I'm sorry for what he did to you."

George stood. "I don't hold anything against you. I'll be in touch if something happens with William. I trust you will let me know if he shows up here again. Feel free to come in the house and use the telephone." He held out a card. "Here's my number."

Frank took the card. He had only used a telephone a few times and doubted he would need to now. "I don't think he would show up here, but I'll call you." His mind dashed to the note. If he told George about it, there would be more trouble. He bit his lower lip. Another secret he didn't like keeping.

George placed his hand on Frank's shoulder. "Why don't we go take a look at the crops? I can give you an idea of when to start harvesting."

Frank followed him to the door. George kept talking as they headed for the barn. "Is your helper still around?"

"Elijah? Yes, he's still here. I'll need him more than ever now." He stopped. George turned around and raised his brows. "Elijah would stay even if you couldn't pay him, but it sure would be great if you could give him a small wage."

George smiled. "I plan to. I'd like to meet him. He should come out to the orchard with us so he knows what's going on."

Frank's tight neck relaxed. A slight glimmer of hope and gratitude seeped into him. One step at a time was all he could manage. When harvest was over, he and Clarissa would have to take a giant leap.

God, help her be ready.

The afternoon sky had clouded over, much to Clarissa's relief. The windows she had opened this morning, hoping for a breath of fresh summer air, breathed with coolness throughout the house. Even 78 degrees was better than the scorching they'd received yesterday. She would welcome fall, except for the fact that they would have to find another place to live and another job for Frank. What she had wished for all along now had a bitter taste.

George's news had struck the last few nerves Frank had been hanging on. She'd tried hard not to absorb the tension as their discussion about the whole mess heated last night. She had prayed to be rid of this place, but seeing how much it hurt Frank to lose the opportunity to manage it sent her guilt to a new high.

"It's not your fault." His words were said with a twinge of anger.

He had to be smoldering deep inside, but she dare not coax him too much to let it out.

The squeak of the living room door opening behind her startled her, until she realized it was Martha and James coming in. James couldn't have grown in less than a week, yet he stood taller than she remembered.

"Hi, Mother." His tone didn't reflect an eagerness to be home.

Clarissa let it pass and met him for a hug. "I missed you." She smiled and took his hand.

He pulled it back and set down the sack he had in his other hand. "Is Elijah out with Dad?"

Clarissa cleared her throat and glanced at Martha, who shrugged. "I don't know for sure, but you can go look for them."

He turned to go around her, then stopped to pick up the sack. Clarissa waited for him to toss it in his room and go out the back door. She cast a desperate look to Martha.

"He hates me."

Martha took her arm and led her to the sofa. "No, he doesn't. Let's take your vitals."

Clarissa's stomach churned as she lay back against the pillow. "Did he do all right at your place? How's Morgan?"

Martha pushed up Clarissa's blouse sleeve. "Why don't you wear sleeveless blouses? It's too warm for heavy clothes. And they both did fine. Morgan is enjoying having a grandmother around to spoil him."

"None of my summer clothes fit anymore. I can't go into town to buy any. We don't have the money anyway." She bit her lip to hear her sharp tone.

Martha dropped her stethoscope into her lap. "Oh. Sorry. I hadn't thought about that."

"No, I'm sorry I snapped at you. There is so much going on around here, I'm barely coping some days. I've been trying to paint a bit. It calms me."

Martha slipped the cold metal under Clarissa's blouse. "Shh for a minute."

Clarissa closed her eyes and let Martha do what was necessary. She breathed deep and slow to settle down. She popped her eyes open when she felt the stethoscope on her belly.

"Let's see if we can hear a heartbeat this time. According to the information you told me, you should be at or around the end of your fourth month, and I can see you've gained some needed weight. We might be able to hear it if the baby is positioned just right. Be as still as you can. I brought a better stethoscope this time."

Clarissa nodded, holding her breath.

Martha moved the scope around her belly for what seemed an eternity. At last she stopped abruptly on a spot and smiled. About the same moment, the rare fluttering Clarissa had experienced turned to more of a thump against her skin.

A kick. A real kick.

Martha must have heard it. She jumped and her smile broadened. She removed the earpieces and slipped them into Clarissa's ears. "I'll try to find the spot again. It will be faint, but I think you'll recognize it."

The wall clock ticked off a minute. Clarissa frowned at Martha and shook her head. Then the slightest move of Martha's fingers triggered a faraway beat, soft but steady. She concentrated to take in as much of the experience as possible while Martha held the instrument. Then she felt movement, the beat fading.

Martha pulled back. "Did you hear?" She buttoned Clarissa's blouse and pulled up her skirt waistband.

Tears spilled over as Clarissa tried to affirm she had indeed. "Thank you for being patient. It was wonderful. I can't wait to tell Frank."

"Tell Frank what?" His voice bellowed from down the hall. James followed behind and Elijah stayed back. "Hi, Martha. You remember Elijah?"

"Yes, hello."

Elijah slipped off his hat and nodded. Frank stepped past Martha to kneel by Clarissa. "Tell me what? Is everything all right?"

Clarissa whispered in his ear. "I heard the baby's heartbeat."

Frank's eyes widened. "Isn't that something?" He glanced up at Martha. "Normal stuff?"

"Yep. Your wife is doing better. She needs to gain more weight and keep resting."

Frank stood after kissing Clarissa's cheek. His mood had changed. She glanced at Elijah, wondering if he had anything to do with it. Or maybe having James home had made a difference. She didn't care what it was, as long as Frank's tension level was eased.

"Okay, I have to go. James, I'll pick you up on Sunday in time to rest up for school on Monday."

"Sure." James gave her a quick wave.

Frank jumped to the door and held it open. "I'll walk you out. I need to round up the hoses for James to repair. Have to be ready for emergencies come harvest. That is, if we have any workers to get it done."

"See you Sunday then." Martha slipped out the door, with Frank following.

Clarissa patted the cushion. "James, come sit here and tell me about the Watkins family. How do you like it there?"

James pulled on one work glove that was too big for him. "I like it fine. They're a real family. Not like here."

Clarissa gasped out loud. Her body jerked as if someone had jabbed her. Silence chilled the room. James turned to leave, but Elijah's big hand pressed against the boy's chest.

"I ain't one for interferin', but you owe your mama an apology. I don't think your daddy would like you talkin' to her that way."

She had never seen this side of Elijah. He was firm and kind at the same time, while his tone held a definite rebuke.

James' mouth dropped open, but his eyes narrowed. Clarissa expected a slew of angry words to flow. Instead he shook his head in a refusal.

Elijah knelt so he was just below eye to eye with James. "Let me tell you what the Bible says about how you're feelin'. It says to honor your father and mother. It don't say they have to be perfect. It says not to judge. It don't say you can take on a wrong that wasn't aimed at you."

James dropped his chin to his chest. Clarissa could only watch, unable to take a deep breath yet. The pain of James' words still stung with a vengeance.

Elijah stayed at his posture. "It also says to forgive and love one another. That's somethin' a child might not be able to do, but a man should. Are you goin' to be a child or a man, James? It's time for you to choose who you gonna serve—hate, or God's love."

He stood, back to towering over James, but lording nothing over him. Clarissa felt the strange and almost foreign wave of peace wash over her. Had James felt it? His slumped shoulders and still hands must mean something.

Elijah walked away down the hallway. James' shoulders shook. Clarissa held the tongue that wanted to cry out to her boy and tell him she was sorry. There was no way to make things right for him. He had to do it for himself.

He edged closer to her and stood at the end of the sofa. "I'm sorry." His eyes moistened.

She could almost hear her heart break for him. "I don't want you to hate your father and me. Not for my sake, but for yours, James. I can't turn back the clock and do everything over again. Elijah is right about choosing. I made a wrong choice, but God turned it to good when he gave me you. Your father, Frank, chose you to love and raise as his own. He didn't have to. I could have given you away, but I chose you."

James wiped the tears from his face and pursed his lips. She had to finish what was on her heart to say.

"It's time to decide if you want to hate us or love us and be a part of this family. I learned the hard way that forgiveness is a powerful thing. I hope you find that to be true someday."

There were no more words. She placed her hand on her chest, willing herself to breathe in and out. James would have to decide now. She held out her other hand. He took it and squeezed. She waited, hoping he would speak but knowing he might not.

The door swung open. "Let's go, son." Frank must not have noticed the monumental emotion in the room. He turned and left before anyone could say a word.

"You go with your dad. I'll be here if you want to talk. We'll have a nice day together tomorrow."

James pulled on his other glove as he headed for the door. "Okay."

He still looked tall to her. She wondered if he felt taller.

Frank sat in the dark for a long time after Clarissa went to bed. James' silence through dinner, and Frank's racing thoughts of what Clarissa had told him about Elijah's words, refused to let him sleep. He had to find a way to release the pain of James' declarations—from today and the night he spoke of his allegiance to William. Putting on a brave front for Clarissa tonight had been convincing. Truth was, he shook inside to remember James talking about being nice to William, to hear him call William his father. Frank secretly hoped James would go on hating William and that it would cement Frank as a father in James' heart.

"He will learn to extend grace," Clarissa had said.

That was what he also needed to do, but didn't he deserve credit from Clarissa too? He had given her all the grace she needed when she was in trouble. He had kept on extending it all the years of their marriage, hoping she would love him the way he loved her. What good had it done him? For all he knew, she still had feelings for William.

He jumped up from the sofa and turned on the porch light before stepping outside. The night air had cooled. He would talk it out as he did the nightly check on the place. A walk around the moonlit night would do him good. His attitude about Clarissa and William had to change. After all, extending grace to his wife was his job. He was tired of the mental roller coaster. Elijah was right—time to choose to love.

He strolled to William's house and jiggled the back door

handle. All secure. The light at the top of the power pole behind the house shone just enough to get him to the barn without a lantern. He breathed in the sweet smell of grapes. In less than two weeks they would be on a truck to a processing warehouse. His nerves sharpened to think he would soon be harvesting the crop William had put his energy into nurturing. He stopped to look up at the twinkling stars.

"I'm sorry, William. I wish things could have been different. Lord, look after him."

He meant it, even though he knew William's heart wasn't in the right place. God could take care of that.

As he turned to the barn, he heard a noise. Elijah must still be up. Didn't that man ever sleep? Up at dawn, working all day, and now busy in the barn late at night. This was the man he wanted to be like. A model of humility and grace. Half man, half angel.

Frank approached the barn door, ready to scold Elijah for being up so late. A lantern sat on the ground in the same corner where William had dug up something. Frank peered around the corner of the door opening, expecting to see Elijah sharpening a knife or other implement. Instead, William's shadowy figure filled his vision.

He stepped back, not believing what he saw. Looking again, he saw William pulling a sack from a hole not far from where the other one had been. An eerie silence hung in the barn. Where was Elijah? Surely he would have heard William digging, as he did before. William's back was to Frank—a chance for him to step inside before William spied him. It was time for a confrontation.

God help me.

"What are you doing here, William?"

William spun around so fast, he faltered, thrusting his hand against the barn wall to steady himself. The bag in his had looked bulky and heavy. Frank put his hands in his pockets and took another step. William didn't answer, so Frank inquired again.

"What do you have there?"

This time William snapped back. "None of your business. Go on back to your family." He shifted his eyes to the other corner of the barn without moving his head.

Frank sensed something more from William than just being startled. He stood his ground as William kicked the shovel away from him, into the pile of old moldy hay on the ground. He picked up the lantern in one hand, holding tight to the bag in the other.

Frank kept his tone civil. "You need to take your buried treasure and leave. I don't want to have to tell the landlords you came back here." Frank listened, wishing Elijah would come out of his room. How strange that his friend would leave him to confront William alone.

William stepped forward into the lantern light. His eyes sparkled as he inched his way toward Frank. "Go ahead. I don't care. I'll be long gone from this county before they could even send the sheriff for me. You're the one who caused all these problems."

Frank bristled, struggling to keep his composure. He didn't want a fight, but he didn't want William to have the upper hand. His brother needed to know once and for all that he had set his own course.

"It didn't have to come to this, William. Your hard heart needs a change. I can't believe Clary would have fallen in love with the kind of man you are now. You must have some kindness and honesty left in you. Why don't you accept your faults and deal with them?"

William's chest heaved. He raised the bag and lunged at Frank, throwing it against Frank's head. A crushing jingle rang in his right ear as the bag smashed against his cheek. He fell to the floor, and as he stared ahead of him, regaining his senses, he saw a figure lying in the corner.

"Elijah!"

A sharp jab in his ribs made him curl up.

"You shouldn't have brought her here. It wasn't fair that you had her. I had forgotten how beautiful she was. I had to watch her with you and then find out she had my child. You cheated me."

Frank glanced at Elijah again. He wasn't moving, and in the dark, Frank couldn't see if he was breathing. Before he could stand all the way up to go to his friend, William twisted to swing at him again. Frank had just enough balance to push William hard.

The lantern flew from William's hand and landed in the hay. The barn darkened for a moment, enough to let Frank stand again. He stumbled toward Elijah but was met with the end of William's boot against his side.

The barn glowed in a sudden burst of light.

"William! The hay's on fire!"

William stared at Frank, his hands hanging at his sides.

"It wasn't fair. Clarissa and James should have been mine."

Frank scooted toward Elijah, watching the fire grow. William threw the bag, his eyes wild. He grabbed Frank by the feet and drug him close to the flames now creeping up the post that braced the loft. Sparks flickered up to the ceiling.

"William, stop. We have to get out of here."

William jerked his head toward the fire and let go of Frank. He stepped back to where the bag lay next to a wooden box of tools. When he picked up the box, Frank stood to move in William's direction. He couldn't let William use the box as a murder weapon. William hoisted the box high above his head and was poised to attack. Smoke filled Frank's lungs, and just as he bent to cough, Elijah came from behind him and launched himself at William.

Frank saw blood spatter onto his pant legs. He heard creaking from the loft as Elijah rolled away from William. Then a deafening snap before the post broke and the loft tumbled. A shock sensation coursed through Frank's head and shoulders as the beam from the loft crushed him.

"Elijah!"

The air he breathed burned his throat. He could see nothing and could only hear the snapping of flames—and moaning. Was it him who cried out, or someone else? His eyes wouldn't open. He wanted to sleep. He was going to die.

Huge hands thrust under his armpits. He felt his limp body move across the ground, and then a blast of cool air hit him.

"Mr. Wildin'—Frank!"

Frank reached up and grabbed the first thing he could. He felt overalls buckles in his palm. *Elijah.*

"I'm all right," Frank croaked

Elijah pulled Frank's grip from his overalls. "I have to get Mr. William." He stood before Frank could grab him back.

"No, Elijah. You'll get hurt!"

Clarissa screamed in the background, then she was at his side, crying. A pair of soft hands touched his face. "Frank, Frank. Are you all right?"

Frank forced his dried eyes open. "Get James away. Call the fire department from William's phone. The key—the key—it's under the mat—hurry."

James fell on his knees beside Frank. "I'll do it. Mother, stay here with Dad." He was gone before Frank could even reach for him.

"Help me up." He pulled on Clarissa's arm and sat. He rubbed his burning eyes and searched the flaming barn. "Clary, get back. The whole thing could fall and spread the fire."

He pushed himself up and found his footing. His head throbbed, and his left shoulder seared with pain. He couldn't move it, but he had to if he was going in after Elijah.

"Frank, look." Clarissa screamed.

Elijah emerged from the smoke, dragging William by the feet. William's clothes smoked, as did Elijah's.

Frank dropped to the ground. "Clarissa! Bring some bandages and water. Hurry!" He coughed up mucus, nearly losing his breath.

Elijah continued to pull William away from the barn, passing Frank along the way. Frank crawled to where they stopped. Elijah rolled onto the ground, breathing hard and convulsing with coughs. The roaring of the fire drowned out any sound from either man. Frank reached for Elijah and checked to see if he was going to be all right. Horror hit as he saw the extent of Elijah's burns and wounds. Pink flesh broke through his black skin.

He turned to William, whose chest rose and fell, but he was unconscious. Blood flowed from a gash on his forehead, and his clothes were charred like logs in a fire pit. His hair was burned off on one side of his head, exposing red skin. Frank's heart lurched. His brother wasn't going to make it.

A strange man rushed by toward the water trough. James collapsed beside Frank, breathless. "The neighbor—is here. He saw the flames and already called in the fire…" His voice fell off when he saw William's injuries.

"Son, go help your mother. We need bandages."

James stood, walked a few steps, and then stooped, retching. Frank couldn't help him now. He had to stay with these men.

What was taking Clarissa so long? In the distance he heard sirens piercing through the night air. He tried to search the stars, but they were blocked by black smoke.

Other men he didn't know ran past him with buckets.

What was the use? If Elijah and William died, saving the barn wouldn't matter.

They should never have come here. The sand piles and waterless plains of Kansas weren't this painful.

Chapter 17

The pre-sun glow purged the darkness from the parlor window. Clarissa's tears had all dried up. There wasn't any point in crying. The time for mourning would begin now, prayers all having been said. She sat very still and watched William's breaths grow slower and shallower.

He had refused to go in the ambulance once the medics had pronounced he was likely mortally wounded. After sending Elijah off to the hospital, another attendant had worked on William for an hour, trying to peel the charred fabric from his skin. He had slipped in and out of consciousness during that time. In one of his lucid moments, he made Frank promise to keep him here.

"I don't want to die in a hospital. I'm not in much pain. Let me die here on the farm."

She knew Frank's heart had broken to grant him his wish. The ambulance drivers made William mark an *X* on release papers, then helped Frank carry him to the big house. Martha had come after a frantic call from Clarissa. She didn't want to care for William alone in his last few hours. It seemed a cruel way to die. She made Martha convince her he would be pain-free.

"He really isn't in pain because of the nerve damage," Martha had said. "But the doctor told me I could administer morphine if needed."

Frank had stayed at the cottage. His injuries were not serious—a dislocated shoulder and minor burns. James had begged to stay in the big house near William. A queer end to a complicated situation.

Clarissa's inner voice screamed. *Where is God's mercy now?* Sparing Frank wasn't enough. She wanted more. She wanted William and Elijah to live and for Frank and James to have peace. She didn't deserve anything for herself. Just having the flutter of life in her body was more than she could hope for.

Martha tiptoed into the room, a cup of tea in her hands, and whispered to Clarissa. "Here. You need this."

Clarissa shook her head, but Martha grabbed Clarissa's free hand and shoved the cup and saucer into it.

"Orders." She put her hands on her hips. "At least do it for the baby. And I've called for a doctor to come. One should be here in case—"

"I know."

"I hope it's all right, but I told my dad to bring Morgan here now that things have settled down. He is near hysterics thinking the worst. Frank will wait for him at the cottage."

Clarissa nodded, unable to speak. She set the saucer on the table next to her and picked up the cup to take a sip of the steaming brew. William stirred, his head shifting on the pillow in her lap. She dare not touch him, even though she would give anything to ease his discomfort.

His eyes opened with a start. "Where am I?" His voice scratched through the quiet.

Martha knelt beside him and took his pulse as Clarissa explained, again. "You're in the parlor at your house. James and I are here with you. Just stay still."

James crept into the room and sat on the floor next to the sofa where William lay. He hadn't looked upon William since that first look. Even now he diverted his gaze.

"Where—is Frank?"

"At the cottage. He's hurt. But he'll be okay."

Martha continued searching for William's pulse, moving from wrist to wrist, her lips pursed. She glanced at Clarissa, then at James, and pulled her stethoscope out of her bag. She held it to his chest and closed her eyes. When she looked up again, she discreetly shook her head and mouthed *soon*.

William's breaths reduced to wheezing, but he tried again to speak. "I want to—talk—to you."

Martha tapped James on the shoulder and motioned him to follow her. He first glanced at Clarissa. She tipped her head toward the door. He pushed himself up from the floor and stood by William's feet, still not looking at his face. He reached behind him and touched William's leg.

His voice cracked one word. "Goodbye."

William blinked a few times. "Goodbye, James Wilding."

James straightened his shoulders and followed Martha out of the room. Clarissa wiggled ever so slightly to nurse her aching back. She had been in the same position for hours. Martha had tried to get her to let William lay by himself, but she couldn't bear the thought of him dying without human touch. Everyone, no matter how bad, deserved to die in someone's arms.

She wiped a tear falling down the side of his face. He winced, then swallowed hard.

"Would you like a sip of water, William?"

"No."

Could she do this thing? She had to. He had no one else to be with him, except his half brother. Frank wanted to stay with him. She'd seen it in his tortured eyes. But Morgan needed him.

"William, would you mind if I prayed for you?"

"Not until—I've told you. It's about the painting." He took a long breath and then let it eke out. "I came to see you—when I got back to town. You were gone. Your father was burning…"

He paused to breathe again, a thin breath at best. Then he winced hard.

She knew what he was about to say. She had heard it from Treena, what her father had done with Mother's paintings. "Father was burning the paintings that were left in the house."

William nodded. "He gave me the one with you—in the picture. I kept it to re—remind me. Then I kept it—for spite. I hated you for—"

"I'm sorry, Will. I didn't know you were coming back. I did love you then."

"No. Forgive me."

"I do, Will. I do."

He held up a finger to point to the wall where she had seen the picture hang. "I took it."

"Yes, I know. It's all right."

"It's in—the trunk of—my car. You take it."

She couldn't hold back the dam of tears. "Will, let me pray with you before—"

"Tell Frank—he was a—good brother."

Clarissa wiped her nose with her robe sleeve. She wondered if her father had wanted the same redemption by keeping her and Treena in his will. It seemed God's hand was in her life even when she didn't realize it. Now He had to come to William.

"I'm going to pray, Will. You listen and believe in your heart." She closed her eyes. "Dear heavenly Father, be with Will in his last breaths. Hold out your merciful hand—"

William's body wilted. She opened her eyes and studied his chest. No more breaths. No movement anywhere until a breeze came through the window and chased the curtains from where they hung. Not even her emotions moved. She had prayed to be rid of William, for Frank to take her away from this place. She had wanted to escape William's face so she didn't have to think about forgiving him. Now his dying face would forever be etched in her mind.

She hung her head. "It's finished, Will. I forgive you. Please forgive me." She placed her hand on his forehead.

Martha poked her head around the corner. "Clarissa, the doctor—"

"Would you help me up, Martha? William's gone."

Martha moved William's head and grabbed Clarissa's cold hand. She led her to the doorway, past the doctor standing on the landing. He patted her shoulder. James came to her side and took her by the arm. She leaned on him. He felt so strong next to her.

They took the stairs one by one, as if in a death march. Her back ached, and her head pounded. Had William heard her pray? Did he call out to God in his mind?

James stayed by her side as they ambled to the cottage. She took one glance at the smoldering remains of the barn. Where would Elijah sleep now? She didn't want to think about the prospect of him not coming home. It would push her over the edge of the cliff she clung to now.

Frank sat in one of the rockers on the porch, Morgan next to him asleep in the other chair. When they reached the top steps, Frank stood and took her from James' hold. She shook loose from him and turned to James.

"Thank you, James. I needed a strong man to hang on to just now." She kissed him on his forehead.

His expression lifted a little and held no sorrow.

She turned to Frank. "What is the word on Elijah?"

"No word. I'll go now if you're all right." He grasped her hand. "They said they were taking him to the public hospital. I protested, but they said… Well, you can imagine what they said."

She felt sick at the thought of Elijah going there, but put

it out of her mind. She had to tell Frank about his brother. "William is gone. His last words were, 'Tell Frank he was a good brother.' He died while I prayed for him."

Moisture brimmed in Frank's eyes. He glanced at the big house. "I know the doctor is over there. I'd like to see William before they—take him."

Her legs wobbled under her. She pushed off Frank and grabbed the handle of the screen door. "I'm going to bed. Martha will have my hide if I don't get some rest. James, will you wait here with Morgan and make sure Martha is all right?"

"Sure."

Frank took the first step off the porch and without turning around, spoke to James. Clarissa stood still.

"Thank you, James. You took good care of your mother."

James sat in the rocker Frank had been in. Clarissa felt the urge to laugh at his short-legged pajamas, until she saw they were covered in dirt and soot.

Sleep was all she wanted. No dreams, no worries, no fires. Just sleep. And later today she wanted to see Elijah. Alive.

The events of last evening haunted Frank all the way to the hospital. The coroner's van had passed him when he hit the main road to town. He turned over images in his mind as he used his one good arm to turn into the public hospital parking lot. The flames still danced behind his eyelids. The silhouette of Elijah's broken and burned body lying in the dirt flashed before him like a scene in a war newsreel. And seeing William's scorched frame on the sofa this morning—his head resting on the pillow that Clarissa held for him—would be branded onto his memory forever. She tended him, and he calmed to her touch. In that he saw a new side of her. And of William.

He stopped the truck and turned off the motor. He leaned

his head on the steering wheel and rubbed his aching shoulder. As he released a breath, particles of dust and soot from the fire flittered off the dash, twinkling in the morning sunlight.

He studied the building before him. The peeling paint on the facade made him cringe. Elijah deserved better than this place. If their friend had passed, it would be the largest toll in the totality of grief for the Wilding family. Elijah had spoken only a few words as they loaded him into the ambulance. He had asked about William.

A sick feeling twisted in Frank's gut. He checked his face in the rearview mirror. Stubbly and red-eyed, but acceptable after scrubbing off the soot. He threw open the door and slammed it behind him. His fatigue had peaked on the way here, but he ran all the way to the front door of the hospital. What if Elijah was fighting for his life in there, all alone? He should have come sooner. He should have jumped in that ambulance and rode with him.

"Hang on, my friend. I'm coming." He pushed through the door and marched to the nurses' station.

A petite woman with long red hair tied back with a ribbon greeted him. She leaned in closer over the counter. "Sir, are you all right? Are you injured?"

He glanced down at his pants, covered in black smudges and splatters of blood. He had changed his shirt, but he forgot about his pants. He smiled at her, hoping he wasn't blushing.

"No, I've been looked after, but my friend is here. He was brought in by ambulance last night with burns and—"

She glanced at her clipboard, but then set it down. "Yes, I checked on him when I got here early this morning. Mr. Green, the colored man with burns and abrasions. He's just come out of surgery."

Mr. Green. A colored man. Frank never knew Elijah's last name, and he never really thought of him as a colored man, especially lately. That was all he was to these people. They didn't know what he had done last night, that he had saved one person's life and tried to save another. Mr. Green, the colored man, was a hero and an angel.

"May I see him? Please?"

"Well, obviously you're not a relative." The nurse half laughed. "He's seriously burned, and I doubt the doctor would let just anyone be with him."

He would stand here all day and plead if necessary.

"I'm—he's my employee. He'd want to see me, really."

"I think it would be best if you sat in the waiting room." She turned to answer the ringing phone.

Frank held out his hand. "He doesn't have any family. I'm his friend."

A man dressed in a white coat and a stethoscope around his neck had approached the counter behind the nurse. He held a clipboard and scribbled on it with a fountain pen. He glanced at them a few times during the conversation but kept scribbling.

The nurse turned her back on Frank and picked up the receiver. His vision blurred through tears. He couldn't possibly leave here without seeing Elijah. He was alive, but alone. He would state his case again when she hung up, and push his way in.

The man tossed his clipboard onto the desk, took off his spectacles, and took a few steps in Frank's direction. "Are you Mr. Wilding?"

Frank cleared his throat. "Yes. I'm Frank Wilding."

The man leaned on the counter. "I'm Dr. Falen. I've just performed some skin graft surgery on Mr. Green. He's been asking for you." He peered back at the nurse, who still had the receiver in her face. "You can see him. Follow me."

Frank tried to keep up with the doctor as he hurried down the stark white-walled hallway.

"I didn't think this hospital did those kinds of surgery. Who pays for that?"

The doctor spoke over his shoulder. "I volunteer my time with patients who are seriously burned."

A kind soul at last. It was about time Elijah was on the receiving end of mercy. He picked up his pace to match the doctor's. Paintings of rolling green hills and golden wheat fields hung on each side of the hall. The effort to make the institution less drab didn't succeed for Frank. He'd always hated hospitals. He smoothed back his hair and checked his wrinkled shirt again. His bloody pants stuck out like a blight against the cleanness of the white floors.

The doctor stopped in front of a swinging door. "He's awake from the surgery, but we have him pumped with pain meds. He will be groggy and fuzzy." He placed his hands on the door, but Frank spoke up.

"Is he going to make it? What's his prog… no…"

"Prognosis." The doctor smiled. "He's a strong man, unusually so, considering my guess at his age. He couldn't recall how old he was." Another smile. "Your friend is a lucky man. But he still has a long recovery ahead of him. That gash on his head will leave him with headaches for a while."

As the doctor pushed the door open, Frank chuckled to himself. Luck would not be Elijah's word for his close call. God had spared him. He couldn't wait to get home to tell Clarissa. First, he wanted to thank his friend. Mr. Green. The colored man.

Dr. Falen led him to Elijah's bed at the end of a row of beds full of sick or injured men. Frank stood close to Elijah's head, unable to speak through his tightened throat. He clenched his jaw to hold back tears of sorrow and joy. He placed his hand on Elijah's arm.

Dr. Falen left. Frank stood still, willing any remnants of

his own strength to flow into Elijah. A nurse moved from window to window, turning up the yellowed blinds to filter the bright sunlight. Other patients groaned and some snored. Frank wished Elijah could have a room of his own. He would need quiet rest to heal.

Frank reached for the chair by the bedside table and pulled it close to the bed. It creaked as Frank sat down, loud enough to rouse Elijah. Frank stilled. He should let him sleep, but if he were almost awake anyway, what harm could there be in speaking to him? He didn't have to, as Elijah shifted his bandaged head toward Frank. His eyelids fluttered open, and he blinked.

"Elijah?" Frank's voice wavered.

Elijah first looked in the opposite direction, then maneuvered his gaze to face Frank. The end of his lips curled up, but his eyes closed again.

"It's Frank. Mr. Wilding."

The man in the bed next to Elijah's coughed hard, and Elijah jumped, grabbing the bedrail with his uncovered hand. He blinked a few more times and looked up at the ceiling.

"Where am I, Mr. Wildin'?"

"You're in a hospital. You're badly burned, my friend. Lay still."

Elijah swallowed a couple times. "Is everyone—are you all right?"

"I'm fine. Just a little banged up. Would have died if not for you."

Elijah closed his eyes. "God did the hard work. I jus' helped Him a bit." He lay still so long Frank thought he had drifted off to sleep. Then Elijah's eyelids lifted again. "And Mr. William? Is he all right?"

Frank held his breath, thinking of what to say.

Elijah reached his arm through the rail bars. "He's gone, isn't he?"

Frank clutched Elijah's swollen hand, the emotion flowing between them prompted a broken dam of grief. He couldn't speak the words of confirmation.

Elijah lay quiet as Frank sobbed. He couldn't stop, but he had a feeling Elijah didn't mind. After a few moments, the nurse touched Frank's shoulder.

"Mr. Green needs to rest now. You can come back later this evening if the doctor approves."

Frank let go of Elijah's limp hand. He had fallen asleep while Frank cried. He stood and wiped his face with his sleeve.

"May I call later to see if my wife can come to see him? She's terribly worried."

The nurse looked puzzled but pulled out a small card from her uniform pocket. "Here's the number to the nurse's station. Call after six."

"Thank you."

He had just enough energy to make it home. His shoulder ached with each turn of the steering wheel. At least the pain would keep him awake while driving. He had to sleep before he came back, and he had to make sure bringing Clarissa to the hospital was a good idea. The ordeal she had just endured must have taken a greater toll on her. And possibly the baby.

It wasn't the first barn to go down on his watch. The first one he had built with his own hands. The one barely standing before him had just been turned over to him. He had plans to make a better place for Elijah inside and to fortify the loft for storage. William had never done any improvements on the farm buildings. That was another difference between them. Frank always looked for a way to make things better.

The inspector approached Frank, having given the burned-out structure a good going over. "Structurally, it's not in the best shape. The roof on the west side is gone, as well as most of the wall on that side. The loft is destroyed, and all that's left to hold up the end is the corner closest to us." He pointed to the charred lumber jutting up on the northeast side. "The tack room is still sound, and I think you can fix it up without too much work."

Frank tipped his head back and closed his eyes. He had to ask the most important question. "Is it safe to be inside—if we want to still use it?"

The inspector paused and shifted from one foot to the other. "I'd say yes. The remaining support lumber is stable and, even though the integrity of the northeast end is poor, there's enough rafters to carry the load of the walls. They won't fall in."

Frank stuck out his hand. "Thank you for coming out. There is no insurance on anything around here, but we will make do with what we have for now. At least none of the machinery was in there at the time."

The man shook Frank's hand. "Still, I'm sorry for the death of your brother. No one around here knew much about him. He kept to himself, except for one or two local businessmen who I'd never deal with. I'll be on my way then."

"Thanks again." Frank walked over blackened dirt and into the remains of the barn. His mind flashed with vivid recall of that night. He could feel the heat on his face and arms and hear the roar of burning hay. The shovel William had tossed in the hay lay on the ground, the wood handle burned off.

"What did the inspector say?"

He hadn't heard Clarissa's footsteps. It would be the first time she had been out in the yard since the fire. At least she and the boys had escaped harm. If the events of that night had gone differently, the cottage might have also gone up in flames. They might all have perished.

He turned around. "It's okay to be in here, and Elijah's room is intact. That's something to be thankful for. I doubt we'll get this mess cleaned up before harvest. Might not matter anyway. We'll likely be leaving here before winter."

"Hard to believe that so much could happen in just a few short months. I thought life would be better here." She touched her abdomen and shuffled over to a charred pile of objects. She leaned down to pick up a stick and poke the unrecognizable items scattered around.

Frank picked up a crushed oil can and tossed it. "What a waste of life and a good farm. William must have been out of his mind to risk it."

Clarissa shrugged. "I think he was a misguided lost soul. I'm sorry he died."

Frank's spine bristled. He was sorry for his brother, but Clarissa's forgiving attitude stepped on his pride. She should be more concerned about him and their future.

She continued to poke the ground while he thought of something clever and gracious to say. Her stick flipped something up in the air. When it landed, the same jingle he heard during his fight with William rang in the air.

He lunged toward her. "Wait. Did you hear that?

"Yes, but what was it?"

He remembered thinking when William hit him during their scuffle that there was metal in the sack. This could be the same one. William had dropped it, if he remembered correctly. He moved slowly in the daylight of the opened roof, searching for the pouch in the blackened debris. Clarissa followed him.

"There it is." He looked up to see her pointing on the ground about a yard in front of him. He moved slowly, trying not to stir up soot and dust. When the sun split the clouds and sent a ray to the ground, something sparkled. Frank reached for it.

Clarissa took one step closer. "Be careful. There could be broken glass around here."

Frank knelt and emptied the burned gunny sack of its contents. The outside of a roll of bills were burned, but the inside, although smoky, was still all right. He handed it to Clarissa. His fingers weaved through the dirt until he found all the gold coins he could.

He stood and held them in his palm. "Two, four—seven altogether." He looked at her, both just staring at the treasure. "We have to give it to George. It's his money William stole." He wrapped it in his bandana.

Clarissa's head moved back and forth as if she didn't believe him. "It's only a small part, I imagine. You're right."

Before she said more, a car door slammed in the yard. Frank ran to the barn door. "It's George. Right on cue." He turned slowly. "He's in William's car."

Clarissa joined him and handed him the roll of bills.

"Well, it's only right. And we don't need it."

She took his arm as they walked out to meet George. Frank hesitated, wondering how his new boss would react to the entire tragedy. Frank couldn't tell by the tone of his voice when he had made the call to him yesterday from William's phone. Now the look on his face as he gazed at the barn told it all. Shock and worry woven with discouragement.

"Hello, Frank. Mrs. Wilding." George stopped, gaping at the sight of his barn in a rubble.

The three of them stood in silence. The contrast of the ugly structure against the glory of the green vines and purple grapes would capture anyone. As the clouds scurried north, the full sun shone on the barn wall facing them. The bitter smell of charcoal in the breeze rose so strong, Frank could taste it on his tongue.

George spoke while gazing at the ruins. "I'm very sorry about William. He wasn't the best of men, but he was a hard worker. No one deserves to die like that."

Clarissa shielded her eyes. "Mr. Tanner, William did love it here. I know that much. Would it be all right with you if we buried him here? Somewhere on the farm, maybe overlooking the river?"

Frank's heart skipped. How could she suggest such a thing without talking to him first? William was his brother, but he had also become a thorn in Frank's side. He had no obligation to take care of him that way, and neither did Clarissa. He dropped the arm she held and pulled away enough for her to let go. She kept her eyes on George.

George glanced between her and Frank, frowning. His mouth opened to speak, but Clarissa broke in.

"He has nowhere else to lay his head, Mr. Tanner." She blinked, still avoiding Frank's disapproving glare.

George looked down. "I suppose it wouldn't hurt anything. You'll have to go deep with the grave and mark it well."

Frank had to be a part of this conversation before he appeared hardhearted. "We will. Thank you, George."

"Yes, thank you." Clarissa turned to walk away.

"Wait, Mrs. Wilding. I have something for you. Wait here." He looked at Frank. "Then I need to take a look at the damage."

Frank nodded, and George marched over to his car. Frank jerked his head to Clarissa. "What in the world was that all about? Why do we have to bury him here?" He clenched his teeth, waiting for her to give him a reason not to change George's mind.

"He would have wanted it that way. He can't hurt us anymore, and it's the kind thing to do."

Frank whispered in her ear as George approached. "Are you sure that's the reason?"

She pulled back and glowered at him.

"I believe this belongs to you." George's smile broke the tension. He handed her a large item wrapped in brown paper.

Frank knew what it was. He wished George hadn't found it. He didn't care that Clarissa would want it. It was just another reminder of her tie to William. Just when he had come to terms with their relationship, a new thorn poked his side. He was determined to pull it out before it poisoned him.

Chapter 18

The day she first saw it, she had been in such a hurry to get out of William's house, she hadn't given her mother's painting a close look. Her heart raced as she dropped the brown paper on the ground. George helped her hold it while she studied every inch.

"In all my mother's paintings, she never added people. Only landscapes—mostly gardens. Yet, there it is—a little girl in the garden, and it's me." The warmth of her mother's love filled her from head to toe. "I wish I had taken it all those years ago."

Frank moved closer to her. "She probably meant for you to have it."

She believed that. "And my father didn't. William told me he was going to destroy it before he gave it to him."

She sensed Frank withdraw, his body ease away from her. She held the frame close to her. "Thank you so much for bringing it to me. I wasn't going to ask for it. I was prepared to let it go, but this is a blessing."

George grinned wide. "What would I do with a beautiful thing like that? My taste is more casual. I'm glad to return it to you. If Frank hadn't mentioned it, I wouldn't have known it was your mother's."

She turned to Frank and nodded toward the treasure in his hands. He seemed distracted. "Frank? Don't you have something for Mr. Tanner?"

Frank lifted his head. "Oh yes." He opened his bandana and held out the bundle of bills to George. "William was after this the night of the fire. He dropped it when we fought. Clarissa found it just a while ago." He shuffled the coins in his hands and held them out. "And these coins were in the bag too. They are just like the one William gave James. I have that in the cottage. I'll get it for you."

George grabbed Frank's arm when he turned away. "It's okay. I can get it later, or maybe not at all."

Clarissa felt the adrenaline flowing through her. "Do you know anything about the coins or why William would have them?"

"The only thing I do know is that there were people who hoarded gold when President Roosevelt passed a law making it illegal to own it. Everyone was supposed to turn it in to the banks, but some folks hid their gold—even the collectible coins. If you were on the dishonest side, you could find brokers who would get it for you."

Frank brushed the soot from the money off his hands. "Do you think that's what William did? Dealt in underground gold? Hard to believe."

"Don't know for sure, but I have seen these coins before, and I can guess where they came from and about how much they are worth." George held the coins closer. "I'll find out exactly how valuable these are and let you know. I wish it were enough to pay the debt on this place, but judging from their condition, that would take a small miracle." He juggled the money from hand to hand. "Let me take this to the car, and we'll tour the barn and check the crop."

He jogged toward the car. Clarissa's heart stirred as she thought about the debt William left for George, and how it was going to affect their lives. A strange idea came to her. She glanced at Frank. It had to be now.

"I want to give George my inheritance to pay the rest of the debt." She didn't have time to ease into the conversation.

Frank froze. "What did you say?"

"It's the only way we can stay here. I know you want that, and we would just use up the money finding a different place. Why not make it so we can stay?" She glanced George's way. He had pulled a towel from his car and commenced wiping his hands.

Frank's mouth hung open. She leaned the painting against her leg.

"I really want to do this for us. Will you let me?" She rested her hand on his arm. He tensed at her touch.

"Why would you want to pay a debt William caused? I don't know if I—"

It was clear to her. He didn't trust her motives. Her adrenaline ran cold. She had been blind to it all along—Frank was jealous and suspicious. She wanted to laugh or hold him or slug him, she wasn't sure which.

"The one and only reason to do this would be to secure our future here, at least for a while. You have to be with me on this, or it's no good. If you don't trust me, that's no good either."

George stepped toward them, unaware of the turmoil rumbling between her and her husband. Frank would have to take the lead. If he didn't say anything, she would drop it forever. She would have her baby in a strange place, but her heart assured her that if they stayed, she would make it feel like home.

Frank toed the ground, and she removed her hand from his forearm. George pointed to the barn. "Shall we take a look?"

Frank held up his hand to George, who stopped and frowned at them both. Frank sighed a long breath. "My wife would like to say something about William's debt." He turned to her and winked. "Honey?"

She would have thrown her arms around Frank if she hadn't been guarding the painting. She eyed George and smiled. "Mr.

Tanner." Her voice shook. Could she really do this? "I recently came into some money from my father's estate. Frank and I would like to put this money toward William's debt if it would be enough to allow us to stay here so Frank could manage your farm." Her hands shook so much she could hardly hang on to the frame.

George's face contorted into a facial question mark. It had to be a shock for him—a small miracle from out of the blue. She mouthed a prayer that he would accept her offer.

"Um—I don't know what to say. Mrs. Wilding, are you sure you want to do this? I mean, depending on how much it is, your plan might be feasible. I would love for all of us to come out of this tragedy with something positive." He scratched his head and stared at Frank.

She waited for Frank to back her. This had to be a joint decision. Seconds ticked off, draining her strength. She would have to sit down soon. *Frank, please.*

Frank straightened and held out his hand. "Shall we shake on it?"

Her knees threatened to give out. She had just presented herself with the opportunity to make everything come full circle. Her father's money, William's hurtful deeds, Frank's identity, and her resentment for all of them melted into an idol she'd just released. The cage she had been living in for so long suddenly sprang open, and the fresh air breathed new hope in her.

The sight of the two men shaking hands and chuckling gave her everything she needed to get through rebuilding a marriage, and an entire family. She was suddenly free to live the life she always wanted. Free to be who she was meant to be.

Fatigue settled in fast and heavy, but it was a peaceful fatigue. "I'll leave you gentlemen to your business. Thank you again, Mr. Tanner, for my mother's legacy to me."

She struggled to stay upright as she turned.

"When are you going to call me George?" He blurted out to her while she walked.

"When you start calling me Clarissa."

She heard them laugh as she made her way to the cottage porch. Her legs felt like lead as she climbed the steps. She gripped the arm of the chair and dropped the frame in her hand. Just as she eased into the chair, the sun drifted behind a cloud.

Her head whirled so fast, she couldn't focus. She leaned back and hung on to the chair arms and realized it wasn't the clouds darkening the sky.

The end of the shovel rang each time it struck a rock hidden in the earth. If it weren't for that, the soil would receive the blade with ease, as it was rich and sandy. Today the immense hole left from Frank's hour of digging would receive a casket, thanks to that shovel. The significance of the process kept Frank's mind off the final piece of his anecdotal puzzle. The piece that would seal William here on this farm forever. Unnoticed by the rest of the world, except for the Wilding family who came here because of him.

He threw the last plume of earth over his shoulder and leaned against the side of the open grave. The effort had caused his face to drip with sweat, his shirt sticking to his back. He tossed the shovel above him and pulled himself out of the dirt pit. If only he could pull himself out of the pit of confusion that had been brewing for days.

He tipped his head heavenward. "Lord, why don't You just tell me the truth about Clarissa's loyalty? Can't You remove this distrust from my mind?"

Everything else seemed to have fallen into place, except the battle with his attitude. His doubt had reared its ugly head again this morning when Clarissa suggested he make a marker for William's grave. He had swallowed his cruel remark when he realized James and Morgan were in the room.

He glanced at his watch and rubbed the dirt from its face. William's body would be delivered in a few hours, and he still had to run to town to pick up Elijah and bring him home. Perhaps Elijah's influence would stabilize the remnants of turmoil for a troubled heart.

"May I go with you to town?"

Frank turned his head to see James standing a few yards back from the grave. The boy looked the other way and had his arms crossed over his chest. Frank pushed himself up off the ground and dusted his pant legs.

"I think that would be all right. Does your mother know?"

"She said to ask you."

"I guess she knows best. We'll need to grab some pillows from the chairs on the front porch for—"

"Already did that. Mom said we want Elijah to be comfortable in the truck. I thought maybe I could be there to help get him in the cab."

Frank walked past James and stopped to wave him on. "Come on then. We have to get back before—"

James nodded, his eyes to the ground. "I know."

A question hung in the air. He could see it on James' face and the fact that he had stood his ground instead of heading for the truck. He studied the posture of the boy he called his own. When James finally met Frank's gaze, he bore the look of a determined young man—no longer a boy.

"Why are you mad at Mom?"

A simple direct question that sent heat to Frank's face. His demeanor from this morning hadn't escaped James. The boy might be growing up, but he couldn't understand the dynamics of Frank's relationship with Clarissa. Still, it was a fair thing to ask.

"I'm not mad at her, James. It's just that there are some things your mom and I need to work through. A lot has happened in the last few weeks, and it would be hard for me to explain how it is between a man and a wife."

James slipped his hands behind him. "I think you blame Mom for how things turned out." He turned to gaze at the vineyard. "It's not fair. Elijah says God is sad when we don't forgive—that when we haven't forgiven others, it's harder to forgive ourselves."

"Well, I suppose that's true in a way, but it's not that simple. Our situation is—complicated." Frank sensed the tug of war in his mind, that part of him that couldn't get over William's part in his wife's life. James had no right to challenge him about the issues facing his parents. He didn't care what Elijah said. His feelings were justified. He had obviously never had all of Clarissa's love.

"Do you think it's possible you're making it complicated? You always said we were supposed to give people the benefit of the doubt. Mom deserves to be forgiven. I forgave her. Why can't you?"

The words jabbed him in the stomach as sure as someone had punched him. He didn't like how they rang true. He needed to hold on to his resentment. It made him master of Clarissa's love.

James turned his head to stare at the mound of dirt Frank had just created. "When I walked up and saw the grave, I tried to imagine how I'd feel if it were you instead of William. I'm not glad it's his grave, but I'm sure glad it isn't yours, Dad. You got to live. Maybe you should be more grateful."

Tears welled up in Frank's eyes to remember how just a few days ago, James had turned against him, confused and angry. Was that how Frank had treated Clarissa in his confusion?

James scratched his head. "I don't mean to be disrespectful, but it would help all of us a lot if you could get over your anger. I did, and I feel so much better."

As James spoke, a breeze tossed soot from the barn through the air, sending it high in a funneling swirl. Frank watched it dissipate over the vineyard, like an illustration to James' rebuke. He had to find a way to get the soot of distrust and hate off himself—give it flight.

He took a step toward James and placed a hand on his shoulder. "I'll try. Be patient with me?"

"Sure. If Mom can be, so can I."

That was his proof. Said from the mouth of the son he'd chosen to raise. Clarissa had been the patient one, not he. She had been the one who sacrificed, not the other way around. He had received everything he wanted—the homestead, Clarissa, two sons, and a life away from a drunken stepfather. She had given up her self-respect, her home, her love of painting, and her beloved homestead. All for him. And he'd repaid her by not trusting her love or her motives.

He threw back his shoulders and headed for the cottage. "Let's go tell your mom how wonderful she is."

James returned his smile and ran ahead of him. "That didn't take long," he called over his shoulder.

Frank spoke low so James wouldn't hear his confession.

"It took too long, son. Too long."

Any other day she would have pushed Frank to let her go with him. Since the secret fainting spell the other day, she had behaved herself and rested as much as possible. It was easier now that she had said goodbye to William, relinquished her father's money, and reconciled with James. Peace was once again her companion after a long absence. The last two pieces of the puzzle would close her need to worry—Elijah's return and William's burial.

She rocked in the chair on the porch and sniffed in the first hints of autumn. The blooms had all fallen in her garden, and the leaves on the trees had turned like a page in a book. If her visit with Martha went well today, the boys would be able to come home next week or the week after. Just having James here for today's preparations had been nice. His pat on her hand as he left with Frank had been the tender acceptance she had longed for from him.

Frank had followed his son's lead and whispered in her ear sweet words of love and renewed trust. What had happened out there by William's open grave she might never know. It was enough to see a glimmer of hope in both their eyes.

The sound of a car bouncing up the rutted drive raised her to her feet. Martha was early as usual, but help for today was a welcome gift. The gathering for William's burial would be small, but she wanted to at least have a bit of food to share with the few neighbors who wanted to come and pay their respects.

"Hard times call for neighbors to band together," Mr. Fortunate had said. His quick response to the fire that night had been a blessing. Two other men from neighboring farms had followed close behind to help douse the flames, but it was too late for William to know anyone cared.

Martha's car pulled up under the lilac bushes, and Morgan jumped out of the backseat. He ran up the stairs and into her arms. "Mama, guess what."

She rubbed the top of his head. "You got a haircut." She laughed at his excitement over such a simple thing. Yet it had been more than a month since she'd felt well enough to snip at his blond mop.

"Mr. Watkins is a barber, and that means he cuts people's hair. So Martha said he could cut mine."

She lifted his chin to look in his eyes. "It's perfect. I hope you told him thank you."

"He did." A man's voice came from the direction of the car. A broad-shouldered balding gentleman stood next to Martha, who held a large box in her arms.

"Clarissa, this is my dad, Ed Watkins."

Ruth emerged from the other side of the backseat, carrying a bulging sack. The three approached the porch as Clarissa held the door open.

"Nice to meet you, sir. Please come in, everyone."

As Mr. Watkins slipped by her, Clarissa touched his arm. "Thank you for Morgan's haircut. He needed it—like me." She tugged on the ends of her long hair.

He winked at her. "Need a trim? I have scissors in the car."

Clarissa laughed, thinking he was teasing her. Martha came up beside him. "He's not kidding. It might make you feel better. And Mom's been sewing. A little hemming and you'll have a new wardrobe fit for a pregnant lady."

They all scooted past Clarissa as she stood with her mouth hanging open. She closed the door behind them. Somehow she had forgotten how fast God could turn things around. A day that was supposed to be sad and depressing, could be a day to rejoice on His terms.

"I don't know what to say. You're all too good to us."

Ruth giggled and unloaded a measuring tape, sewing supplies, and articles of clothing made from bright material. "Do you have an ironing board and iron?"

Morgan jumped up from the kitchen table, where Martha was feeding him cookies. "I know where they are."

Before Clarissa could catch her breath, Morgan had dragged the padded board Frank had made for her and plopped it and the old iron on the table. She felt her face heat to think she hadn't used it since they'd arrived.

As Ruth set up shop, Mr. Watkins unloaded the box. Two pies, a plate of sandwiches, and a bowl of something filled the counter. He gathered up the empty box and headed toward the front door.

Martha looked around the room. "Morgan, why don't you take my mom and dad for a walk around the farm. They would love to see it. They always wanted to live on a farm."

Morgan ran to the front door and opened it. "I know where everything is. But we can't go in the barn, right, Mama?"

"Right." Clarissa glanced at Martha, who motioned for her to move to the sofa.

"Mom, you can measure Clarissa when you get back. I should be done by then."

Ruth answered in her familiar soft tone. "I can do that."

Ruth embodied the quiet type, going about her tasks without much conversation, just like she had the last visit. She wasn't anything like Clarissa's mother, who routinely dressed up and sometimes talked everyone's ear off.

Once the door shut, Martha dove into her duties. After each test, she smiled this time. Even the stethoscope on Clarissa's belly garnered a hefty nod. Clarissa could barely hear the faint thumps of the baby's heart, but it was there.

"So Elijah is coming home today?" Martha packed her black bag.

"Yes. I'm so glad. I've been so worried about him. And some other things that have recently resolved."

Martha patted Clarissa's hand. "You're improving, I'm happy to say. I think the boys can come home end of next week, if you like. I'd just like Frank to get you back to the doctor for a checkup before we decide. He'll give you a complete exam and give you a due date." She squinted. "It's getting on late August, so I figure maybe around mid to late January."

A due date. Somehow it was now real. The several times

she had felt movement inside excited her, but knowing the week her child would be born struck joy and fear at the same time.

"What is it? Don't you want to know a date?"

"It's hard knowing a date that could bring tragedy. Sort of like knowing the day something bad will happen and you can only sit and wait."

Martha leaned in to whisper, "Don't let yourself think negatively."

Clarissa leaned back. "At least I'll have some things to look forward to in the meantime." She paused and wrinkled her nose. "Frank wants to move into the big house. The landlord suggested it. What do you think?"

Martha rested her elbows on her knees, Clarissa needed an excuse not to accept the landlord's offer and held her breath that Martha would provide one. By the look on her face, her nurse was about to let her down.

"If you don't do any lifting, and if there is a bedroom on the main floor. I think it would be nice. I can help get it cleaned up and ready. But don't ask me to give decorating advice." She stood just as the tour group came through the door—all except for Morgan.

Mr. Watkins smiled as though a secret was about to be revealed.

"Dad?" Martha tipped her head. "Where's Morgan?"

He chuckled. "He's counting his jars."

Martha shot a glance to Clarissa. "Jars?"

Clarissa gasped. "Mason jars?"

Mr. Watkins nodded. "He has a bunch of them filled with water by the pump house. Said he was making sure you had enough water for when the drought came."

Her hands flew to her cheeks. "Oh no."

Everyone's face fell somber. Clarissa stood and held her

hand out to Martha. "I need to talk to him. I'll be back. Make yourself at home."

She didn't give Martha a chance to protest before she marched out the back door and through the garden. Morgan sat on a turned-up bucket under the oak tree, breaking a twig into pieces. He had tears dripping off his chin. Clarissa crept to his side and knelt.

"How many jars did you count?" She tried to sound indifferent, but her voice wavered.

"Not enough. I should have gotten more, but I was afraid Uncle William would be mad if I took another jar. Then he died, and I was scared to go over there."

Her poor little man had more imagination than she'd ever dreamed. She wanted to cry, but held back. "Well, you did your best, and we appreciate it. I don't think William would be mad. You were just doing what you thought was best." She wrapped her arm around his shoulder. "You should have told me or your daddy what you were up to. We were worried each time you ran off when it rained."

"I know." He sniffled and dropped what was left of the twig. "I wanted to surprise you when we got the drought."

"And that was sweet, but they don't have droughts here—not like in Kansas. You don't ever have to worry about that again. This is a place where it rains enough for everyone to have crops and water to take a bath in. Isn't that nice?"

He looked up, his eyes brighter. "Really? I don't have to catch the rain anymore?"

"Really."

"I need to go tell Mr. Watkins. I think he was afraid I didn't have enough." He jumped up and was gone, leaving her to sort through conflicting feelings.

Another lesson from one of her children. Wait until Frank heard this one. He could finish explaining what she surmised—that folks didn't need to ask for trouble, but when they did, they couldn't possibly take on the task of complete provision. God provided the manna from heaven.

"No. We don't have to catch the rain."

Chapter 19

By human standards it was astounding. That a man who was a thief and a would-be murderer should have as his casket bearers the very people he'd victimized. It seemed to Frank as he listened to everyone singing *Amazing Grace* that the reenactment of Christ and the thief on the cross was happening here and now.

I once was lost, but now I'm found. Twas blind, but now I see.

It was true for him, for James, and for Clarissa, but would it be true for William? As the song rang on, he thought back to his childhood with his brother. Their mother had taught them the Bible truths and prayed with them every night. He had to trust that William had chosen those truths for himself.

Than when we've first begun.

It was his cue to bring William's burial to a close. Only one thing left to do, and he knew the best man for the job.

"Elijah, would you say a prayer?"

Elijah looked up from the chair James had carried over for him. His bandaged left hand lay in his lap. More white gauze peeked out from under his new hat. James had insisted they stop at the general store on the way home from the hospital and buy their friend a replacement for the one burned in the fire. He was quite dapper in his finery.

"Yes, sir, Mr. Wildin'. I'd be happy to."

He struggled to stand, but Morgan and James rushed to his

side. He placed one hand on each of them to steady himself and spoke a prayer of intercession for the man who tried to kill him, for the family left behind, and for a bountiful harvest. His words filled everyone's eyes with tears. Each head nodded in agreement.

As Elijah prayed, Frank questioned his own ability to forgive. Somehow, he had to figure out how to forgive a man who wasn't here anymore. William's death had only cemented the bitterness that plagued him.

Elijah wrapped up the prayer.

"Help us to find in our hearts mercy for the lost and compassion for those who have done wrong." Elijah patted the heads of both boys beside him. "Amen."

Morgan echoed, "Amen!"

This was the answer. If he could find mercy and compassion for William just like he had for others in his past, he would be free. After all, hadn't he been shown mercy by God and Clarissa and James? He could do no less. William had given him a precious gift—James. He had no right to hate him.

"Honey?" Clarissa slipped her arm through his. "Are you all right?"

He wrapped his arm around her. "Sure. I'm fine."

"It's just I've never seen you cry before." She snuggled in close to his chest.

Crying? He felt his face. A stream of tears had been flowing without him noticing. That must be what happened when you regained your soul. And a brother. How terrible William couldn't know he had been loved and forgiven.

He pushed Clarissa away. "I need to check on James."

She nodded her head in James' direction.

Frank hadn't expected the sight before his eyes. He crept through the dispersing crowd to reach his son. Along with two other men, James shoveled dirt from the pile Frank had made, onto William's coffin. The clatter of dirt and rocks hitting the hemlock box jarred Frank's nerves, until he saw James' tears.

The scene pierced into his mind, a picture of redemption and maturity of heart wrapped in pain and sorrow. Frank felt his own burden lift as he picked up the last shovel and stood side by side with James. William was gone, needing nothing anymore, but James was here and wholly in need of a father's support.

James stopped shoveling, elbowed Frank, and pointed to the sun nearing the horizon. Frank leaned on the wood handle, feeling the splintery grain in his palm. The gold and amber hues scattered east and west were the perfect send-off for William. James saw it. How much he had grown in such a short time.

James shook his head. "Perfect, isn't it?"

"Yes, son. Perfect."

Just when he had victory over his fears and failures, they robbed his sleep once again. He would have to call down extra strength and confidence from above today. His attempt at harvesting the first, and possibly last, apple crop of his life was about to commence. With or without the manpower he desperately needed. The trip to town to find help in the camp had been interrupted by tragedy.

He tied his second boot and stood to do some deep breathing before he faced the overwhelming task before him. With Clarissa unable to help, Elijah still on the mend, and James not quite a grown man, Frank would have to shoulder the majority of the work—even if it meant working around the clock.

The smell of pancakes and eggs wafted under the bedroom door. His churning stomach might not accept a big breakfast this morning, but if Clarissa had put forth the effort to cook it, he would try to eat it.

He felt the stubble on his chin. No time to shave. It wouldn't matter anyway. He might just grow a beard in honor of harvest. Then again, Clarissa would never stand for it.

When he turned the handle on the door, he hesitated, thinking he heard voices and the shuffling of larger feet than should be in the house. Perhaps Elijah had felt good enough to join them for a meal. He pulled the door open and shuddered at the roomful of people. Something wasn't right. Or was it?

"Breakfast is ready!" Morgan and Clarissa shouted together.

The living room was full of faces—some he recognized, some were strangers. Mr. and Mrs. Watkins sat at the kitchen table eating pancakes. Martha stood next to Clarissa, stirring something in a pan on the stove. James closed the icebox door and held up a glass pitcher with orange liquid.

"Fresh-squeezed juice from Mr. Fortunate."

The neighbor bowed from where he stood against the living room wall. On the sofa, two people Frank didn't know turned and waved with one hand, holding a plate of food in the other. He nodded to them.

"Those are our neighbors down the road to the south, Frank. Meet Tomas and Nancy Garcia."

Frank managed to speak through his confusion. "Hello."

Why had Clarissa invited all these people on a day he needed to get to work? A nice gesture, but there was no time to entertain, especially at this hour of the morning.

Elijah sat nestled in the corner in the rocking chair from the porch. His grin and shining eyes hinted at something mysterious. Clarissa laid down her spatula and sauntered up to him.

"Martha arranged it all. They are here to help with the apple picking." She pulled a handkerchief from her apron pocket and dabbed at her eyes.

Martha shoved a plate in front of Frank. "I should have invited all my old boyfriends. We would have had a much bigger crew."

Everyone laughed, including Frank, his plate shaking in his hand. "How can I thank you all?"

On his way to the sink, Mr. Fortunate hollered, "Breakfast like this is good payment." His Italian accent livened up an already festive room.

Martha wiped her hands on a towel. "We have it all organized. Elijah will keep us running efficiently from his chair in the yard, with Morgan as his assistant, of course. And the rest of the jobs are mostly designated as pickers and drivers and haulers. If you just do what you're told, it will all run smoothly."

Laughter and then a hush filled the room. Clarissa cried into her hanky. Morgan hugged her around her growing waist. James stood with one foot propped up on the stool by the window. He shot a mischievous rise of his brows to Frank.

He had to say something to these kind individuals, or his heart would burst.

"The Wildings have had some rough times lately. I suppose most everyone in America and abroad is being tested these days. Even the news from our native countries is bleak with wars and rumors of wars. In the scheme of things, my troubles are small. Without generous people like you, I'd be tempted to lose faith in humanity." He chuckled, and others followed. "Pulling together is what makes us stronger. We have to get through one day at a time and pray our children and grand-children will pass down the values you display today." He pulled Clarissa close.

She finished up with the only sentiment possible. "Thank you all, from the bottom of our hearts. And God be with us and keep us safe."

George Tanner slapped Frank on the back. "A three-day harvest. It's wonderful. I didn't think you could pull it off. I tried to find workers myself, but even the camp had disbanded. You must be living right."

Frank laughed inside. Living right? If that were all it took for success, he wouldn't have been inundated with friends and neighbors who'd helped him bring in the best harvest in years. Only a few boxes of rotted fruit and a couple small accidents. The small assembly of Wilding helpers had managed a miracle, with God's help.

The rains could come, the temperatures could drop, and the soil could rest. All that was left was to prepare the vines and trees for winter. James and he could manage that alone. They both had experience at pruning now—at the core of themselves. It hurt for a season, but Frank was ready to see the new growth that would come of it.

George wouldn't stop praising Frank. "I hope you'll stay. You're as good or better farmer than your brother ever could have been. Thanks to your wife's contribution to William's debt, I can keep the land. Move your family into the big house, and I'll pay you a wage over the winter months too. Sound right to you?"

"It does."

"I'll be in touch." George squeezed into his fancy car.

Frank walked all the way around the big house. Could he do it? It would be a reminder of William. A reminder of that day when Clarissa held him as he died. A reminder of what William could have taken from him.

He stared at the cottage for a long time. All those memories would from now on hold other feelings for him. He was proud of Clarissa for staying with William that night, and he would be glad to remember William in a positive way. It was the least he could do, for himself, for James.

"And for you, sweet Clarissa."

Chapter 20

December 25, 1935

*H*e tasted like peppermint. It was no wonder, since the crumbs of the frosted cookies Ruth brought still lingered on that blasted beard of his. She didn't really fuss much about the wiry kisses he gave her. As long as they kept coming, she would drink them in. The lights twinkling like diamonds on the enormous fir tree and the crunching of discarded wrapping paper under Morgan's feet cornered the sights and sounds of Christmas—a Christmas like no other in the history of the Wilding family. If she could capture the essence of tonight on a canvas, it would be her greatest masterpiece.

Moving into the big house had been like a changing of the guard. No longer William's house, his things, his smell, but a cleaning out of all the desperation and depravity that was his. Replacing it with joy and hope had taken a month or two, but with Martha's help, Frank's patience, and her own artistic touch, the house had become the home it cried out to be. Her mother's painting had been returned to the place she'd first seen it. Another one hung beside it—her own rendition of the barn before it burned.

"Are you just going to sit there, or are you going to tell us what's in that package by your chair?" Martha called from the sofa, where she sat with Elijah.

Clarissa chimed back. "Oh, the nursing school graduate is getting bossy?"

"Just dying of curiosity."

Clarissa had wanted to wait to the last, but if the mob was clamoring for her secret to be revealed, she would give in. "All right, all right. But I need James' help."

James turned his head and frowned but jumped up to join her beside the tree. She struggled to bend down, since her belly had grown past her ability to see the floor. James grabbed the package up for her and held it while she pulled the twine from the plain brown wrapping.

"Are you sure you're all ready for this?" She giggled when they all shouted an affirmative yes.

"James, hold it up higher."

He stabilized the package in his arms and stood tall. She pulled the last of the paper from the front. The room silenced, except for Mr. Watkins' spoon dropping to the floor.

"Shh," Ruth chided him.

All eyes fixed on the painting she had kept hidden from everyone, working on it a few hours a day since the first snowfall the first of November. Her heart had been in each stroke, as if she were comforting a child. She had been the one to be comforted by the images that came from the ends of the brush.

"Honey, it's beautiful. Your best yet." Frank approached and helped James bring it closer to the rest of them.

"Mama, it's our family." Morgan clapped and jumped, crushing more paper.

Frank held the frame while James stood back and smiled at his mother. "You finally painted us. All of us."

All eyes moved to Elijah. He stared at the portrait, which included himself, hands in his overalls pockets, standing next to James and smiling up at heaven. Now, his lower lip quivered as tears flowed freely down his dark face. He stood to come closer. Clarissa met him halfway.

"I hope you don't mind. You *are* part of our family. A special part." She extended her hand, and he grasped it in his. She studied the pink scars left from his courageous ordeal. Was God crying now? Everyone else certainly was. Tears of gratitude for the mercy and grace this man had brought to their lives.

"I don't mind. You're very kind to think of me that way. Haven't had a family for some time before I met y'all." He wiped his tears.

Ruth blew her nose and wagged her finger at Clarissa. "Young lady, you're very talented."

"Thank you, Ruth. Now that you, Ed, and Martha have moved into the cottage, I'll paint something for those tired old walls."

Martha laughed and nudged Ruth. "Believe me, Clarissa, just being here and a part of this farm is joy enough for them. You and Frank have made a dream come true for this old barber and his wife."

Ed teared up but didn't speak. He pulled his handkerchief from his overalls and wiped the bottom of his red nose. Ruth just nudged Martha back.

Movement returned to the room.

"Okay, all you crybabies. I have one more gift to give." Frank set the painting under the tree and reached far behind all the boxes and wrapping to pull out a bright-colored paper bag tied with a red ribbon. "Morgan, this is from your mama and me."

Morgan grinned and ran to grab the gift. "Another one?" He tore off the ribbon and reached into the bag. His grin faded when he pulled out an empty mason jar. A quick look to his father and then to Clarissa begged an answer. Perhaps they had offended him and it seemed like a joke, especially when James laughed.

298

Clarissa knelt beside him. "We wanted you to know that you taught your dad and me a valuable lesson. We're thankful for you and for your thoughtfulness about saving the rainwater."

Morgan's face lit up again and he held the jar close.

Frank knelt on his other side. "We learned from you that we can't always stop the hard times from coming and that we have to trust each other and God to make things okay. Our time is better spent not hoarding up treasures but sharing them with each other. That's what you taught us, son."

His little face beamed, competing with the candles lit all over the room. Elijah called Morgan over and hugged him before passing him on to Martha, who also wrapped her arms around him.

Ruth meandered over to the old out-of-tune piano and played a Christmas carol. Clarissa took the opportunity to gather up a few dishes to take to the kitchen. She hummed the tune as she set them in the sink. Tomorrow would be as good a day as any to clean up. Tonight was for rejoicing.

"Ma'am?"

Elijah stood behind her when she turned around. She held on to the back of a kitchen chair. "Don't worry about offering to help with the mess. Not tonight."

He shook his head. "I have somethin' to say to you. May I?"

She pulled out the chair and sat. "Of course. Sit down."

Again he shook his head. "I'd like to stand."

Her heart collided with her chest wall. His countenance told her all she needed to know. She had seen it coming, but each time the thought entered her mind, she buried it deep, not able to deal with the sadness it brought her. What she knew about most people, she had guessed from looking from the outside in, like through a glass, trying to judge their character. Her guess about Elijah had been spot on.

"Are you going to leave us, Elijah?"

A tear dropped. "Yes, ma'am. My time here is done. The Lord wants me to move on and see what He has for me to do. I've been blessed more than I deserve to be with y'all this long. Don't usually do it like that. I know y'all will be doin' jus' fine now. God says so."

She closed her eyes. Elijah always spoke the truth, and like the gentleman and angel he had been, he knew when to leave. Her breaking heart would mend, as would the hearts of the rest of the family. It was time to stand on their own feet.

"We'll cherish everything you taught us, dear friend. And if you should ever get a hint from the Lord to come back—"

"I know where you'll be."

Joy to the World played in the parlor, with voices raised in harmony. Elijah reached over and gently touched the top of her head. Her whole body flooded with warmth, and the baby kicked stronger than ever before, as if the child had been tickled.

After a moment, she stood and took Elijah's hand, leading him to join the family for the last time. She tried to reason whether she had taken him in all those seasons ago or whether it was the other way around.

No matter. It was ordained either way.

She ignored Frank's raised brows when she came into the room. He would guess about Elijah soon. She stood at the window and wondered if the same stars twinkled over Kansas. Were the homestead and the little graves in the yard covered with sand or snow on this Christmas night?

As she stared into the night sky, a few white flakes danced by the window. In a few short weeks, a new Wilding would be born, never knowing all that had happened while she was tucked safe inside the womb. When she arrived, all would be as if nothing bad had ever invaded their world.

Frank snuggled up to her from behind. "Are you sad or happy?"

"Both. And excited for new vines come spring, if you know what I mean."

He squeezed her shoulders. "I do."

The infant inside kicked in agreement. Ruth played another carol as voices joined to sing along.

Oh, holy night.

Jan Cline is a firm believer in late bloomers. She began her writing journey at a young age, but didn't venture into fiction writing until 2009 when a friend dared her to write a novel. Her love for relics and history pointed her to America's untold stories of the 1930s and 40s, and her first published novel, *Emancipated Heart*, tells the story of a Japanese American family living in an internment camp during WW2.

To Jan, researching is just as fun as putting pen to paper, especially when it requires travel to places she's never been. Her current women's fiction series, *American Dreams*, takes readers from the dust bowl years of America's heartlands through WW2.

Her writing credits include magazine articles, devotionals, anthologies, and a women's self-help book. She is a former writers conference director and enjoys teaching at conferences and writers groups.

Jan lives in northern Idaho with her husband and spoiled dog, and enjoys golf, crafting, painting, and spending time with her nine grandchildren at the family lake cabin.

Visit her online at:

JanCline.net

Facebook: https://www.facebook.com/JanClineAuthor/

Twitter: https://twitter.com/Jan_Cline

Pinterest: https://www.pinterest.com/JanClineAuthor/

$\mathcal{W}$hen I was about seven years old I traveled with my mother, sister, and grandmother to Nebraska, where many of our relatives still lived on the same impoverished homesteads that survived the depression and dust bowl years. It seemed as if time had stood still, freezing them in a life of simplistic tolerance to hard times. They had lived through some of America's most difficult years, but never lost the strength of family and love for the land.

The Wilding family, born from inspiration of that trip, has been through much of the same hardships. I fell in love with the characters as I wrote the first two books in this series, and I hope you have seen in them the courage, hope, and faith they demonstrated in the midst of the struggles common to many Americans in this time period.

The vineyard setting in this book is actually inspired by the vineyard my grandparents (the Watkins family) lived on. Martha is modeled after my mother, and you will learn more about her and her story in Book 3.

I encourage you to research your own family's stories of America's Midwest during the 1930s. You will see what solid stock you come from!

I would love for you to leave a review for *The Pruning* on your favorite social media forum, or retail website. Reviews are important for authors—helping our rankings and increasing visibility for our work. You can visit the book's page, click on reviews/leave a review, and write a few words about how you enjoyed the book. Short and sweet is good—even if it's not a 5-star review.